CLAIMED BY
LOVE

THE RYDERS

LOVE IN BLOOM SERIES

MELISSA FOSTER

ISBN-10: 1941480292

ISBN-13: 978-1-941480-29-8

Cover Design: Elizabeth Mackey

WORLD LITERARY PRESS

PRINTED IN THE UNITED STATES OF AMERICA

A NOTE FROM MELISSA

I had so much fun writing Duke and Gabriella's story! Duke has been with me through several series, and I'm so glad to finally give him his happily ever after. When I met Gabriella, I knew she'd give him a run for his money. I hope you enjoy their wild ride as much as I do. Please note that Elpitha Island is a fictional location, created specifically for Duke and Gabriella. If this is your first Love in Bloom book, all of my love stories are written to stand alone, so dive right in and enjoy the fun, sexy adventure!

The best way to keep up to date with new releases, sales, and exclusive content is to sign up for my newsletter.
www.MelissaFoster.com/news

ABOUT THE LOVE IN BLOOM BIG-FAMILY ROMANCE COLLECTION

The Ryders are just one of the families in the Love in Bloom big-family romance collection. Characters from each series make appearances in future books, so you never miss an engagement, wedding, or birth. If this is your first Love in Bloom novel, you have many more loving, loyal heroes and sexy, sassy heroines waiting for you!

Download a free Love in Bloom series checklist here:
www.melissafoster.com/SO

Get **free** first-in-series Love in Bloom ebooks and see my current sales here:
www.MelissaFoster.com/LIBFree

Visit the Love in Bloom Reader Goodies page for downloadable checklists, family trees, and more!
www.MelissaFoster.com/RG

For my fabulous fan club member Christine Dyc
because there's no way I'd ever
leave you out of Duke's book and live through it

CHAPTER ONE

DUKE RYDER BALANCED his cell phone against his shoulder, listening to his buddy and investment partner Pierce Braden talk about their newest potential investment property as he followed the rickety wooden dock onto the white sandy beach.

"The dock just might be the most stable thing on Elpitha Island," Pierce said. "Try to soak in a little sand and sun while you're there. That's the best part of the island."

Duke's eyes were immediately drawn to the sprawling oak trees he'd read about, standing sentinel over the forested acreage beyond. Long, thick branches spread like languid arms draped in moss, reaching for...*what?* One glance told him that there wasn't much to reach for, save for a building that looked more like a forgotten Mediterranean villa than the welcome center of the small Southern island. The stone and wood building had a deep porch that spanned the entire length of the left side with stone pillars. A wooden trellis laced with the most captivating flowering vines shaded the area. Although the structure itself was in need of repair, it was surrounded by perfectly manicured, ornate gardens, which contrasted sharply with overgrown and unkempt bushes littering the far edges of the property.

"The proximity to the mainland isn't bad," Duke said to Pierce. He set his suitcase on the sand and looked back at the Atlantic. "It only took an hour fifteen to get here." Elpitha was the smallest of the vacation islands off of South Carolina, and more than half of the land had been owned by the Liakos family for centuries. It was just over eight square miles, and not many investors wanted such a small tract of land, or to deal with families that were as entrenched as the Liakos family was thought to be. Some families might sell out, but they would fight tooth and nail against change, which could cause discourse on an island this small. Duke and Pierce weren't deterred. The restrictive size of the property would only increase the value, making it an exclusive vacation spot for the elite.

"With Hilton Head and the other islands so overrun," Pierce said, "Elpitha is ripe for development. Although we'll have to work around that name. Who wants to go to an island called Elpitha? It sounds more like a disease than an island."

Duke squinted up at the blazing sun and loosened his tie. "I don't know. I kind of like it." He noticed a plantation-style home tucked behind the trees in the distance. "They weren't kidding about the strange mix of Mediterranean and

Southern feel of the place. This should be interesting." Duke knew some of the island's history, and though he still didn't understand why Greeks would immigrate to the South and try to re-create their country's feel, it didn't much matter. If he and Pierce decided to purchase the land, they would bulldoze every structure and give the island a complete Southern overhaul, making it the most desirable resort area in the South.

"Chuck called earlier and said Liakos's granddaughter Gabriella is an attorney," Pierce explained. "He thinks they might bring her in on things. Apparently their family keeps things tight. So if you meet her, play nice."

The hollow clank of a screen door hitting its frame drew Duke's attention. A woman stood on the porch of the old building, shading her eyes from the sun as she looked out at the water. Her long dark hair hung halfway down her back. Duke was too far away to see her features, but there was no missing her curvaceous ass and full breasts, not to mention legs that seemed to go on forever beneath her short summery dress. Duke watched with interest as he listened to Pierce relay the most recent information from the attorneys and engineers.

The woman glanced at her watch, then settled her hand on her hip. A voice rang out from inside the building, and the pretty woman hurried back inside.

"I just found proof of life," he said to Pierce as he stepped onto the sandy path. "I'll call you once I've done some recon."

His black leather shoes quickly lost their shine from the dusty road as he approached the building. Voices filtered out the open windows as he mounted the steps. He glanced through the screen door, spotting the brunette he'd just seen. She was facing away from him, speaking heatedly in Greek, hands flailing as her exasperated voice pitched higher.

A thick-waisted man with salt-and-pepper hair sat at a table near the counter, amusement shining in his dark eyes as the brunette ranted to an older woman, and then the man said something Duke couldn't hear.

"*Ugh!* Baba!" The younger woman threw her hands up in the air and flew out the screen door, nearly smacking Duke in the face.

He stumbled backward, giving the angry woman a wide berth as she paced the front porch. She mumbled something in Greek and then crossed her arms, raised her shoulders, and dropped them quickly with a loud *harrumph*. Duke couldn't help but drink in the flush on her smooth, sun-kissed cheeks. Her nose was small and straight, and her almond-shaped, dark—and currently angry—eyes were shadowed by lashes so long they brushed her cheeks.

Having grown up with a younger sister, Duke bided his time in announcing his presence, not wanting to take the brunt of her reaction to whatever the man had said to upset her.

She inhaled a deep breath, her breasts rising and pressing against the sheer fabric, then falling as she exhaled loudly. Her shoulders lowered, and the tightness around her mouth softened. She turned a full-lipped, mind-numbing smile to Duke, as if she hadn't just come out in a firestorm.

"My father believes that no matter what he says, I hear something else." She tilted her head to the side in a thoughtful pose, and in the space of a second her eyes filled with rebellion, making her even sexier. "Hearing and agreeing are two different things."

Duke wondered what her father had just said that got her panties in a bunch. *Christ.* Now he was thinking about her panties.

"I'm Gabriella Liakos. Welcome to Elpitha Island."

The granddaughter? Playing nice would not be a problem with this feisty beauty. Duke shook her hand, holding it a beat longer than he probably should, still mesmerized by the whirlwind of energy radiating from her. "Duke Ryder. It's nice to meet you. I didn't mean to intrude."

"No one intrudes on Elpitha," she said sweetly.

Duke shifted his eyes to the screen door, and she laughed softly. It was the rare type of laugh that floated like the wind and wasn't easily forgotten.

"We're Greek," she said with a shrug, as if that explained it all.

He arched a brow.

"When you combine a Greek father and a Southern mother, who learned *all* the best Greek ways, that's what you get. Food, yelling, guilt, more food. Sweet love. Crazy love. More food. That's who we are." She dragged her gorgeous eyes down his suit to his shoes and put one hand on her hip as she had earlier, tapping her lips with the other.

Duke wouldn't mind getting his mouth on those succulent lips for some *crazy love.*

"You're the investor, checking out our island so you can line your pockets, right?"

He couldn't tell if the look in her eyes was teasing or serious, but her sharp tongue piqued his interest even more. Duke respected confidence, and even though it wasn't the greeting he'd hoped for, he liked knowing that Gabriella wasn't a pushover.

"Something like that," he answered casually.

As a real estate investor, Duke knew his clients were vulnerable and, more often than not, taking a deal they didn't really care for because by the time he swooped in to save the day they had gotten a strong dose of what failure tasted like. A hard pill to swallow. Which was why Duke didn't flinch as Gabriella measured everything about him, from his appearance to his answers. While other investors were cold as sharks, Duke had never quite mastered making ice flow through his veins. But he always got the job done.

Her eyes flicked toward the water, where another boat was nearing the dock. Her smile turned genuine at the sight of a handful of children waving from the boat. She waved both arms over her head and yelled something in Greek, then settled her hands on her hips as she watched the children file from the boat.

"It was nice to meet you, Gabriella," Duke said, hoping he'd see her later. The island had a population of just over two hundred and fifty people, so he imagined it would be hard not to see the same people throughout his stay. "I'll just step inside and see about my room and a tour."

"Lucky you," she said, turning a steady gaze back to him, "I'm your tour host." She didn't wait for him to reply as she opened the screen door and hollered something in Greek to the people inside. Over her shoulder, she said to Duke, "Give me a sec to get your keys and the cart, and I'll show you around and drop you at your place."

It took a moment for him to remember that they drove golf carts or used bicycles on the island and that cars were prohibited.

She hurried inside and headed directly to her *Baba*, which Duke now knew meant he was her father, and said something that made the man laugh. She leaned in to kiss and hug her father, and her dress crept up, exposing the backs of her thighs and hugging her ass. He tried to ignore the stroke of awareness racing through him. She walked around the counter and grabbed a set of keys from a hook, then draped an arm around the shoulders of the woman with whom she was speaking earlier.

"Mama," Gabriella said to the woman. Her mother's hair was a shade lighter than hers. "Talk some sense into him, will you, please?" She whispered something, then kissed her, too.

The woman wiped her hands on an apron and smiled at Duke, catching him observing them. "Welcome to our island, Mr. Ryder. I'm Peggy Ann, and this is my husband, Niko."

Her warm Southern drawl took Duke by surprise after hearing her speak fluent Greek, and he realized it shouldn't have. They were in the South, after all.

He stepped inside. "It's a pleasure to be here, and to meet you both."

Gabriella's father nodded. "Nice to meet you, Mr. Ryder."

"I'll meet you out front," Gabriella said as she grabbed a large basket from the counter, then disappeared through a door in the back of the room.

As he stepped onto the porch, Duke had a feeling Pierce was wrong about the sand and sun being the best part of the island. Those things had nothing on the intriguing woman who'd just slipped out the back door.

CHAPTER TWO

GABRIELLA HAD BEEN back on the island for only a few days, but she'd already settled right in. It was funny how quickly that happened every time she came home. She'd happily fallen back into her old routine, waking early to watch the sunrise over the ocean, cooking with her family, drinking more wine than she should, helping with her nieces and nephews and wherever else her family needed. She was so happy here, she desperately needed a reminder of why she was wasting any time at all helping sell the island. She made a quick call to her close friend and assistant, Addison Dahl, who was holding down the fort in New York City.

"You're doing the right thing," Addy assured her.

"Am I, Addy? Or am I helping to ruin my family's legacy?"

"Listen, Gab. You deal with assholes all the time. Men and women who don't give a shit about tearing apart their families because they found someone younger or cuter to satisfy their needs. You fight for what's right in each and every case," Addy reminded her. "You're doing this because you have to. Take a good look around you."

Gabriella took in the cracks in the foundation of the building, the missing shingles overhead, and when she looked down the street, she saw more of the same. Even from a distance she could see broken windows and the harsh state of disrepair that fell upon the shops along the main road, half of which had been closed for years. The other half struggled to keep income flowing. It was time to make a change, but she cared deeply about the people who lived here, and she feared what an investor would do to the island. Would they make Elpitha Island into a high-rise metropolis? Ruin the close-knit and casual feel? Would they make rent so high that business owners had to close down shop? Gabriella had grown up here, been part of these people's lives, and every chance she got since she'd left for college she'd come back. The residents were more than a mishmash of cultures and personalities. They were family. The buildings might be in disrepair, but the people inside them? They were just as whole as ever.

"Oh, Addy," Gabriella said. "I know you're right. Being here to show the potential investor around and sell him on the island is the right thing to do. Besides, it's not like I could have refused my grandfather when he asked me to handle it. But once he lets go of the resort and his property, then what? This has been his life, his home, forever. His family immigrated here when my great-great-grandfather was younger than me."

Gabriella knew that her life was a world away from what her ancestors' lives were at her age. Many of her male ancestors had been sea captains or involved in some way with the seas in Greece. Their immigration here to start a shipping company that never came to fruition was born of their hopes and dreams for a better future. She'd never lost sight of how her family came to reside in the States, or the determination and courage it had taken to get there, and she didn't take her ancestors' resilience for granted the way so many people often did. Selling the island felt like she was negating all her family had ever worked toward.

"*Then what?*" Addy repeated. Having been Gabriella's assistant for four years, she would give Gabriella hell as easily as she'd have her back. "You say it like your grandfather is going to wither away in an apartment somewhere. I thought your goal was to try to weasel your way into convincing the investor to offer more than just a sellout, to keep your grandfather involved in some way. Have you changed your mind?"

"No," Gabriella said quickly. "Of course not, but I'm not sure I'll be able to negotiate anything. I'm not here for that purpose. I hope, but…" She'd hoped for a lot in her life, and she knew from experience that hope alone never got people very far. What she didn't tell Addy was that she didn't really want her grandfather to sell the resort or any of the property, despite the fact that she knew he had to do *something*. She held on to the hope that somehow things would get better.

"Well," Addy said, "at least it'll take your mind off the McGrady mediation."

They had been working on the McGrady divorce for months. Mr. McGrady's attorney was a slick bastard, and Mr. McGrady was a high-profile cheating husband with a holier-than-thou attitude and numerous assets he stood to lose in the divorce. Gabriella didn't have high hopes that anyone could get through to him, but mediation was a necessary step in the process. Not for the first time, she wondered how she'd gotten sucked into such an unpleasant field. She'd wanted to ensure children's lives were managed well through the stressful process of divorce and to help families with adoptions and surrogacies. Unfortunately, she'd quickly realized that in too many cases children were used as pawns.

"Ugh, don't remind me. Hopefully I can forget about them for a few days."

"Crap, I totally made you think of something horrible when you need me to pep you up. Sorry."

"Hey, that's my life, right?" Gabriella pictured Addy's big hazel eyes narrowing as she mentally sifted through ideas to pick up Gabriella's spirits. Addy was good at that, like a ray of sunshine when the assholes of the divorce world rained down on Gabriella.

"Only *part* of your life," Addy said. "You'll have fun with your family. And remember, Gab, your grandfather asked you to handle things because he knows how much you love the island and that you're an incredible businesswoman, so go get 'em, tiger."

After ending the call, Gabriella tried to stop the recurring, childish thought from slipping in, but it was no use. She'd never fully shaken the hurt. *If I'm the best there is,* Gabriella thought, *why didn't he fight to keep me on the island?*

She wondered why her grandfather hadn't had his attorney, his real estate agent, or even another family member who still lived on the island show the investor around. But in their family, respect for their elders was everything, and she would do as he asked out of respect, and out of love.

Gabriella placed the basket of bread she'd baked for her grandfather on the seat beside her and started up the golf cart, thinking about the overly starched mainlander waiting for her. He was big, at least a foot taller than her five three, and strikingly handsome, in a cityish sort of way. He'd probably read up on the perfect number of days to grow out the sexy scruff that covered his chiseled cheeks and strong chin. *And those eyes.* He had the kind of warm dark eyes that made a woman feel like she was the only thing he saw.

She totally had his number. How many men like him had she slaughtered in divorce court? He probably had at least one ex-wife mixed with other skeletons she didn't want to know about. She drove around the building, thinking about how easy it was to see the difference between a city boy and an islander. Sure, city boys like Duke introduced themselves with friendly words and a handshake, like they were as easygoing as a summer breeze. But it never took long for the lack of reliable Internet, or the heat, or the sand, or early-morning birds singing to greet the day, or any number of the other things Gabriella adored about the island, to bring out the arrogance and attitudes that followed savvy businessmen like shadows.

She rounded the building and was surprised to see Duke sitting on the front step beside her twelve-year-old niece, Vivi, and a handful of Gabriella's other nieces and nephews and their friends, who had just returned from school on the mainland.

There was only one school on the island, with two multigrade classrooms. Kids in grades six through twelve were transported to the mainland by ferry, then picked up by a school bus to attend middle and high school. Gabriella used to rue those hours away, and when her parents insisted that she attend college, she'd hated that even more. She had never liked the selfishness that clung to city people like a second skin, or the way they never slowed down enough to enjoy the glorious earth they lived on. They were destroying it with their carbon footprints, raping the land of trees and greenery, and don't even get her started on the way so many people took family for granted, putting work above all else.

"Do you have more pictures of your sister? She's so pretty." Vivi's dark eyes were wide and excited as she waved to Gabriella. "*Thea*, his sister is an actress!"

Figures. Images of pin-thin, entitled women came to mind, and she wondered how much of that mind-set ran in his family. Duke was savvier than she'd given him credit for. He was trying to win over the kids, too. She forced a smile for her niece's sake.

"How exciting." She knew Vivi, like many of her younger relatives, was enamored with life on the mainland in a way that Gabriella had never been and had aspirations of leaving the island.

Gabriella and other relatives her age had been lovingly forced to move off the island after graduating college to *have a life*. She couldn't think about that now, not when she had a tour to give.

Duke flashed a panty-melting smile that, in combination with his sexily tousled dirty-blond hair, she was sure charmed him into the beds of plenty of women. Despite herself, she could totally see how it would work. While marriages seemed to not only last, but flourish, on the island, as a family-law attorney, Gabriella battled the pain of divorce for her clients on a daily basis. She didn't date often, and it had been a long time since she'd been flirted with. Obviously her body was craving a little flirtation, because it was betraying her intelligence and enjoying the attention.

Way to go, Gab. He's not even flirting. He's smiling.

Duke turned his attention back to the kids. "I have only one sister, and she's nowhere near as pretty as you." He tapped Vivi's nose, earning another grin from her niece and making Gabriella curious at his easy nature with the kids, which was a complete contradiction to what she'd expected.

"I think it's time for me to take a tour of the island, but it's been nice talking with you." Duke shifted his attention to Gabriella's nephew David, and his tone turned serious. "Hey, buddy. It takes a bigger man to shrug it off when people call you names rather than shooting them right back. Think about it. Maybe try that next time."

David's eyes shifted to Gabriella. His dark hair was thick and tousled, and his eyes pleaded for lenience. She wondered what Duke had heard. If David had been in trouble at school, the kids were probably talking about it. There were no secrets in their big, extended family. She knew he'd been in some trouble for mouthing off. Even if she wanted to tell David that everything would be okay, no matter what had happened at school, she knew she shouldn't. Their family believed in standing up to their messes and facing them head-on. They didn't hide from them or pretend they didn't happen. Although the look on her nephew's face told her that he'd like to do just that.

She focused on her nephew once again and spoke in Greek, so as not to embarrass him in front of Duke. "Is your mother going to get another call from the principal?"

David shrugged.

"Now that you've eaten the bull, you want to leave the tail? *Tsk.* I don't think so. Go tell your mother what happened." Gabriella picked up the basket of bread she'd set on the passenger's seat, marveling at how easily the words her father had said hundreds of times spewed from her lips. *See, Baba? I do listen.*

"Are you joining us on the tour?" Duke asked Vivi and David.

"I can't, but thanks," David said.

Vivi's dark eyes widened. "May I, *Thea?*"

"Absolutely. We'll just stop by and tell your mama." Gabriella was relieved. Vivi would be a great distraction from Mr. I Want to Ruin Your Island. She said goodbye to the other kids and watched them walk toward town, not for the first time reveling in the contrast between the safety of the island versus the city she now called home.

Their grandfather had been talking about selling for years, but Gabriella didn't believe for a minute that he would actually go through with it, despite their diminished economy. But she wasn't about to leave it open to chance. She'd give Duke a tour, all right. She'd make sure he got the *whole* island experience, from the sweltering heat of the afternoon sun to the sand that would ruin his pricey shoes and pants. Throw in a few overly talkative residents who would bore him to death, and he'd probably be gone by sunset.

Duke lifted Vivi's backpack from her shoulders and waved to the passenger seat. "Ladies ride up front."

Vivi giggled as she climbed in and took the basket from Gabriella, while Gabriella tucked away her surprise. Most men like him, impeccably dressed, with a suitcase that probably cost more than the golf cart, would sit in the front, away from the dusty plume of sand that would follow them down the road.

"Thea?" he asked.

"It means *aunt*. I'm not really her aunt. She's my cousin's daughter. But in my family, we call cousins who are significantly younger, nieces and nephews. It's weird, I know, but it's what my family has always done."

"I like that," he said, and nodded toward the basket. "A tour and a snack? Looks like we're pretty lucky, Vivi."

Vivi laughed. "That's for *Papou*. *Thea* makes the best bread on the island."

Their grandfather was in his eighties, and as the owner of the majority of Elpitha, he was the man who made their wonderful island life possible.

Gabriella answered the question lingering in Duke's eyes. "*Papou*, grandpa. We don't use descriptors like *great*-grandpa, or *first* cousin." In her family, there were no delineations of lineage, and that Greek tradition carried over to her mother's side of the family as well. A second cousin or a great-aunt was simply known as *cousin* or *aunt.*

Duke nodded. As he went around to the back of the cart and set his suitcase on one of the seats, he said, "*Papou.*"

His curiosity about their language intrigued her. Most visitors never cared enough to ask.

Vivi lifted the cover from the basket and turned pleading eyes to Gabriella, asking in Greek, "May I share?"

Gabriella had a soft place in her heart for her nieces and nephews. As much as she'd like to tell Vivi she couldn't share their grandfather's bread with Duke just for the sake of squeezing out the guy who wanted to buy the island, she would never squash Vivi's giving nature.

"You may," Gabriella said.

Duke caught Gabriella's eye as he reached for the bread Vivi offered him. Gabriella's stomach fluttered nervously, surprising her, and she quickly turned her attention back to driving and pulled onto the sandy road, hoping he liked the bread she'd made.

Ugh. Why does that matter?

DUKE HAD SEEN plenty of pictures of the island, but as they drove down sandy roads, shaded beneath large trees draped in moss, he thought he'd never seen anyplace as serene. As they neared the residential area, the view of the ocean disappeared, replaced by lush greenery as far as the eye could see. They passed homes nestled among the trees, some with grassy lawns, overflowing with gardens, and others barely visible amid the trees.

It was a strange feeling to see cottages, stately plantations, and Queen Anne–style houses mixed in with Mediterranean-style villas. The only thing that seemed to tie the homes together were the colorful shutters, giving each house its own personality.

Gabriella turned down a long driveway and parked in front of a boxy white villa with bright blue shutters.

"This will only take a moment," she said as she and Vivi stepped from the cart.

Duke carried the backpack as Vivi ran into the house.

"She seems like a sweet kid." He followed her up the walkway.

"She is." Gabriella reached for the backpack.

"It's okay. I've got it, unless you'd rather I wait in the cart?"

Confusion filled her eyes, in the same adorable way it had when she'd pulled up and seen him sitting with the kids. "You *want* to go inside? Most people would be put off by the inconvenience."

"Inconvenience? If anything, I'm inconveniencing you." He put a hand on the small of her back as they started up the walk, and felt her bristle beneath his touch.

"Sorry." He pulled his hand back. "I wasn't trying to be forward. It's a habit. A protective one, I guess, carried over from when I'm with my mom or my sister."

Before she could respond, the front door flew open and a very pregnant woman carrying a little girl with curly dark hair hurried across the lawn toward them. The woman's hair was piled on her head in a messy knot, and she was speaking loud and fast in Greek. Her hand went this way and that as she pulled Gabriella into a hug, kissing each of her cheeks, and then she stood, hand on her hip, as her eyes feasted on every inch of Duke.

He waited for her to say something he could understand, but she continued speaking a mile a minute in Greek. Between the way her eyes were taking him in and the rosy blush rising on Gabriella's cheeks, he had a feeling she was talking about his looks. At six four, Duke knew he had an imposing presence, especially to petite women such as these two, who couldn't be more than a few inches over five feet.

"Duke Ryder," Gabriella finally said, "meet my cousin Katarina."

Before he could say a word, Katarina placed one hand on his shoulder, went up on her toes, and kissed each of his cheeks.

"And this is Ermione." The little girl's name sounded like *Er-mee-oh-knee*. Katarina kissed the baby girl's cheek and whispered, "Say hi, Mione."

The little girl buried her face in the crook of her mother's neck and said, "Hi."

Duke loved children, and Mione looked like she was maybe three or four years old, and cute as a button. "Nice to meet you both. You have lovely daughters."

A spark of mischief appeared in Katarina's dark eyes and she bumped Gabriella's shoulder. "And a lovely cousin, too, yes?"

"Katarina!" Gabriella shook her head and shielded her eyes with her hand. "Ignore her. She's had so many children she's lost her mind."

Katarina patted her burgeoning belly. "Hopefully this one will be a boy."

"*Baba* says we'll keep having them until he gets his boy," Vivi said, reaching up to pat her younger sister's back. Katarina leaned down and kissed the top of Vivi's head.

"How many daughters do you have?" He tried to place Katarina's age, and didn't think she could be much older than thirty.

"Four, *so far*." She patted the side of her hair and said, "I started young."

"Mama had me when she was first married, at twenty," Vivi said. "She's thirty-two now."

Katarina yanked playfully on Vivi's ponytail and said something in Greek that made Vivi cover her mouth with her hand and laugh.

"You're very blessed. I come from a large family and hope to have one myself someday." Duke was the eldest of six. His brother Cash had recently married, and Blue, another of his brothers, had recently gotten engaged. He'd always thought he'd be the first to marry, but he had yet to meet a woman whom he could see himself spending the rest of his life with. He gave his brothers a hard time about settling down, but the truth was, Duke had had his share of women, and he was ready for the next chapter of his life.

Katarina elbowed Gabriella, and Duke pretended to ignore her matchmaking efforts, though he was secretly hoping that Gabriella was as attracted to him as he was to her. What man wouldn't be? A feisty brunette with a killer bod and a spark of rebellion? *Perfect.*

"We should go. I'm on tour duty today." Gabriella hugged her cousin, and Vivi reached for her aunt's hand.

Katarina lowered her voice. "Are you *sure* you want Vivi tagging along?"

"Yes, of course," Gabriella said vehemently, and headed for the golf cart with her niece in tow.

Duke swallowed the sting of Gabriella's brush-off at the chance of spending time alone with him. "If I don't see you again, I wish you luck with your new baby, Katarina."

She grabbed his forearm. "Are you coming to the celebration tomorrow night?"

"Celebration?"

"We're celebrating my father's birthday. Practically the whole island will be there, and you should definitely come." She leaned in closer and said, "It's at the big house by the lighthouse, seven o'clock."

Duke glanced back at Gabriella, wondering if she'd be there, too. Normally if a woman blew him off, he'd take the hint and turn his attention elsewhere. But there was something about Gabriella that intrigued him, and that made her impossible to put out of his mind.

"Thank you. That sounds like something I'd enjoy."

He climbed into the golf cart, and they spent the next hour touring the residential areas. Everyone they passed waved. Duke noticed that there were no fenced yards, no divide between one family and the next. Women talked in their yards while children played nearby, giving him a warm feeling about the island.

As they drove back into town Gabriella said, "None of the roads are paved. There are only a handful of cars on the island, and they're used for emergencies, mostly." She brought the cart to a stop in front of Liakos Taverna, a small restaurant built in the same Mediterranean style as several of the villas he'd just seen.

"We travel by golf cart, bike, or these." She pointed to her feet. "The island is only eight square miles. You could walk it in a day if you wanted to."

"Can I run in and see *Theos*?" Vivi was already out of the

cart and heading for the door.

"Sure." She stepped from the cart, and Duke took the cue that they were done riding.

"*Theos?*" he asked as he came to her side.

"Uncle." She had that curious glint in her eyes again.

"Ah. I can't wait to be an uncle." He stripped off his suit coat and tossed it over the back of the seat, then rolled up his shirtsleeves. When he lifted his gaze, there was no mistaking the heat in Gabriella's eyes.

"Yes, well…" Her cheeks flushed, but she held his gaze, which Duke found impressive, given that he'd just caught her gawking at him. "We have a very big, very close-knit family." She took a step toward the restaurant just as a thick-bodied man with jet-black hair and a goatee stepped from the restaurant. His eyes moved between Gabriella and Duke.

He held a hand out to Duke. "Niko."

"Duke." He shook the man's hand. "Nice to meet you."

Gabriella said something in Greek as she kissed the other man's cheek, and Duke wondered if he was her boyfriend.

Niko responded in Greek. Gabriella answered with a sharp tone and a narrow-eyed glare. Duke decided it was high time he learned the language. He owned resorts and casinos all over the world, and he was used to having the upper hand. He didn't mind being on an even playing field, but he wasn't about to be the underdog.

Worried that he'd upset a jealous boyfriend with his presence, he said, "Gabriella, if you tell me where I can find the resort, I don't mind walking. I can tour the rest of the island on foot."

"Don't be silly. Gabriella loves to give tours." Niko didn't look like a man pushing his girlfriend into another man's arms. He looked like he was up to mischief, teasing her maybe.

"I actually do enjoy giving tours. I just don't usually get assailed by my brother for turning down a date with one of his friends."

Brother? Turned down a date? Relief, far stronger than what he should feel after her brush-off, rushed through him. He was beginning to see a matchmaking pattern among her relatives.

"Ah, well, you're a very different type of brother than I am," Duke said. "I do everything I can to keep guys *away* from my sister."

"Wow. Do *all* brothers butt into their sister's lives?" Gabriella asked as Vivi came outside with two other girls her age.

"Didn't you know? In order to be a brother, one must first prove himself to be overprotective and nosy beyond acceptable measures," Duke said.

She laughed, louder than the last time, and it might have been the sexiest laugh Duke had ever heard.

"*Thea*, I called Mama and she said I could go to the library with my friends," Vivi said. "Do you mind?"

"Of course not. Have fun." Gabriella hugged her niece.

"It was nice to meet you, Mr. Ryder," Vivi said to Duke.

"You too, Vivi. Do you need us to swing by and take you home on the way back?"

She shook her head. "No, thank you. The library is right there, and we walk home together afterward." She pointed down the street to a small brick building. "Have fun on your tour." She and her friends ran across the road huddled together and giggling.

Duke took a moment to check out Main Street. No two storefronts were alike. While the restaurant was richly Mediterranean in appearance, and the library was a nondescript brick, the bank was a stately Georgian-style building boasting wide stone steps leading to double wooden doors. An intricately carved triangular pediment graced a concrete porch. A market with colorful baskets of fruits and vegetables out front was flanked by a pharmacy and an empty brick building. Several shops were closed, or in severe states of disrepair, which he'd expected, but they looked out of place against the backdrop of the peaceful Atlantic and all the beautiful foliage surrounding them.

"She'll be okay walking home later?" Duke asked.

"Life's different here," Gabriella said. "Niko, I'll see you tomorrow." She kissed his cheek and nodded toward the road. "Shall we?"

Duke shook Niko's hand again. Niko pulled him into an unexpected manly embrace, surprising him.

"Enjoy Elpitha," Niko said.

"Thank you." Thinking of Gabriella, he added, "I already am." Duke fell into step beside Gabriella. Without the noise of cars, he noticed other sounds, like the sounds of bike tires and footsteps on the dirt as people passed by and the birds chirping above. There were a dozen or so people coming and going. Nearly everyone smiled or said hello as they passed. It was quite different from the hustle and bustle of New York, where he lived, or for that matter, from just about anywhere else he'd ever visited.

"You said life is different here. How so?" he asked as they walked through town.

"It's...better," Gabriella answered. "Life is simply better here."

"Better than...?"

She shrugged and looked up at the blue sky. Her eyes took on a dreamy quality. "Better than anywhere else on earth."

Her simple answers—*We're Greek. It's better*—told of her love of the island and of her family, but it was the breathlessness of her answer that made him want to experience the island through her eyes.

CHAPTER THREE

AS THEY TOURED the town, Gabriella made a point of introducing Duke to shop owners and residents, acting on her plan to quickly overwhelm and bore him. He'd tire of their small-town ways and realize that this wasn't the type of place he wanted to sink his money into.

Lyman and Dottie Eastman, the couple who ran the local market, were out front stocking the fruit boxes when they walked by. They were as Southern as a couple could get, and *real* talkers. The perfect annoyance for a busy city man.

"Lyman, Dottie, this is Duke Ryder. I'm giving him a tour of the island."

"Nice to meet you, Mr. Ryder." Dottie's Southern drawl was as thick as her graying blond hair. She was short and stout, with plump rosy cheeks. "How long're you stayin' on the island?"

Gabriella realized she'd been so confident she'd be able to push him back to the mainland by nightfall, she hadn't looked at his booking close enough to know how long he planned on staying.

"Oh, a few days, maybe. I'm not really sure." Duke shook Lyman's hand. "Nice to meet you, sir."

Lyman nodded. "You've got the best tour guide around." His face was mapped with deep grooves from the sun. He winked one squinty eye at Gabriella, then pulled her into a hug against his rail-thin frame. "Gabriella knows every nook and cranny of this place. Why, I remember when she was yay high." He held his hand about two feet off the ground. "Cutest little thing."

Duke laughed. "So you've lived here quite a while?"

"Oh, yes," Lyman said. "We moved to the island right after we got married." He went on to describe what life was like when they first married and how it changed with the birth of each of their three children.

Duke talked with them for a long time about their family, the storms they'd seen roll through over the years, the trials and tribulations of getting supplies by boat, and just about everything else under the sun. Gabriella grew bored before Duke seemed to, and she finally urged Duke away to complete the tour. Was he trying to win them over, too?

"Nice folks," Duke said as they walked down the hill toward the bait and tackle shop, owned by Gabriella's uncle George.

"*Gabrielaki mou*," George said as he opened his arms and embraced her. His eyes went to Duke, and after a quick appraisal, he gave Gabriella *the look*. She was used to *the look* and sick of *the look*. The look that said, *He's attractive, male, the right age. Well?* How long would her family try to get her to find a man, marry, and have babies? Why couldn't they have given her grandfather a look that said, *Let her stay. She'll be happier here.* She pushed those thoughts aside and focused on giving Duke a boring *and* overwhelming tour. The problem was, he didn't seem to be either, and if she was honest with herself, she was enjoying his friendly, down-to-earth side, which had emerged as their tour progressed. Had it been there when she'd first met him?

"*Theo*, this is Duke Ryder. I'm giving him a tour of the island."

Duke shook his hand, and just as she'd known he would, George pulled him into a tight embrace. There was no such thing as too much love in her family, and they liked to share. Another sure turnoff for city people. Although Duke didn't seem to mind it at all. He embraced George right back.

"Come." George motioned for Duke to follow him down the fishing rod aisle. "Do you enjoy fishing?"

Gabriella leaned against the counter, watching the men talk, and laugh, and…Her plan was definitely not working. Duke seemed sincerely interested in hearing about George's children's fishing expeditions and the newest lures he was carrying. She took the opportunity to look at him a little more closely than before, now that he was busy and unaware of her checking him out. He ran a hand through his thick hair, then leaned closer to her uncle and said something that caused George to laugh. Duke patted her uncle's arm, then slid his hand into the pocket of his slacks, which were now boasting four inches of dust at the hem. He glanced in her direction and her pulse quickened. He lifted his chin, as if to say hello, and flashed the panty-melter again. She liked that panty-melting smile a whole hell of a lot, but it was his dark eyes that currently held her captive. Her body was acutely aware of his gaze as it lingered on her for a few seconds, causing her nipples to stand at attention and her skin to prickle with awareness before he turned his attention back to George.

After leaving the bait shop, they headed down to the fishery.

"Does everyone here play matchmaker?" Duke asked.

Embarrassment flushed her cheeks.

"I'm sorry if that's too personal. It's just that you seem to be getting looks from your cousin and some of the people here, and after what your brother said, I was curious." He was quiet for a minute or two, and the silence suddenly felt heavy.

She hoped he was just making conversation and not thinking that she was a loser who needed a matchmaker. She might not date much, but she wasn't in need of help in that area. She just didn't come across very many down-to-earth people in the city.

"They're not very discreet about it, are they?"

He laughed. "Does it bother you?"

"A little. My family thinks they need to find me a husband. No one seems to understand that I'm perfectly happy as I am. Well, except for living off the island."

"I hadn't realized that you lived off the island," he said with a note of surprise. "Why do you, if you would rather be here?"

She was glad he focused on that instead of thinking she was in need of help finding a husband—or that she was looking for one. Which she wasn't. God, what was happening to her mind? She never overthought everything like this. She focused on answering his question instead of the strangeness going on inside her head, or the awareness of how near he was walking to her.

"By the time I graduated from high school, tourism was really slowing down, and my grandfather decided that all of his descendants my age and younger should get college educations and have the chance to have more in their lives than what the island had to offer. While other residents on the island *chose* to move away, my grandfather really didn't give us a choice. In our culture respect goes a long way. It's not like the 1950s or anything. Women work, we have power, but our respect for our elders goes above and beyond all else." She thought about the truth in that statement and added, "Actually, if you really delve into the homes, the women rule the roost. But after I got my degree, I got scholarships and went on to law school, and it's not like we needed a family law attorney here on *Bliss* Island."

"Bliss Island?"

She sighed and looked around with a dreamy warmth in her eyes. "No one here ever gets divorced. And divorce is only one aspect of family law. I handle surrogates, adoptions, and a number of other legal issues, which I really do enjoy. But that's not the point, really. It's that I didn't have the chance to choose what I wanted. Everything I want is right here on the island. I don't care about money, or building a big career, or making a name for myself in an industry I find a little…hypocritical."

His eyes narrowed.

She cringed inside, wondering if he had an ex-wife in his past. "I'm sorry. I don't mean to rant."

His gaze softened. "I like hearing about you."

You do?

"Your family seems so close. Wouldn't your grandfather put family above the rest and be more interested in keeping the family together than in sending you off to live somewhere else?" He slid a hand casually into his pocket, as if he had all day to chat about her life, and seeing that warmed her toward him even more.

"Yes. He does, don't you see? He adores us, but he's getting older, and he worries about what will happen to us after he's gone, what will happen to the island. The dating pool on the island is practically nonexistent, and he worries about what that'll mean for our family lineage, too."

"That seems valid. Wouldn't that have worried you? Do you want to have a family? Do you want Vivi to have the option to one day get married and have a family?"

She was surprised that he was asking these personal questions, but it also pleased her. No one ever asked her about what she wanted.

"I *did* worry about that, but I would have pushed those worries away, because I love the island and my family and the communal lifestyle more than I could ever enjoy the legal field." She could hardly believe she was sharing so much of herself, so easily, but obviously Duke wasn't the rushed, self-centered businessman she'd thought he was. She wanted to get to know him better.

"I do want Vivi and all of my relatives to have wonderful lives, but to me the *island* is wonderful. I think my grandfather thought that if I got a college degree, I'd want to stay on the mainland." She shook her head with the memory. She'd cried for weeks after she'd gone away to college, but her family had insisted she stay in school. "But he was wrong. I only built my career to appease them. Family. Love. It seeps into every part of our lives." She shrugged, intrigued by the genuine interest in his eyes. "This island *is* my life. The rest is…Well, it is what it is. When I'm here, I'm happy in every way."

A look she couldn't read passed over his face.

"I admire your passion, and I think that's a perfectly legitimate reason to return. But don't you worry about how quickly the island is losing money *and* residents? I read that the population has gone from three hundred and ten to two hundred and fifty in the last three years."

"I know the statistics, and it's true. The island, the residents, they're in dire financial straits because we have almost zero tourism income these days, and without income, we lack funds to fix the resort and villas. My entire family is in favor of selling. But you need to know that I'm not." She paused, realizing how childish her next sentence would sound, but for whatever reason, she didn't care. She needed Duke to know where she stood.

"I have to believe that somehow we'll make it without anyone's help, and more importantly, without the island becoming host to a plethora of high-rise hotels and flashy casinos, with cars and paved roads and selfish attitudes to match."

Duke stepped in closer, bringing a heat wave with him. Despite their being on opposite sides of the fence, she found herself admiring everything about him, from his sexy gaze and lips that looked like they were made for kissing to his kindness, willingness to talk, and to see both sides of the coin.

"I understand completely, Gabriella, and I'm not sure I disagree with your concerns. With development comes risk.

Do you really believe you can make it without the help of investors?" He searched her eyes. "And I do love to hear you say 'we' when you speak of the island. It's obvious how much of your heart remains here."

She hesitated, because she knew that making it without investors was impossible. But that didn't mean she was giving up hope. Something in the way Duke was looking at her tore the truth from her heart.

"I hope so."

Neither spoke for a long moment, as her heart lay bare between them. Duke gazed thoughtfully into her eyes, and she could see, could feel, that he understood how deeply she cared about the island, and she swore she saw something else in his eyes. As if he cared, too.

He touched her arm, nodding toward the fishery. "How about we meet the next matchmaker?"

Mal Hacknee was a balding man with black-framed glasses and a body still carrying more muscle than fat, even though he was in his late fifties. He'd owned the fishery for more than twenty years, and when he saw Gabriella his green eyes widened and his thick arms opened. Oh, how she missed these types of greetings. In New York, she was lucky to get a glance of recognition, even after shopping in the same stores for years. Mal hugged Gabriella so tight she worried she'd smell like fish for the rest of the afternoon. He and Duke talked for a while, and then Duke and Gabriella circled back toward the center of town.

She couldn't stop thinking about his earlier response to her not wanting to leave. And that look? Oh, what that look did to her! Did he truly understand her love of the island? She was beginning to feel a connection to Duke and felt a little guilty for trying to turn him off to the island, but she resolved to stay on course with her plan. She'd show him to his villa and leave him be to wrestle with the spotty Internet.

Once they reached town, Duke asked if she'd mind if they went inside the library. She was surprised but agreed, and was happy to have a little more time to delve deeper into the mystery of Duke Ryder.

"You now know my life story. What about you? Is there a Mrs. Ryder or a fiancée back home?"

"No," he said as they climbed the stairs to the library. "I hope there will be one day. I haven't found the right woman yet."

That was the second time he'd mentioned something along the lines of wanting marriage or a family, and it piqued her curiosity even more.

They lingered in the library, looking through stacks of books, until Duke spotted Vivi and her friends. He stopped by their table to say hello, and Vivi patted the chair beside her. *Huh. He really has won the kids over.*

Gabriella reflected on their conversations. Every so often Duke looked up at her and smiled, and she shifted her eyes away, not wanting him to catch her studying him again.

After he finished talking with Vivi and her friends, he joined Gabriella, leaned in close, and said, "They're discussing boys, not reading."

"You think?" She laughed. "They're twelve-year-old girls. What else would they talk about?" She saw Georgette Swan nearing and waved at the sweet librarian. Georgette was in her early seventies, and she had worked at the library longer than Gabriella had been alive.

She introduced Georgette to Duke, and just as he had with everyone else, he fell right into an easy conversation, asking Georgette all sorts of questions about how long she'd worked there—*forever*—and who her favorite authors were—*Harper Lee, Dorothy Allison, and Kathleen Grissom*. Georgette and Duke agreed that the classics were always good fallbacks.

When they left, Duke carried a book by Kathleen Grissom, borrowed from the library, under his arm.

He'd taken so much time with each person she'd introduced him to, Gabriella wondered if he'd done it just to be cordial, like he was somehow obligated, or if it was part of his plan to win over the residents in his pursuit of the island. But he'd seemed too interested in each of them for that to be true. She was beginning to think she'd completely misjudged him.

"Thank you for taking so much of your time to give me a tour," he said as they headed back toward where they'd left the golf cart.

"It's actually been a nice distraction. When I was a teenager I showed tourists around just for fun."

"You really do miss living here, don't you?"

"I do. I know the lack of tourism is an issue for many reasons, but to me it's better now. I love the solidarity of the community, and when it's quiet, I get more time with family and to just…*be present*, you know?" She waved to a few of her friends across the street.

"Your love of the island definitely shows, and the people here obviously adore you," he said with a smile. "My life rarely slows down enough for simply being present, but it sounds like a wonderful idea."

She realized he'd been smiling all afternoon. It wasn't the panty-melting seductive smile she'd seen earlier. This smile was easy, casual, like he hadn't a care in the world, but it was having the same effect as the panty-melter. She didn't know what to make of that, or of the fact that she'd spent the last few *hours* giving a tour that usually took about an hour max.

He stopped walking by the Sip 'n' Chat coffee shop. "Can I buy you a cup of coffee as a thank-you for the tour?"

Her goal had been to turn him off to the town, and he was asking her out for coffee? Her plan was definitely *not* working. As she met his kind gaze, she realized that her plan wasn't working for *her*, either. She *wanted* to have a drink with him. She wanted to learn more about the man who dressed like he belonged on Wall Street but was as gentlemanly as a small-towner. She felt like she'd known him for much longer than just a few hours, but she could see that he had that effect on everyone. And when his lips curved up, waiting for her answer, her stomach dipped and flipped. This wasn't good. She needed to pull out all the stops and bring in the big guns, for both their sakes. It was time for *Liakos overload.* Surely a good dose of her family would send him running back to the mainland.

But did she really want him to leave? *You need to scare him away, no matter what your body is thinking.*

"I'm not a big coffee drinker, but I could go for a glass of wine." She pointed down the road to her brother's restaurant.

"Ah, the *taverna.* Now, that's a Greek word I know." He lowered his hand to her back again as they walked the short distance.

She didn't flinch against his touch. In fact, she found herself warming to it and enjoying the heat a little too much.

They walked past the crowded *taverna* patio, where customers ate at tables covered with red and white tablecloths. As one of the few restaurants on the island, Liakos Taverna was always busy.

Duke held the door open for Gabriella, and she was greeted by the scents of her youth—grilled meats and *patatas. Patatas,* she thought. *French fries.* She'd practically grown up on them. She heard her brother's deep laugh coming from the kitchen and spotted her uncle behind the bar. She missed being here, missed her family, missed the scents and warmth of family and love.

"Let me grab a carafe and we can sit out on the patio." She felt the heat of his stare burning a hole in her back as she went behind the bar. She kissed her uncle Chris on the cheek and grabbed glasses from a rack, stealing a glance at Duke. Her heartbeat quickened when she saw that he was still watching her.

"Who is the stuffed shirt watching you with eagle eyes?" Chris asked in their native tongue. He was her father's brother, in his early fifties, and like the rest of her family, he hardly ever kept his thoughts to himself.

"Investor." She was glad Duke couldn't understand the language. "We're going to sit on the patio."

"It's warm out there," Chris said. "Sit in here, in the air-conditioning. Or you'll run him off."

"I'm counting on the full Liakos family treatment, the late-afternoon heat, and the loud customers to do exactly that." As she said the words, her chest tightened. She might not want her grandfather to sell, but she was definitely attracted to Duke. *I wouldn't mind if he stuck around for other reasons.*

She glanced over her shoulder, and Duke lifted his chin, as if to say, *I'm right here.* She felt herself smiling as she filled the carafe with wine, unable to look away from him. The sun had already kissed his face and heavily muscled forearms. She wondered if the rest of him was as well defined and delicious-looking.

Duke's eyes widened seconds before she felt wine spill over the top of the carafe.

"Shit," she said sharply.

Chris swooped in and wiped it up with a chuckle. "Someone's taken with our handsome investor."

"*Tsk.* No, I'm not." She grabbed the tray and stepped around the bar before her uncle could read the lie in her eyes. Duke took the tray from her hands, carrying it single-handed, while his other hand found its new home on her lower back.

God, that felt good. He felt good, with heat rolling off of him as they walked toward the door to the patio.

"You okay?" he asked quietly as they headed outside.

Not even close.

"Sure," she managed. "I was just thinking of a hundred things in there." *Like how when I look in your eyes I see so much more than a stuffed shirt.*

Out on the patio, Duke set the tray on the table and pulled out Gabriella's chair for her.

"You look really beautiful today. That might not be appropriate for me to say to my tour guide, but…"

Holy cow. He was doing it again, looking at her like she was the only person around, when there had to be at least twenty other people on the noisy patio.

"Thank you." She studied him with interest as he settled

into the seat across from her and filled their wineglasses. For a moment his eyes swept over the street and the people walking by, and then that calm focus returned and settled solely on her.

His lips curved up as he lifted his glass.

She swallowed a sigh. *That smile.*

He held up his wineglass. "To being present."

As their glasses touched, electricity sparked up her arm, and she swore the temperature rose about a hundred degrees.

CHAPTER FOUR

EVERY SIP OF wine Gabriella took left her lips shiny and wet, and when her tongue swept across her lips, she got the most seductive look in her eyes. Duke could watch her all night long. Or, even better, he'd like to kiss her, taste her, *feel* what was really going on beneath that tour hostess facade. But as Mr. Liakos's granddaughter, Gabriella was off-limits, at least until the deal was done.

Niko came through the doors from the restaurant and set another plate of food on their table.

"Gemista!" Niko pronounced the dish *yemista*. The colorful dish boasted stuffed eggplants, tomatoes, and peppers. It was overflowing with rice, small pieces of meat, and vegetables and garnished with cut-up potatoes and an orange-red-colored sauce. The tops of the peppers and tomatoes rested on the stuffing like colorful crowns.

"You spoil us, Niko," Gabriella said, smiling up at her brother with adoration in her eyes.

"I don't know how we can possibly eat all of this," Duke said. Niko had already brought them plates of grilled meats, vegetables, French fries, as well as large bowls of soup.

"I'll help you." A dark-haired man who looked to be in his late twenties leaned down and kissed Gabriella's cheek. Then he sat at the table and grinned like a Cheshire cat at Duke.

Gabriella shook her head. "Duke, this is Dimitri, my younger brother. He's also Niko's business partner."

Duke extended a hand in greeting. "Nice to meet you. The food is delicious."

Niko said something in Greek before returning to the restaurant, and Dimitri laughed. Duke had already met several of the locals, as they stopped by the table to chat with Gabriella.

"So, you're the potential investor?" Dimitri said. "What do you think?" He loaded up a plate with food, then took a sip of Gabriella's wine.

He reminded Duke of his brother Jake. Young and brazen, with a smile that softened his approach.

"I'm impressed, actually." Duke couldn't help watching Gabriella sipping her wine. Aaaaand…there was the tug in his gut and the awareness beneath his zipper. "The island is far more interesting than I had thought it would be."

As Dimitri's eyes ran between Duke and Gabriella, a shout came from the other side of the patio, where two men and a woman were heading toward the table. They all turned, and Dimitri waved them over.

"My uncles and aunt," Gabriella said.

Duke opened his mouth to respond as the three of them arrived at the table, and suddenly there was a flourish of hugs and loud conversations in both Greek and English, as another group of people joined them. And seconds later, a family with three young children was talking with them, too. Duke was lost in introductions, watching the mayhem and enjoying every second of it. The friendly visitors pulled chairs up to the table, and for the next hour or so, Niko continued to bring out dish after dish. They emptied one wine bottle after another, all while the kids ran around playing on the patio. Even the friends and relatives who were clearly not Greek spoke Greek, and learning the language climbed even higher on his priority list. He didn't want to miss a second of what was being said, because Gabriella had already blushed about a dozen times, and each time she'd sneak a peek at Duke.

He loved watching her with her friends and relatives. She was so easy to be with, so sweet and confident, and her love for her family was evident in everything she said and did.

By the time they left, they'd been plied with enough food and wine for a week. Everyone hugged Duke, just as they hugged Gabriella, and he'd been invited to the birthday celebration so many times he'd lost count. It was no wonder Gabriella loved the island and the people so much.

It was nearing ten o'clock, and the moon cast a romantic glow over the island. With no hotels and no casinos breaking the night sky, the scents of the sea mingling with the aroma of the tavern had Duke feeling like he was on a Mediterranean island, rather than a hop, skip, and a jump from South Carolina.

"This is my favorite time of night," Gabriella said with a sigh. "When the sun's just set and the air cools and the night sounds of the island come out to play."

He'd like to *play* with her. Duke had learned so much about Gabriella over the course of the day, and it made him want to know more. She'd clearly tried to wear him out, but she had no idea who she was dealing with. Duke didn't get worn out.

When they reached the golf cart, he held out his hand for the keys. She stared at his hand as if she didn't understand the gesture. He guessed she wouldn't, since it appeared that they didn't drive much around the island. He curled a finger beneath her chin and lifted her face, searching her gorgeous eyes. His heart stuttered as the moonlight danced off her eyes. Up close he could see she wasn't wearing any makeup. Her long, thick lashes were all her own. Everything about her was natural and comfortable, unlike the women he was used to in the city. Her dress was pretty and simple, and her sandals were covered in dust from their afternoon walk, as were his shoes and the hem of his slacks, but she didn't seem to care.

"I would like to explore your thoughts on this glorious evening," he said. "But you drank as much as I did, and I've got about a hundred pounds on you. I'm thinking it's not safe for you to drive."

"Is this that big brother thing again?" she asked with a hint of flirtation in her eyes.

He stepped closer, unable to resist placing a hand on her hip, and shook his head. How could he tell her that his thoughts were anything but brotherly toward her? Her hip filled his large palm in the most delicious way. He should move away before the heat working its way through his core became noticeable, but he was powerless to resist tightening his hold on her.

"Something like that," he answered, reminding himself that he was on the island for business, not to pick up the most beautiful woman here.

She looked down at his hand as he reluctantly dropped it to his side.

"The key is in the ignition," she said as she met his gaze again. "No crime. It's better here, remember?"

"I doubt I'll ever forget." He glanced in the cart and noticed the basket of bread and his suitcase. "Gabriella, shouldn't we deliver this to your *papou*?"

She gasped and grabbed his forearm. "Oh no, *Papou*! He's going to wonder what happened to me."

"We'll take it now," he reassured her. "I'll explain to him that it was my fault."

"You don't have to take the blame. It's my fault." She

gave his arm a quick squeeze. "But if you don't mind driving me there, I'd appreciate it."

Gabriella guided him through town and up a hilly road. "You remembered the Greek word for 'grandfather.'"

He didn't think before reaching over and squeezing her hand. "I doubt I'll forget anything you've said."

Their eyes held for a beat before he turned his attention back to the road, their hands still linked. His heartbeat quickened in a way it hadn't in years. He tried not to overthink what that might mean. He'd held hands with women before. Hell, he was no saint, but he found himself acutely aware of everything about Gabriella, including the way she was currently making an effort not to look at him. He'd never been as aware of, or as interested in, any other woman. He slid his hand from hers in an effort to give her space, but he didn't want space. Every second they spent together made him want more.

They rode in silence, save for the hum of the cart and the swishing of the trees. A few minutes later the road opened up, giving way to the resort grounds and the most spectacular view of the moon hovering over the ocean.

Duke had read so much about the resort that he had practically memorized the details. The stunning Mediterranean-style estate included seven smaller villas, of which he could see two off to the left. He knew the others were more secluded, accessible only by footpath.

"Your grandfather lives in the resort?" That was something he didn't expect.

"No. You need to make that hard right up that road there." She pointed to a dark gap in the trees.

Duke turned the cart, and the lights illuminated another narrow dirt road. They followed it around a bend, and a small villa came into view, much like the others he'd seen. He parked in front, and Gabriella stepped from the cart and reached for the basket.

She smoothed her dress. Her eyes traveled swiftly, and nervously, down Duke's body. They'd done nothing more than spend an afternoon walking around and had shared a meal, but hell if he wasn't attracted to everything about her. He'd already jumped ahead in his mind to their first kiss good night, how sweet she'd taste, and where it might lead. The worried look in her eyes coupled with the heat rolling off her body brought him back to the numerous comments and looks she'd been given by relatives, which were clearly meant to nudge them together.

They didn't need any nudging. In her gaze he saw the sobering effects the hand-holding had had on her. She clearly worried that her grandfather might read her desires as easily as he just had. His brain shifted into gear. Gabriella was the granddaughter of the man he was going to be negotiating with. That was messy and complicated. He needed to get a grip on his desires.

"It's late," he said. "I don't want to disturb your grandfather. You go ahead, and I'll wait for you here."

"Thank you." Relief flooded her eyes.

As she pushed open the door and called out, "*Papou*," in a tender voice that spoke of her love for her grandfather, Duke knew he'd done the right thing. He was there on the island for only a few days, and obviously the residents were a nosy crew. The last thing he wanted was to put Gabriella in an uncomfortable position.

When the door closed, he paced the yard, trying to regain control of his emotions. Duke lived his life weighing the risks and benefits of investments and of his actions. As he tried to regain control of the heat stoking him from the inside out, he tried to convince himself that the risk of losing the investment wasn't worth the reward of being with Gabriella. Never before had his mind and body called him on his bullshit louder or more clearly than they were right then. He was hard as steel, and his mind was drenched in thoughts of Gabriella.

A shadow passed by the window, catching Duke's attention. Gabriella came into focus as she approached an old man sitting in a leather chair. She set the basket on a coffee table and knelt by his side. Placing her hand on his arm, she kissed his cheek. He had a bushy gray mustache, with hair to match. Duke couldn't make out his other features, but that was enough to recognize him from the photographs he'd seen. When he covered Gabriella's hand with his own, Duke could feel the love between them. He had the strangest desire to be with her in the room, to meet her grandfather and be introduced as part of her life, rather than as an investor. It was rare to witness the open affection that Gabriella and her family doled out so effortlessly, and it reminded him of his family.

She laughed, and her gaze turned to the window. His pulse quickened, and he told himself that she couldn't see his face in the dark, but somehow he knew she didn't need to. Even as he tried to convince himself that he needed to back away, to end the night without so much as a taste of her lips, the rush of emotions soaring through him were too big, too raw, to deny.

THEY DROVE BACK toward the resort in silence. Gabriella was lost in thought. Her grandfather had been happy to see her, but he'd seemed as distracted as Gabriella felt. She hadn't realized just how deeply Duke had gotten under her skin until she caught sight of him standing outside the window of her grandfather's den. It had been too dark to make out his features, but she'd felt his gaze boring through her. His silhouette emphasized his squared shoulders, slim waist, and powerful legs, displaying his confident attitude and somehow just as clearly conveying an air of studied relaxation. The energy between them had shifted from friendly to sizzling, and it was those sparks that had her thinking...*wondering*...if she should allow herself to discover what else she might like about him.

When they arrived at the resort, she directed Duke to the covered parking area around back. It was dark, save for the moonlight streaking over the inky water. The sounds of the ocean mingled with the piercing chirping of crickets and the distant cries of tree frogs and other insects. These were the sounds that usually calmed her, but sitting with Duke, Gabriella was aware of more than the sounds of nature. The energy vibrating between them heightened the internal symphony of blood rushing in her ears, accompanying the thundering of her heart.

"We'll leave the cart here," she said, in an effort to distract herself from her desires. "I'll show you to your villa."

Duke covered her hand with his before she could step from the cart. When he'd held her hand earlier, it had taken all her focus not to pay attention to the wanton thoughts he stirred in her. Now, in the darkness of the night, with the end of their time together nearing, she didn't want to fight the heat simmering inside her.

"Why don't you give me directions? I'm sure I can find it on my own."

It had been a really long time since she'd been with a man, but was she *that* out of practice? Had he not been flirting with her over dinner? Treating her like she was the only person he saw, listening to every word she'd said? Was his hand on her back really just a habit? She'd thought it was at first, but then, as the afternoon had worn on, hadn't she felt the press of his fingers a little more firmly? When he'd touched her hip, hadn't he gripped it tightly, like a man who wanted more?

He gently squeezed her hand, bringing her focus back to the moment.

"Gabriella."

Her name rolled from his tongue laden with desire. She hadn't misread his signals after all. The darkening of his eyes and the tension rolling off of him were confirmation that he was fighting the same internal battle she was. She didn't know exactly what she wanted from him, but she knew she wasn't ready to say goodbye.

He brought her hand to his lips and pressed a kiss to it. "Let me get you home safely, and then I'll find my way."

Her pulse raced at the idea of him taking her home, then sank at the thought of him leaving and finding his own way to his villa. Not that she was ready to jump into bed with him. Was she? Her mind raced in directions she hadn't anticipated.

He brushed his thumb lightly over her knuckle, sending a shiver of heat up her arm and forcing her lungs to work. "My villa is down that path."

He seemed to mull that over for a minute, nodding slightly before releasing her hand and holding up the keys. She instantly missed his touch.

"Do you take these with you tonight?" he asked. "Or leave them here?"

"The key to your villa is the blue one. If you take that off, you can leave the other here."

He separated the keys and slid the blue key into his pocket, then set the other key on the dashboard.

"I guess there's no place for thieves to hide on the island," he said as he stepped from the cart and retrieved his jacket and luggage.

They made their way along the narrow footpath. Gabriella longed for his hand on her lower back, but he was carrying his suitcase and jacket, and he had to follow a step or two behind her. Tall trees blocked the moonlight, and plants buffered them from the sounds of the sea, amplifying the cacophony of the forest.

"Do you ever get frightened staying out here alone?" His mouth was so close to her ear, when she slowed to listen, he bumped into her back. His hand landed on her waist as she turned to tell him she was sorry. Their bodies aligned, his hand searing her skin right through the thin fabric of her dress.

"Sorry," he said in a low voice. "I shouldn't follow so closely."

It took all of her focus not go up on her toes and kiss him. Just one blessed kiss. One taste.

She must be losing her mind. She wanted to make out with a guy she'd known less than a day. An incredibly handsome, charming gentleman who wanted a family of his own and smelled of musk and something spicy and hot and who was more masculine than any man she'd ever known. A man who was looking at her like he wanted to devour her—and was taking a step backward.

His hand slipped from her waist. "Sorry, Gabriella. I'll try to keep my distance."

"Why?" The word came without thought, and she pressed her lips together to keep from saying anything more. Embarrassed, she turned and walked quickly down the path, hoping he hadn't heard her. A minute later, she sighed with release. If he'd heard her, at least he wasn't calling her on it.

When they reached the end of the secluded path, her villa came into view.

"That's my villa." She turned, and he was right there again, towering over her, smelling like sinful seduction and making her knees weak without saying a word.

"And mine?"

His voice was tense with restraint, and it took her a moment to realize what he was asking.

"I'll walk you to yours." She took a step, and he gently wrapped his hand around her upper arm and drew her back, close enough that she could smell the wine on his breath.

"I said I'll get you home safely and then find my own way."

His tone was possessive, his gaze penetrating, as if he could see right through her efforts to hide the lust coiling deep inside her. He ran his hand gently up the length of her arm and brushed his thumb over her heated skin.

"Your...your villa is over there." She pointed up a path that led up a hill. "In daylight you can see it from here."

"I'm sure I can find it." He picked up his suitcase and then placed his hand on her back as they crossed the grass toward her villa.

She stepped beneath the trellis over the front door, reveling in his touch, memorizing the feel of it as she fought the urge to throw caution to the wind, turn around, and kiss him.

"Do you have your key?" he asked, breaking her from her fantasy.

She wondered where he thought she'd keep a key in her dress with no pockets. She turned, and *Lord have mercy*, he'd done it again. Her hands landed on his firm abs. She swallowed a noise that threatened to give her desires away.

"No key," she answered.

"Right. Because it's *better* here." He glanced at the door. "I know you feel safe, but I've never been here before, and leaving you to enter a home that has been unlocked all day feels wrong. Would you mind if I come in long enough to make sure there aren't any creepers waiting for you?"

Would she mind? She didn't have time to process the many ways she most definitely wouldn't mind him checking out her house, her bed, before he added, "I promise to behave," stopping her fantasies cold.

"Sure," she said.

He walked inside, and she closed her eyes for a split second to remember *why* she shouldn't want to kiss him. If she didn't want him to buy the island, why was she even considering kissing him? There were so many things wrong with her desires right now that she couldn't think straight.

He flicked on the lights and walked through the foyer of her cozy villa. His formidable presence made the villa feel much smaller. His eyes rolled over the stone floors, sofa, coffee table, and corner fireplace. She wondered what he was thinking as he turned and took in the bar dividing the kitchen from the living room, where her legal case files were stacked in a neat pile beside her laptop.

"This is lovely," he said. "Do you mind checking your bedroom for me? I don't want you to feel uncomfortable with me poking through your things. Check the closets, and I'll be right here."

"Sure." Her vocabulary had suddenly diminished. He was gentlemanly enough not to check her bedroom? Wow, she should be ashamed of the images she had running through her mind, of him trapping her beneath him in the bedroom and keeping her up all night as he made passionate lo—

"Everything okay?" He was leaning on the doorframe, his feet crossed at the ankle, looking devastatingly handsome. His body filled the doorway, and her mind jumped back to his body filling *her*.

"Uh, yeah," she said nervously. "No creepers."

"Can't ask for more than that."

Obviously he didn't realize how long it had been since she'd kissed a man. She could ask for a hell of a lot more than that.

"Thank you again for taking your whole day to show me around," he said as she walked him out front again.

"It was nothing."

"It was a whole hell of a lot of something." He cupped her face and stroked his thumb over her cheek. "You are truly a beautiful woman, Gabriella."

Her fingers curled with the need to touch him.

"I know you don't want anyone to buy this island," he said as his eyes drifted over hers, to her mouth, lingering there before meeting her gaze again. "I also know that you're smart enough to understand what will happen if someone doesn't step in to help. I'd like to be that person, so maybe tomorrow if you have time before or after picking up Vivi and working at the welcome center, you can show me the most important parts of the island that you want to preserve."

"Tomorrow's Saturday. There's no school, so I don't have to pick up Vivi." She tried to focus on what he'd said about showing him around, but her mind clung to one thought, and it wasn't the one she would have liked. "So, you're definitely interested in the island?"

She'd known it would eventually come down to selling, hadn't she?

"Yes, very much so. Why else would I want to keep my distance from you?"

Why else? Her head spun. "You heard that, huh?"

He leaned in closer, and she thought he might kiss her. She licked her lips, readying for it, wanting it.

"I heard everything you said." His breath ghosted over her lips. "And everything you didn't say."

Gabriella had never been spoken to with innuendos like that before. He had noticed her, *all* of her. She swallowed hard.

"I have to keep my distance," he explained with a wanting look in his eyes, "because every time you're near, I want to kiss you. And I have a feeling that one taste of you would never be enough."

His words slithered inside her, burning a path south. If he had that power with only words, what would it be like if he ever kissed her? Touched her?

As he disappeared into the night she played his words over and over in her mind, knowing he was right. Acting on such an attraction would be perilous for both of them. She fell into bed, hot and bothered and in need of release, fighting the urge to recall his face, to recall the deep seduction of his words. But when she closed her eyes, there was only him. His scent had seeped into her senses. It was his hands slipping beneath her panties, his voice whispering in her ear, his fingers giving her pleasure as she gave into her desperation and spiraled, blissfully, into oblivion.

CHAPTER FIVE

AFTER A FITFUL night's sleep, where Gabriella starred in every dream, every fantasy, every wakeful thought, Duke called Pierce and filled him in on the details of yesterday's tour, hoping that might keep him from thinking of Gabriella every single second.

"Entrenched doesn't begin to describe the families here." His mind turned to his time with Gabriella yesterday, their walk, their talks, dinner with her family and friends. "They're practically sprouting roots from the sand, but I think we can work with them." Duke had never met a business owner he didn't like. He might not like their attitudes, or what it was they were selling, but when it came to people, Duke looked deeper than what people wanted him to see. Most people wore their insecurities on their sleeves despite trying so desperately not to. Gabriella's emotions were present in everything she did, everything she said—and more loudly, everything she kept trapped inside.

"It's clear that the residents are either older families who put down roots generations ago, or younger generations of the Liakos family. There's almost no one between eighteen and thirty left on the island. When the economy tanked, the younger residents fled. Of the ones who are still here, if they aren't part of the Liakos family, then they're leftovers who were too set in their ways to move off the island when hard times hit."

"And Mr. Liakos? When are you meeting with him and feeling him out on his intent to sell?" Pierce asked.

"I'm on my way in to meet with him now. I met his granddaughter Gabriella yesterday, and she does not want to sell."

Pierce laughed. "That's never stopped us before. You'll find a way to ease her into it."

"Easing her into the sale is the least of my problems. She's smart. She knows they need help." *And I want her so badly I can't see straight.* He'd gone down to the beach for a run this morning just to keep from watching her villa in hopes of seeing her.

"But?" Pierce asked. When Duke didn't respond, he said, "Duke, clue me in, buddy. Otherwise I'm going to jump to a conclusion here about you and the granddaughter of the man we're trying to make a deal with."

Duke ran his hand through his hair and looked out over the Atlantic. He tried to quell the smile that tugged at his lips, but he was a terrible liar—even to himself.

"You wouldn't have to jump far. But I didn't…I'm not

going there."

"You don't sound very confident about that, and *that* doesn't sound like you. You never cross the line between business and pleasure."

"Nope." Duke was just as baffled by his desires as Pierce was. Never in all the years he'd been investing had he crossed those lines. "I'm not sure why the line's gone blurry, but I didn't act on it, and it's not like I don't know the risks of getting involved with her. I'll keep it together."

"Uh-huh. Maybe you should let me handle this one."

"Don't be silly. You've got a wedding to plan, and I can handle this." Or at least he'd try. What he wasn't telling Pierce was that their previous plan of bulldozing the existing structures and creating a consistent Southern feel for the resort had already begun to change. The mix of cultures here was unique. He could see that being part of the allure of the island, and after getting to know Gabriella and learning how much she truly loved everything about the island, he couldn't fathom the idea of tearing it all down. But he didn't have the solution, or even know if it was possible to change directions and still get a solid return on their investment. So he kept those thoughts to himself.

"Listen, I'll do my best. Anything new you want me to bring up with Mr. Liakos?"

After they discussed their strategy and ended the call, Duke headed into the resort for his meeting.

"Y'all set, Mr. Ryder?" Dreama Beaumont greeted him when he arrived at the resort. She was a sweet, stout woman with thick blond hair and a friendly demeanor. She had offered Duke coffee earlier when he'd been sitting on the patio, and now she stood before him with a welcoming smile, ready to take him to meet Mr. Liakos.

"Yes, thank you."

"Mr. Liakos is eager to meet with you," she said as she led him into an office with a large conference table and windows overlooking the water. "Can I get you some more coffee or sweet tea?"

"No, thank you. I'm fine."

Before she could close the door all the way behind her, it pushed open again and Mr. Liakos walked in, holding a cane in one hand. His receding hairline was surrounded by thick tufts of silver hair that looked finger-brushed. The silver made his bushy dark brows seem even darker, and the combination made his eyes appear squinty far beyond the deep crow's-feet fanning out from them. His silver mustache was full, curling over his upper lip and curving up at the ends. His shirt was unbuttoned nearly to the center of his chest, exposing silver curls of chest hair and sun-drenched, wrinkled skin.

Duke offered a hand in greeting. "Thank you for taking the time to meet with me today."

The old man looked at Duke's hand and smiled before

shaking it. Still holding his hand, Mr. Liakos leaned in and embraced Duke. "In my family, we greet as if you are part of our family." He spoke English, though the accent of his ancestors couldn't be missed.

Duke laughed. "What if you don't like the person you're greeting?"

The old man motioned for Duke to sit. "What makes you think we like all our family members? We are either loving, yelling, or eating. Love? Like? Dislike? It's all the same." He set his cane beside him and relaxed into the leather chair, folding his hands over his slightly rounded belly. For a moment he nodded silently, as if answering a question or, Duke thought, assessing Duke just as Gabriella had.

"You met my sweet Gabrielaki, yes?"

"Yes, sir." *And sweet she is.* "May I ask about the way you said her name? I'm trying to learn about the culture of the island and its residents, and of course learning the Greek language is part of that. I'm working on my Southern-speak as well. I've got y'all down pretty well."

Those bushy brows lifted in surprise. "You're interested in learning about the culture of the island?"

"Yes, of course. Gabriella introduced me to a number of the residents. My intent is not to wipe out the very roots that sustained the area for all these years."

"I see. I like your philosophy, Duke." He leaned forward, and his voice turned serious. "You asked about my granddaughter's name. My people are all about love. The use of diminutives is one form of love. We add *aki* or *mou*. *Gabrielaki mou*, or *my little Gabriella*. *Gabriella* is not a traditional Greek name, but we are not in Greece, are we?"

He went on to explain the variations of nicknames and how the Greek and Southern families had blended together, each learning the ways of the other, over the decades. An hour later they were laughing over hypothetical names his children might have had, had they been named for their personalities.

"Mr. Liakos—"

"Niko, please."

"Niko, thank you." Duke recalled Gabriella's father and brother's names and realized there were three *Nikos* in the Liakos family. He wondered how the family kept them straight. "What is your vision for the island? Your goal for this sale?"

The old man sat back with a heavy sigh. "My vision—" He gazed out the window for a full minute or more, as if he were scrolling through memories like movies playing out before him. "What I want is to keep my family whole and provided for. I'm an old man. I have lived my dream." He shrugged, and his gaze turned thoughtful. "The island, what we once hoped for, what we worked toward, and what we had for a very long time, was my ancestors' dream. It's time for a new dream, Duke. Surely you know this."

As an investor, Duke's business was all about new visions and new dreams, but ever since Gabriella mentioned that she'd left the island to honor her grandfather's wishes, he'd wondered if there was more to the move than she'd let on. Now he could see that her grandfather would do anything to ensure his family was well cared for, including selling off their legacy.

"What if I come back with an offer you can't refuse and then bulldoze everything and build a factory?" Niko was acting as if he'd take a monetary offer to secure his family's stability, but Duke could tell that that wasn't the case. If it were, he would have had a real estate attorney handling the tour, and this meeting would not be taking place without his legal advisers present.

"Then I have misjudged your character." Niko sat back and folded his hands over his stomach. "We have a unique island. The old ways of the Greek have combined with the ways of the South. And now it's time to interject bigger visions in order for the families who have made this island what it is to be able to remain here. It's time for a change." He paused, then lifted his hands and said, "What is that change? I don't know. But I think you do."

By the time Duke left, he'd been given a history lesson on the immigration of the Liakos family and extended yet another invitation to the upcoming birthday celebration for Katarina's father.

THE AROMA OF casseroles cooking, lamb grilling, and the unique scents of the people Gabriella loved most blended together in the most comforting way. Gabriella worked side by side with her mother, cousins, aunts, and uncles in the kitchen of what they called the *big house* by the lighthouse while children darted in and out of the open patio doors. The big house was a large villa overlooking the ocean. It was where they held all of their celebrations.

The excited tenors of the women's voices filled the air as they prepared for the evening's festivities. While slicing colorful red, orange, yellow, and green peppers, Gabriella watched her mother's capable hands cutting, chopping, and layering foods in an enormous casserole dish, as she'd done Gabriella's whole life. Her brown hair had a few strands of gray, and she wore it pinned back in a ponytail. She moved more like a thirty-year-old than a woman in her late fifties, all energetic gumption and warmth. Gabriella had always thought her mother was pretty, and as she took in the various shapes and sizes of her relatives and friends, she saw unique beauty in each of them.

Her aunt Alexandra was tall, with wavy dark hair and an inquisitive nature. She stole glances at Gabriella while she sprinkled cheese over the dish she was making.

Gabriella had taken more care dressing today, hoping she

and Duke would meet up at some point since they hadn't made any firm plans. She had a feeling that was the cause of the glances her aunt and a few of the others had been sneaking at her all morning. Her great-great-grandmother on her father's side had had seven children and twenty-two grandchildren, each of whom had between three and six children of their own. And her mother's side of the family was just as large. Needless to say, there were more celebratory gatherings than not on the island, and she missed it, she missed this—the coming together of generations for something as simple as preparing meals for the people they loved. The ache of missing these connections, creating these memories, balled together and stuck in her throat.

"Vivi said the investor's sister is an actress," Alexandra said to her sister Eleni. This caused all the women to gasp and discuss how exciting her life must be.

"I wonder if she knows Brad Pitt," her cousin Salina said with wide eyes.

"Or Matthew McConaughey. His Texas accent is so yummy," Katarina added.

Eleni held her hands up, silencing the others. "I wonder if she knows Giannis Anastasakis!"

Gabriella laughed. Giannis Anastasakis was John Aniston, an incredibly handsome Greek actor best known for his patriarch role of Victor Kiriakis in *Days of Our Lives*. Younger generations simply knew him as Jennifer Aniston's father, but to Gabriella he would always be her very first crush.

"Why do you laugh, Gabrielaki?" her aunt Loy asked.

"I remember all of you watching that show while you cooked and swooning over him. You made me adore him."

"My little princess had a crush on an older man," her mother said with a wink. Her mother's sweet Southern charm softened the boisterousness of the others.

Her aunt Loulou glanced up from where she was chopping mushrooms and said, "And now our little Ella has a crush on another man."

Gabriella's heart skipped a beat at how easily Loulou had read her thoughts. As the other women reeled off a string of hopes, their hugs swallowed her embarrassment whole, leaving only warmth and love. Endearments fell like drops of rain from their quick tongues—*Ella, Gabrielaki, Lala.* Her family never agreed on just one nickname, but they agreed on one thing—she *needed* a husband.

She felt a heavy arm fall over her shoulder seconds before Dimitri whispered against her cheek, "Come help me cook outside. I'll save you."

Their mother shook her head. "Dimitri, you would do well to find yourself a wife, too."

Dimitri held his hands up in surrender and backed away. He was twenty-seven years old, which meant their older relatives saw him as prime husband material.

"Oh, no, you don't." Gabriella pulled him back to the

table. "You'd leave me out to dry?"

She followed Dimitri's gaze to the entrance from the porch, where Duke stood in a pair of jeans and a black polo shirt, his dark eyes piercing the distance between them.

"Am I interrupting?" Duke asked as he stepped inside.

Gabriella was vaguely aware of her aunts swarming him, drawing him into the room, fussing over him in the way only they would. Touching his arms, his collar, kissing his cheeks so many times he had a dozen shades of lipstick on them in seconds, all while doling out compliments and questions in equal measure. But their commotion paled in comparison to the rampant beating of Gabriella's heart at the invitation in his steady, smoldering gaze.

"DON'T BE SILLY. Come, come," Gabriella's mother said as they ushered Duke into the room.

"Thank you." Duke had waited to seek out Gabriella until he'd convinced himself that he could control his desire to be closer to her. He'd even managed to convince himself that his attraction to her was fleeting, born from opportunity rather than something more meaningful, a deeper connection. She stood before him now, the careful strain of composure written in her squared shoulders and the slight lift of her chin. As he stepped closer, drawn to her like metal to magnet, the mixture of surprise and desire in her warm dark eyes was unmistakable.

He'd been a fool to tell Pierce he could handle the sparks flying between them, especially with the way his heart turned over in his chest at the mere sight of her. This was not an attraction of convenience. Nor was it fleeting. This was a type of connection he'd never experienced before. The risk manager in him searched for a plausible explanation, but the man in him knew it would come up empty, because a connection like this could only come from a well too deep to reveal.

"Hi," she said with a hint of question in her voice—a far cry from the in-control woman he'd met yesterday.

He liked this softer, more feminine side of her, which seemed to be having just as much trouble understanding the energy drawing them together as he was. Did that mean she'd thought about him last night the way he'd thought about her? Did she feel the intensity of this unspoken thing between them as powerfully as he did?

"I hope you don't mind, but I thought you might show me around." He was vaguely aware of the hushed whispers and conversations taking place around them.

Gabriella's eyes darted to the table, where she had obviously been preparing food. He glanced at the stove, the tables, the counters. Every surface was covered with dishes, cutlery, and food midpreparation, and he realized how inappropriate his suggestion was.

"I'm sorry. I didn't realize you were busy with your family. I shouldn't have assumed—"

Suddenly the women's hands were on his arms again, pushing him toward Gabriella. The women here gave a new meaning to *space invaders*. They all spoke at once, and it was all he could do to smile and nod.

"Oh, honey. Go, have fun. We can manage the rest of this," her mother insisted.

A woman with frizzy blond hair ushered Gabriella a step forward. "Go. Take her. Take Ella. See the island." She motioned to the other women, who pressed in closer with more words of encouragement.

"Yes, go. Show him the orchard, darlin'. Go on, now, y'all," a plump brunette said as she nudged Gabriella closer to him.

Another blond touched his cheek and said, "Have Lala show you the cliff."

Duke enjoyed hearing their endearments. Gabriella laughed softly. The sweet sound brought his hand up, reaching for hers.

"The beach, Gabrielaki," a petite blonde said. "Go for a swim."

As Gabriella laid her fingertips in his, a rosy blush quickly spread over her high cheekbones. "I guess I'm showing you the rest of the island today."

"Go on, now," her mother urged. "Y'all get out of here and go have some fun."

The women ushered them out of the house.

"Thank you," Duke said to the women. As they walked outside, he wasn't surprised to see the men who had been gathered around the spit when he'd arrived watching them with interest.

He waved. "How's it going?"

Half a dozen of them answered at once, but the approval in their eyes told Duke he wasn't about to get the typical overprotective treatment his sister's dates endured when he and his brothers were around. He enjoyed seeing how much Gabriella's family adored her, but he breathed a little easier knowing he'd soon have her all to himself.

A heavy hand landed on his shoulder, and he turned to Dimitri, who wore the same amused expression Duke had seen on their father the day he'd arrived on the island.

"They all want to marry her off. I just want her to have some fun." Dimitri squeezed Duke's shoulder. "Not too much fun." He winked.

"Dimitri!" Gabriella rolled her eyes.

"I'll keep your guidelines in mind," Duke assured him.

Gabriella kissed her brother's cheek before saying something in Greek that made everyone—except Duke—laugh.

He *really* needed to learn the language.

CHAPTER SIX

AS DUKE AND Gabriella walked away from the big house, he reminded himself to view the island through professional eyes and not through the eyes of a guy who was taken with a beautiful woman. But the harder he tried, the more difficult it became. After a few minutes of walking with him hand in hand, Gabriella slid her hand from his.

"What exactly did you have in mind?" she asked as they came to the end of the dirt road. "Do you want to see the areas with historical significance? The community gardens, the—"

Just like that she'd switched into tour-guide mode. How could it possibly be that easy for her, when he was struggling to keep from taking her in his arms and kissing her?

"Gabriella." He waited until she looked at him, and the desire swimming in her eyes brought him closer. He touched her cheek, and she blinked up at him from beneath her long lashes. It took all his strength not to lean down and press his lips to hers. But when he dropped his gaze to her luscious lips, they pressed into a firm line, and he knew she was struggling just as he was. Tour-guide mode was her safety net.

"I know all about the historical sites on the island. As I said last night, I want to see the places that mean the most to you, that you'd like to see remain intact if we move forward with this investment." He searched her eyes as her lips curved up and that sexy blush rose on her cheeks again.

She nodded and dropped her eyes for a moment before meeting his gaze again with more confidence in hers. "I'm sorry about everyone being so pushy."

"Don't be. It's such a great feeling to see all those people caring so much for you. My family is really close, and I often wondered if I'd ever meet someone who would feel the importance of family on the same level that I do." He glanced back the way they'd come. "It's obvious that the people who live here feel that way, too."

He threw caution to the wind and reached for her hand. "I can see that you do, too."

"Duke…" She slipped her hand from his grip again, pitching his gut into a nose dive. "I've been thinking about what you said last night, and you were right. Giving in to whatever is going on between us could lead to trouble. I think we should keep things professional."

Duke fought against his baser instincts, which were to take her in his arms and kiss her until she came to her senses. But he knew he was the one in the wrong, letting his emotions get the best of him. He'd been the one to draw the line in the sand last night, but hell if that line hadn't blurred with every look, every stroke of his hand on hers, every single smile she shared.

He forced himself to do the right thing. "You're right. I'm sorry." He slid his hands in his pockets to contain the urge to reach for her. "I'd still like to see the places that are important to you, if you don't mind." He scrambled for a reason other than the truth—that he wanted to know everything about her—and came up empty.

"Okay, sure." Her voice cracked a little.

As they walked across the road toward the beach, Gabriella stood up taller, schooled her expression, and lifted her chin. She'd done that a few times now, and Duke recognized her actions for what they were. He knew all about the invisible walls people hid behind in order to keep from being hurt or becoming the object of ridicule. Or any number of other reasons they felt the need to hide. Duke had never bought into the idea of hiding. He knew his strengths and his weaknesses, and he faced challenges head-on. And as far as being hurt went, well, he'd never do a thing to hurt Gabriella, and he'd rather open himself up to being hurt by her than not have a chance to see what might come of their attraction.

He'd spent a lot of time thinking about Gabriella over the last twenty-four hours, and about more than just how sexy, sweet, and smart she was. Her family loved her *so much* they'd sent her away so she'd have a chance to build a better life.

Duke had left home on his own, thrilled to go to college and get out into the real world. He wondered how he would have felt if he hadn't wanted to leave but was forced to. He sensed she wore those scars just beneath the surface, and he had a burning desire to be the man she shared those feelings with.

"Let's go to the shore first," Gabriella said. "One of the best things about the island is that it *is* an island."

They left their shoes at the edge of the beach and walked along the warm sand to the water's edge. Gabriella closed her eyes and tilted her head up toward the clear blue sky. She looked radiant with the sun glistening against her olive skin and a gentle breeze blowing her pretty dress. Duke imagined her basking on this very beach as she was growing up, *being present.* He wished he would have known her as a curious, rebellious teenager and been there to watch her grow into the amazing woman she'd become. But what he really wished was that he could have been there for her when she was nudged off the island. The idea of her facing that sort of tough love without someone there to hold her on the other end of her family's good intentions pained him.

"Mother Nature's greatest gift to mankind," she said, looking at him with the most peaceful expression he'd ever seen, as if she'd just experienced a perfect moment.

Duke wished he could go back in time and share it with her. A moment later he realized that he was doing just that.

"Nothing beats the clear ocean water, sand between your

toes, and unpolluted air. Try to get *that* on the mainland."
She walked with her feet in the water.

"I can see how easy it is to be in the moment here." *To be
present.* Duke stepped beside her into ankle-deep water.
"Thanks for reminding me how nice moments like this are."

"It is nice, isn't it?" she said with a sigh.

"I'd be lying if I didn't say that being here with you
didn't make it even nicer." He caught himself reaching a
hand to her lower back and slid it into his pocket instead.
"Professionally speaking, of course."

She rolled her eyes. "Of course. So if you've done your
homework, then you know my ancestors came here with the
hopes of building a shipping company."

"I actually didn't research the reasons your family immigrated to the States, although your grandfather did fill me in
on some of that. My research went back to when the property
passed hands to your grandfather from your great-
grandfather. I found it interesting that the resort had been
passed to the eldest son of the previous owner rather than
portioning it out to each of the heirs. Isn't it typically
customary in the Greek culture to divvy up property among
each of the heirs?"

"Yes, that's customary." She stopped to look out over the
water. "We all own pieces of our ancestors' properties in
Greece, which have been passed down and portioned out for
generations. I think I own a fourth of a fifth of a plot of land

somewhere. I'm not sure why they didn't do that with the island."

"Let me guess. Land is love, too?" he teased.

"Actually, yes." She laughed and squinted up at him. "Love, love, love. From hugs to scolding."

"That's not so different from most families, though, is it?"

"I don't know many other families well enough to compare." She began walking again, and her tone turned thoughtful. "We seem to follow the guidance of our ancestors even long after they're gone, and I'm not sure that is typical in most families. So I guess you know the original intent was to have a Liakos shipping company here on the island."

Duke remained quiet as they walked out of the water and up the beach.

"Where there are ports, there are Greeks," Gabriella said as they slipped on their shoes and stepped from the beach onto the dirt road. "We're very industrious people, even though the failing economy here may make it appear as though we're not."

"I haven't met anyone here who doesn't appear to be industrious. The lack of tourism doesn't have anything to do with how hard the people here work. It has to do with what is offered to tourists. The lure, or appeal, to the masses."

She was quiet for a while. They walked down another road to a path in the woods. "I guess you're right about that," she eventually said. "Do you know why there is no Liakos shipping company here?"

He shook his head.

"I don't know all the specifics, because you know how stories get convoluted over time. But supposedly they brought in trucks and materials to build the shipping company, and one of my relatives—and I use that word loosely, because in my family, aunts and uncles aren't always related. Talk about having an identity crisis? Can you imagine sitting around every Easter with Uncle George, Uncle Mike, Uncle Niko, and a slew of other 'relatives'…" She met Duke's gaze. "The men would drink their beers, take turns rotating the lamb on the spit, like they do now, and tell stories. Well, that's how I learned that there was no blood bond between many of us. That little discovery gave me quite an identity crisis at twelve. I mean, what *is* family? What makes a family?"

"I think a family can be any group of people whom you've come to love," Duke said, thinking about Pierce and his siblings. He ducked beneath a branch and couldn't resist pressing his hand to the small of her back again. He craved the closeness and would take any connection she'd allow.

"Thankfully, I figured that out, but I digress." She laughed.

Duke was glad she didn't shrug off his touch, because he had a feeling she needed it for whatever was to come. Her voice was a little shaky.

"Back to the story of the shipping company, which is

also, by the way, the reason we have no paved roads, no cars." Her smile faded. "They brought in the trucks and equipment, and I guess one of my relatives was out in the late afternoon taking a walk through town and one of the workers was drunk and driving a truck…" She slowed her pace, and Duke could feel her breathing deeply.

They came to the edge of the woods and stepped into a beautiful meadow. Her eyes swept over the grass and flowers. "Legend has it that the elders who had purchased the property saw her death as an omen. They stopped all work and declared that there would be no cars on the island, and of course, no roads. Ever."

"That's a very sad story. I can only imagine the devastation your family must have felt after purchasing all this beautiful land, with hopes of a future that you could pass down for generations."

"I know, but the thing is," she said as she walked through the meadow toward a cemetery surrounded by an ornate iron fence. "I think the island is actually better this way. Not that I'm happy that someone lost her life. Of course I'm not. But can you imagine huge ships coming in at all hours? Or cars driving all over the island, with all that noise and exhaust?"

Yes, he could imagine, only in his vision they were ferries bringing tourists several times throughout the day and day cruises leaving from the island. The line between investor and man blurred, and Duke worked hard to keep his perspective as an investor.

They stood at the gate to the cemetery, looking out over the sea of headstones, many faded so badly the etchings were illegible. There were fresh flowers on a few of the graves, and Duke was suddenly struck with the powerful connections Gabriella and her family had to their ancestors. He thought of how little he knew about his distant relatives, how removed he felt from them. He could see by the serious look in Gabriella's eyes how much a part of her life the memories of those who came before her remained.

"When my grandfather first asked me to show you the island, I wasn't sure I could do it. I mean, honestly, you know I hate the idea of selling."

He knew, all right. It was evident in everything she said and did.

"This was the first place I came when I returned a few days before you arrived. I was hoping to get some sort of a vibe, you know? Like my ancestors would give me a sign about whether I should run you off the island or not."

"I guess I don't blame you, but I'm glad you didn't push me away too hard."

"Not for lack of trying. But…I *might* have wanted to ruin your suit and bore you with the simplicity of the life here and the small-town attitudes of the residents so that you high-tailed it back to the city."

He stepped in closer. "It's going to take a lot more than

that to make me run."

Heat flared in her eyes, telling him that she knew he wasn't talking about staying for the investment alone. Unable to deny himself the chance to catch all that heat, he stepped even closer as he asked, "And what did you feel, Gabriella, when you came up here that day?"

She licked her lips, and for a moment Duke thought she'd give in to the pulse of energy filling the space between them, drawing him closer, but she turned away, breaking their connection.

"Nostalgia, mostly," she said just above a whisper. "I thought I'd be here with them. Live and die right here on the island."

The longing in her voice made Duke want to gather her into his arms and hold her, tell her that she should move back to the island if this was where she was happiest. It made him want to forget he was there on business and put all his energy, all his emotions, into Gabriella. But she'd drawn the line in the sand, and he was trying—*oh, how he was trying*—to respect her need for distance. He was already wrestling with how to tell Pierce that he didn't want to keep fighting his feelings for her, no matter what it might mean for their investment.

"My mom and the other women from town bring flowers to the graves pretty often." Her change of subject didn't diminish the longing in her voice, but it did convey her slipping behind her walls again instead of talking more about her feelings about not living on the island.

"Your mom seems very sweet," he said. "I was surprised that she knew Greek so well."

"Can you imagine being a member of my family and not knowing Greek?"

She turned and stumbled. Duke caught her around the waist, and she laughed. He was falling for that sweet laugh of hers, and as he gazed into the simmering heat in her beautiful eyes, he knew he was falling for so much more than just her laugh.

Chapter Seven

GABRIELLA WAS SMOOTH as butter in court, going up against the wolves of New York City, but she had a tingling in the pit of her stomach just being near Duke, her pulse quickened with every look, and she felt anything *but* grounded. He was looking at her in that same way he had in the big house, like it didn't matter if she floated off the ground—which she just might around him—he'd be right there with her, following her up to cloud nine and bringing her back down to safety when she was ready.

"I'm sorry. I don't know why I'm such a klutz today." She took a step back, but his grip remained, searing through her flimsy dress. She gazed up at him and his eyes darkened. His lips were so close she could kiss them if she went up on her toes.

"I'm thinking about setting up obstacles along every path of our tour." His voice was thick with desire, making his words more of a promise than a tease.

Gabriella's chest warmed with the idea of falling into his arms again. *I'm supposed to be working with an investor, not falling for one.* She forced herself to step back, out of his arms, and try to pull herself together.

She didn't know how to respond, so instead she continued their walk and headed back into the woods. At least here she'd have more to distract her from her thoughts. But even as she tried to focus on the sounds of squirrels scurrying on the forest floor, she felt like she was scurrying, too. Scurrying closer to Duke with every minute they spent together and then pulling away once again.

She stepped over a log, and he touched her arm. It was nothing more than a gentle, steadying touch, but somehow it felt intensely intimate and filled the silence with more questions. *Should I let this happen? I want to let this happen. I can't let this happen. But oh, sweet baby Jesus, I want this to happen.*

"This reminds me of where I grew up." Duke's voice tore her from her thoughts. "My folks live on a few acres. My brothers used to spend hours in the woods."

"How many brothers do you have?" she asked, thankful for something else to concentrate on besides how his lips would feel on hers.

He reached over and brushed a leaf from her hair, and his gaze moved slowly from her eyes to her mouth, making her salivate for a taste of him. *Yes, kiss me. No, don't. Yes, please. Oh shit.* Her heart raced with anticipation of the kiss she shouldn't want. The kiss that could be her undoing—and lead to trouble for her family's negotiations. She couldn't remember a single time when she'd felt so drawn to a man, or so completely and utterly like she was any man's sole focus. Maybe it was the magic of the island, the peaceful afternoon, or being alone with Duke that was making her romanticize their time together. But as his gaze made its way back up to her eyes, warm and inviting, she had a feeling she could be anywhere with him and the thrum of desire would be just as overwhelming.

Her question forgotten, "You're not what I expected," slid from her lips. She had no idea where the confession came from. He wasn't full of pomp and circumstance, too busy to get to know the residents or get to know the island—or her. He was intelligent and careful, sweet and strong at once, and unhurried in their time together.

"I had no expectations," he said as he slid his strong arms around her and tugged her in close. "You are…" He searched her eyes, as if they held the words he was searching for. "A lovely surprise. One I might not be strong enough to resist."

She bit her lip to trap the sounds of want filling her lungs.

"We shouldn't…" Her whisper sounded weak, even to herself.

"You're right." He touched his forehead to hers. "Do you want me to let you go?"

No, no, no, no, no!

She opened her mouth to answer, and Duke lowered his face to hers, staring into her eyes with the hunger and urgency she wanted to feel inside her, around her, consuming her. She went still, waiting, hoping, that his next breath would become hers, and then his mouth captured hers. Their tongues crashed together, exploring, taking, filling the need that had been swelling between them. He fisted his hand in her hair, setting the moan she'd trapped earlier free. He swallowed it down, and as his hard body pressed against hers, he released a guttural moan of his own, setting her entire body aflame. He cupped her ass with one hand. It had been so long since she'd felt even a stir of passion, and this—this kiss, his body, his heat—overwhelmed her, engulfed her, made her want more, more, more. His thick thighs moved between her legs, and their bodies came together. *Good Lord.* The delicious friction caused her head to tip back.

"You're so…God, Gabriella, you're beautiful," he said against her neck, pressing kisses to her heated flesh.

Her leg hitched up his hip, and he pressed his hard length against her core, tearing another greedy moan from her lungs. Her hands pushed into his hair, over his muscular back, holding his hard, broad chest to her aching, taut nipples. He claimed her mouth again, and she wanted his big hands to touch more of her, to feel the wet heat between her legs. The way his hips moved, with perfect precision, slow and sensual, hard and intense, she knew he'd be an intensely passionate lover.

"Gabriella," he said against her lips, then pressed his lips to hers in a chaste kiss. "God, Gabriella, you ignite everything inside me."

She couldn't respond, couldn't think beyond her wild, crazy need to have him, and when he took a small step back, the whoosh of air between them felt as vast as an ocean. She clutched at his shirt, wanting him back against her.

"That was…" She had no more words to give.

"Incredible." The heat between them lingered, turning his gaze sinful, and just as quickly, thoughtful. "You didn't want this," he said quietly. "I'm sorry."

"I did." A nervous laugh mixed with the desire tumbling out of her.

He tugged her close again, grinding his thick arousal against her as he said, "I'm sorry. I need you close. I can't…You undo me, baby. But you didn't want the complication. We shouldn't go further. It'll muddy the waters. But I can't seem to let you go."

"Yes," was all she could manage, because damn it, he was right. She wouldn't do her family any favors by sleeping with the man who held the purse strings to their future. But his heart was beating fast and hard against hers, and his hand was still tangled in her hair, causing a pinch of titillating pain, while his other hand was splayed across her back, searing a five-fingered burn into her skin.

In the next breath she was up on her toes and he was meeting her halfway. They feasted on each other's mouths, taking what they so desperately wanted, despite knowing they shouldn't. He sank deeper into her, all those hard muscles against her willing body. And she knew—*God, how she knew*—she would strip off her clothes and lay down on the forest floor for him.

DUKE DEEPENED THE kiss despite knowing he shouldn't, but everything about Gabriella drew him in, from her vulnerability to her strength. He was powerless to resist her. Gabriella clung to him like he was her buoy, and he clung right back, knowing she was his storm, the woman he had no business touching but couldn't deny. She kissed him eagerly, tearing a need from the depths of his soul. He was drowning in her, but this kiss—*holy hell, this kiss*—was ravaging his last shred of self-control.

"Gabriella," he panted out, hearing the desperation in his voice, before their mouths collided again, dragging him under as she moved with him.

Her luscious curves conformed to his hard flesh, and when she lifted her leg against his hip again, rocking all that sweet heat against his aching arousal, their connection ignited. But this was Gabriella, the woman whose family had welcomed him to the island, offered him the chance to make something more of it. The woman he didn't want to only fuck—though he had absolutely no idea how or why he knew that, he knew it was one hundred percent true. He wanted to fuck her, yes. What man wouldn't want to bury himself balls deep in such a gorgeous, glorious woman? But he wanted more. He wanted to consume her, to cherish her, love every inch of her with the tenderness and roughness she desired. He wanted to be the man who made her sigh dreamily, whimper, and cry out his name in the throes of passion. He wanted to steal the sadness he saw in her eyes when she talked about being forced to leave the island and never let sadness touch her again.

He pulled back with the need to see the woman who was turning him inside out at breakneck speed. Her eyes fluttered open, heavy with desire. Her lips were pink from their rough kisses, and he knew the rosy flush of her skin covered every inch of her beautiful flesh. He could feel her heat against him, beneath his hands, searing into him from her hungry gaze, and he was done. Completely, utterly wrecked.

"Fuck," he whispered, cringing at the curse. His body was trembling with the need for more as badly as hers was. "Sorry. For the curse, not the kiss."

CHAPTER EIGHT

AFTER A LONG while of gathering their wits about them, they eventually began walking again, without talking any further about the lust that consumed them. At first their hands brushed as they walked, like teenagers feeling out their first date's willingness to commit to a simple hand-holding. But nothing was simple about the heat simmering between them. It was fraught with potential complications. Gabriella wanted to grab his hand, to guide it to her breast as she kissed him again. She could see from the tightening around Duke's jaw that he was fighting it, too. She didn't know how things had changed so quickly, but as she wrestled with slowing down the heat between them, Duke claimed her hand and squeezed, as if he could read her thoughts.

"We should talk about this," he said.

Gabriella tried her best to slip into lawyer mode, to protect herself. But it was a halfhearted effort at best. "Agreed."

"There's something strong between us, Gabriella, and I'd like to explore whatever it is, but not at the expense of your relationship with your family. Or at the expense of the investment going bad. I want to explore that, too."

"I understand." She did, because she felt the same way, but she didn't have an answer beyond that.

He stopped walking and faced her, looking like everything she could ever want, and scaring the hell out of her because of it. He reached for her hands.

"My business is risk management, and I know you're worth the risk for me. What I'm not sure of is if I'm worth the risk for you."

That was not at all what she'd expected to hear, and for a moment her thoughts stuttered.

"What does that mean, exactly?" She couldn't think straight while he was touching her, so she slid her hands from his. "Are you trying to tell me that this is a fling? Because, Duke, I'm a big girl. I know how these things go, and it's not like I'm looking for marriage." Strangely, just saying the words made her stand up a little taller. She wasn't a weak woman who didn't know the risks of getting involved with a man, but she *was* a woman. And she was fully aware of the way her body reacted to him, which was a world away from what she was used to, and she wanted to explore that so badly she ached.

"No, Gabriella, that's not what I meant at all. I can't make promises of where this is going, not after only two days, no matter what my body is telling me."

He paused, and even though she wasn't expecting him to

profess his love for her, disappointment filled her chest.

"But I'm not approaching this as a fling," he said softly. "If I were, I would have slept with you the first night we met, wouldn't I?" He tucked her hair behind her ear and pressed his hand to her cheek. "A beautiful, smart, strong woman like you? I'd be crazy not to try."

Her stomach got all fluttery.

"I *was* crazy not to try, Gabriella, but that's how I knew you weren't going to be just a fling, because honestly, I'm not a saint. I've had plenty of flings. I know the difference."

"Is that your best line? Because it doesn't make me feel any better." She took a step away, and he closed the distance between them, his eyes dark and serious.

"I don't use *lines*, Gabriella." His words fell fast and angry. "Don't you think I've seen your heart all over this island? Why would I take you like any other woman in the one place you adore? Wouldn't that ruin it for you forever? To have some guy come along and screw you just to appease his own carnal desires?"

Her mouth dropped open.

"I have respect for you, and I'm trying to let that respect guide me." He tugged her in close again, sending her pulse into a frenzy, and when he spoke, his voice was low, controlled, demanding. "I won't lie to you. I want to have you beneath me, to sink into you so deep that you feel me the next day. I want to see you shivering with need, then exploding with passion, but I'm *not* approaching this as a fling."

Her breath left her lungs in a rush. His heated words made her knees weaken. Shouldn't she be wary of a man who was so blatantly honest? Who spoke so dirty? She'd never been talked to like that. But she wasn't wary. She was blown away, turned on by his need to tell her in such sensual details what he wanted.

"I…" She tried to speak, but her mouth was bone dry.

He closed his eyes for a moment, and she watched as the determination riddling his body and the tension around his mouth eased, and when he opened his eyes, his gaze softened again.

"This is difficult for me, as you can tell. I'm not used to feeling anything like what I feel when I'm with you." He stepped back, and she knew that was for his benefit as much as hers. "I'm used to seeing what I want, weighing the risks, and moving forward. But this is complicated."

Now she was the one eating up the distance between them. She placed her hands on his waist, felt his muscles tense beneath them.

"Duke…" She didn't know what she wanted to say. She just knew she wanted to be there, touching him, not letting him get too far away.

"I can't make promises about the island, Gabriella, and that's messing with my head. I'd like to set the business aside and just see how we play out, but I can't do that. There are too many people relying on me."

Her mind snapped back to the island. "What *are* your plans for the island? You must have come here with some idea of what you'd build."

"I did." He held her gaze, but she saw a hint of something there—regret? Secrecy? Uncertainty?

"What was it?" She crossed her arms over her chest, needing to stand on her own two feet for his response.

"What it was and what my thoughts are now are two different things. But I can't commit to either yet. There's too much that needs to be done, too many aspects that need to be analyzed, if any pieces to the puzzle change." He stepped closer again, and she remained rigid.

"Gabriella, that is exactly what I'm talking about. The two of us together might be spectacular, but add in the island you love and what I'm here for, and it might spell disaster."

She knew this. Of course she did. She had since she'd first seen him sitting with Vivi and David outside the welcome center, when her heart had instantly taken notice of him.

"Agreed," she finally said, wondering what happened to her vocabulary. This was important, and she needed to put her thoughts on the table. She wanted him. Really, really wanted him. To feel his thoughtful caring side mix with his darker, passionate desires, and before she could stop herself, she offered herself up on a silver platter. "What are you suggesting? We're both consenting adults. I just want to throw that out there."

He reached for her hand again. "May I?"

She nodded, placed her fingers in his.

"Well, Counselor. I don't think you're the type of woman who has flings."

She opened her mouth to dispute his assessment, but his serious gaze shut the lie down. She *wasn't* the type to have flings. Hell, she was barely the type of girl to make out in the woods with a guy after having known him for only two days.

"That's a good thing, Gabriella, although I wouldn't have cared if you'd had a hundred flings. Whatever you did before this moment is your business, and it made you the woman you are. I don't want to change who you are. I like who you are, and I'm sure as hell not looking for a fling with you. I don't know where we'll go, but a fling isn't anywhere in the realm of what I'm thinking. I'm suggesting that we go into this with our eyes open, knowing what's at stake, knowing that we might butt heads when it comes to the island. And most importantly, letting the people who matter most in this deal know, too. Because I'm not a liar, and if we decide to move forward, I won't hide my feelings for you."

Oh God. She wanted that so badly she could taste it. She felt more confident now, knowing where he was coming from. But with that confidence brought a sense of clarity, and she wanted more before she brought her heart out to play.

"Why don't you tell me what your intentions were when you came to the island? Then you can tell me how they've changed. That way we'll have a starting point."

"Are you sure you want to do this now? We could—"

Before she could chicken out she said, "Yes."

He nodded and gripped her hand tighter. "Only if you promise to hear me out without storming off."

She rolled her eyes. "That tells me what I'm in for, doesn't it?"

"No." He stepped closer, bringing that heat that undid her with him. "It tells you that I want a fair shot at explaining."

She held his gaze, measuring her own ability to remain standing there if he said what she didn't want to hear. Her grandfather trusted her, and negotiating deals she didn't enjoy was her job. She could do this.

"Okay."

"You need to take emotions out of the equation. Can you do that?"

"I'm a professional. Of course I can." She'd take that lie to her grave.

"The island has a lot to offer, but it needs a draw to gain tourism, and that draw has to be a money maker." He watched her carefully, as if she'd suddenly tell him to stop, that she didn't want to hear any more.

"Go on." She ground her teeth together. What he said

wasn't a revelation, but she hated hearing it just the same.

"Our initial thought was an exclusive resort with multiple golf courses, a casino, hotels on the beach, boats—"

She held her palm up, silencing him and trying to reel in her spinning emotions. "After everything I've told you, *that's* where you're headed?"

"You asked me what our initial ideas were, Gabriella, and those were our initial ideas. Certain revenues have to be realized in order for this island to succeed." His tone was professional, stern even.

She had to admit he was right about what she'd asked. "And now, Duke? How have your visions changed?"

He rubbed the scruff on his jaw. "That's the answer I don't have yet. I have ideas, but I can't commit to anything until I know if they're feasible." He slid his hands into his pockets and sighed. "I told you this would be complicated, and if it's too difficult for you to deal with, I understand."

Maybe he could understand if she walked away, but could she?

CHAPTER NINE

GABRIELLA WATCHED DUKE for a long time, reading the honesty and the underlying worry she saw in his eyes and trying to calm the insistent frustration eating away at her insides. What had she expected? Why was knowing the sale of the island was coming and actually hearing it come out of his mouth so different and so freaking hard for her to accept?

"If you want to forget what's happened between us," Duke said softly, "then that's your prerogative. I don't want to forget anything about you, Gabriella, and even if I did want to, I know I couldn't. But I don't want to hurt you, either."

"I don't want to forget it, either," she answered honestly.

Relief washed over his face. "You're sure?" He reached for her hand again, and when his thumb stroked over her skin, it felt more intimate and right.

"I don't. It's all so hard. Being back here when I know the island is going to change. Knowing it needs to change and not wanting it to. All of it, from how it will impact my family to how it will impact the future of the people here makes it so complicated. But you? *This?* Whatever this is between us?" She stepped closer. "I don't want to throw away the one thing that makes me feel alive and happy."

"You can't imagine how much I needed to hear that. But, Gabriella, you know I can't make promises about the island. I have an investment partner, and—"

"Duke, I'm a lawyer. I know all about negotiations and broken promises. When I got into law, I knew there would be things I wouldn't want to deal with, but I also knew it was all part of the job. Dealing with the liars, the cheats, the incessant arguing of people who knew nothing about communicating." She paused, not wanting to let the darkness of her job creep into her mind.

"You're working so hard to be honest and up-front, and that means something. Actually"—she gazed up at him— "that means more than almost anything else. You're not using me to make the deal or placating me to get me in bed. You're keeping me at arm's length and allowing me to make my own decision with all the facts, and I appreciate that."

"Thank you for recognizing that." He lifted her hand to his lips again. She loved when he did that. It was so sweet, so unassuming. "Still want to know about my family?"

She was relieved that he didn't try to discuss the island any further. She had a knot in her stomach the size of the island, but she'd done harder things in her life than hoping things wouldn't go south with a handsome, intelligent, thoughtful man like Duke.

"Yes, I would like that," she said honestly, wanting to know whatever he was willing to share.

He unlinked their hands and draped an arm around her waist.

"Good," he said, before kissing the top of her head. "Because after seeing you with your family, it makes me miss mine."

She loved hearing that, and it made her heart swoon even more.

"I've got four younger brothers, and of course, my sister, Trish, the actress I mentioned to Vivi."

The mention of his sister made her cringe at her earlier assessment. Duke had already proven that he wasn't the stuffed shirt she'd thought. Chances were, his sister wasn't the snotty elitist she'd imagined either. She was curious about his family, and more specifically, his parents, who had raised him to be so warmhearted. She knew from experience that apples rarely fell far from the tree. She had all her mother's sensitivity with her father's stubbornness. But he'd only offered his siblings, and she'd take that for now.

"Are any of them investors, like you?" she asked as they walked along a rocky trail.

"No." He laughed. "My brothers don't have the patience for what I do. Gage is a sports director at a youth center in Colorado. Blue is a skilled craftsman. He builds houses, custom cabinetry, anything, really. And Cash—he recently married—is a New York City firefighter. He and Jake, my youngest brother, who does search and rescue like my father did, are the two who would spend hours out in the woods together. Gage and I were into other, nerdy things."

"Nerdy? I *cannot* see that. I picture you as the big man on campus, the studly football player."

He laughed as he helped her over a pile of rocks.

"Well, not like a pocket-protector-carrying nerd, but the kind who always had his nose in a book or in the computer. I was the kid who studied the next chapter so I'd have a leg up on the other students. I still played football and baseball, but…" He tapped his head. "I liked to stimulate my brain as much as my body."

She thought of all the ways she'd like to stimulate his body.

As Duke shared the details of his family, openly and without hesitation, she realized that she'd been keeping him from seeing *her* favorite parts of the island. She'd shown him the sites that were important to all of the residents instead. She'd feared that if she showed him her most treasured areas, she'd be opening herself up to him in a way she wasn't ready for. But now, as they jumped over the precipice of *I want to kiss you* and *Please don't ruin the island*, she didn't want to hide anymore. She wanted to share something, too, and she headed down the path that led to one of her favorite spots.

"How about you? Just the two brothers? Niko and Dimitri?"

"Yes. They both own the *taverna*. No sisters, but Katarina and the rest of my cousins and I are as close as sisters. Sadly, as I mentioned, most of my relatives my age have also been ushered off the island to pursue better lives."

"Growing up so close, you must miss them."

"I do, mostly when I'm here, though. My life in New York is so busy I don't have time to think about how much I miss everyone, well, except at night. But I spend summers on the island, and holidays. At least I have Addy. She's my assistant and about as close to a sister as I'll ever have in New York. I wish I could pack her up and move back here."

"You've mentioned wanting to be here so often. Why don't you move back?"

Her heart squeezed as she admitted the truth. "I think my grandfather knew what he was doing when he urged us off the island." She tried to ignore the fresh opening of the old wound. She knew it was the dreams of her youth tugging at her, making her stomach knot.

"I talk about wanting to live here again, and a big part of me does want to, but I have to be realistic, and the more time we spend talking about the island, the more I realize what that really means. As much as I don't want to see the land leave our family, or for the island to change, I do understand that what the island has to offer *has* changed over the years.

And my grandfather was probably right. Our family legacy won't survive if we all stay. I mean, unless we want to start marrying cousins."

As they left the woods and crossed the grassy meadow, M'lady's Home Bridge came into view, giving her something else to focus on.

"This is one of my favorite places." She pointed to the rickety, wooden bridge. "It's called M'lady's Home Bridge, although we usually just call it M'lady's Home. This is another story that's been passed down through generations, so take it with a grain of salt. Supposedly Mr. Banks, the man who owns that white house behind the trees on the other side of the bridge, built this bridge, and…This sounds silly when I say it aloud, but I think it's kind of cool. I've heard that there used to be a big iron bell on this side of the bridge, and his wife was a midwife. When she'd return from delivering babies, or checking on the women in town, she'd ring that bell and he'd tell whichever of his nine kids was around, *m'lady's home*, and come out to greet her."

"That's sweet."

"Everything cool about this island is from the past, right?"

"I don't know about that," he said as he drew her in close and pressed his lips to hers. The kiss was unexpected and tender, not demanding, and it felt natural to kiss him back.

"I think the coolest thing about the island is right here

with me," he said. "And she's all about being *present*."

She squinted up at him. "If anyone else had said that, it would sound cheesy."

"That's because you're not listening with your attorney ears. You're listening with the ears of a woman who knows this isn't just a fleeting moment between us. You feel as connected to me as I feel to you."

He pressed his lips to hers in a kiss that was seductive and tender, instead of feverish and overwhelming, making it that much sweeter.

She didn't even try to respond as their mouths parted, and was thankful when he linked their fingers together and said, "Let's walk," as he led her onto the bridge.

He stopped midway across and leaned on the aged railing. "It's beautiful out here, so secluded."

She watched his eyes sweep over the water, across the grassy clumps by the piers, and then back to her. He shifted his weight, so their bodies touched from shoulder to hip, and Gabriella felt her world shift and define, as if they weren't standing out in the open but had somehow been transported to their own private oasis.

"Why is this one of your favorite places?" He settled his hand on her hip.

Oh God, that feels too good.

His fingers pressed into her skin.

That feels even better.

She tried to remember what he'd asked, but she was lost in how hot he looked, with the sun setting behind him and a flash of bare skin visible through the open buttons of his shirt. He was so much taller than her, so broad and masculine. She had the urge to throw caution to the wind, scale him like a ladder, wrap her legs around his waist, and make out with him.

"Gabriella?" he said softly.

For the life of her she couldn't remember what he'd asked. *The bridge? Oh! Favorite place!* She shook her head to clear the tangles of lust from her brain.

"I used to come here with my grandfather. We'd talk for hours, and he always built me up, you know? He made it sound like I could do anything in the world, and I believe he thought I could. He'd say, 'When you're older and you leave the island…'And I'd tell him, 'I'll never leave the island.'" Emotions clogged her throat, and she tried to swallow them down. "This is where he brought me when he told me about his plans for the younger Liakos generations. I should probably blame my father, right? For not fighting to keep me here on the island. But in our family, decisions like that really do come from my grandfather, and my father knew it was for the best."

Duke gathered her in closer, bringing the memories to the forefront of her mind. She'd thought she'd buried them so long ago, tamped them down deep, covered them with layers of success in the hopes of never feeling the pain of them again. Duke stroked her back, not asking for anything, not kissing, or taking, or claiming. Just holding her warm and safe and comforting against him.

"I'm sorry," he whispered, before pressing his lips to the top of her head. "I hate that you had to leave the place you love so much." He pressed another kiss to her head. "Maybe one day you'll find your way back."

So many people had said that to her over the years, and she'd brushed it off every time. Why was part of her daring to hope he was right?

LATER THAT EVENING Gabriella paced the patio behind her villa while talking to Addison on a FaceTime call. The call had already dropped twice, but in this one location, it seemed to be holding strong.

"Addy, telling me you Googled him and he's hot does *not* help me."

"Maybe not, but wow, Gab. I know you've dated some good-looking guys who were pretty jerky, but Duke Ryder? He's smokin' *and* you said he's nice."

"That's only part of the problem." She sat on the edge of the knee-high stone wall that bordered the patio and sighed. Addy's happy eyes were smiling back at her, taunting her like only a best friend could get away with.

"He's also honest, warm, thoughtful, and intense in this sexually magnetic way that makes me want him far too much. I'm supposed to be a competent negotiator, and I turn to mush around him," Gabriella said.

"Sounds like you negotiated some high-power chemistry!" Addy laughed and tucked her dark hair behind her ear.

"Yeah, well, I can't deny that. Can you please remind me that I'm supposed to be talking to him about his plans for the island, not thinking about how great he looks in his under-crackers?"

Addy fell back laughing at the use of their name for men's underwear. "I think tonight you should negotiate for some mattress action." She waggled her perfectly manicured brows. "I saw a picture of him in his bathing suit on Facebook, and I can tell you with complete confidence that the man was made for walking around in his undercrackers. Hell, that man's body was made for taking them off."

"Lord, Ad." She half laughed, half sighed, thinking about Duke in his underwear.

"Oh yeah, I can see it now." Addy waved her hands, as if presenting the image of what was to come. "You're sitting beneath that tree where you got your first kiss, the moon is hovering just above the ocean, and Duke's doing a sexy striptease—"

"Stop it! Don't you think I've already pictured him in

every position, every state of undress, that I possibly can? That's the problem."

"Sorry, boss, but I'm not seeing the issue. What's the worst that could happen? You sleep with a sexy investor, swing a sweet deal, and hook me up with his brother Jake. He's the one with the Facebook page. Did you know he has *several* hot brothers? I swear, Gabriella, if you do tangle in the sheets with Duke, please get me Jake's number."

"You're such a ho." Gabriella laughed, then trapped her lower lip between her teeth, thinking about what Addy had said. Thoughts of tangling in the sheets with Duke made her hot all over. "Maybe I should come back to New York early. What's happening with the McGrady mediation?"

"Dickhead didn't show. He said he's not going to sit in the room with some, and I quote, 'asshole mediator who doesn't know shit.' His attorney is trying to push the court date up to next week."

"Not surprising," Gabriella said with a sigh. "He's really well connected, so if anyone could make this trial happen fast, it'll be him and that slimy attorney of his. I prepped his soon-to-be ex, so she's prepared that this could go directly to court. How did she take it?"

"In stride. She's as cold as he is. She said next week couldn't come soon enough."

"Why do divorcing couples completely forget that they were ever in love?" Gabriella thought of her parents, her aunts, uncles, cousins, and the other married couples there on the island. She'd seen heated discussions, even witnessed what looked like it would be the end of a marriage or two, but within hours the couples were back in each other's arms. Passionate people loved *and* fought passionately. But she'd never worried that her parents or relatives would get divorced, whereas she analyzed every couple she met off the island. She assessed their body language, how often they touched, how they looked at each other, just like she'd done with Duke all day. It was the attorney in her, she supposed, but unlike the couples she met off the island, Duke touched her, spoke to her, looked at her like she was all that mattered. Of course, they'd known each other only two days.

"And why doesn't anyone on the island ever get divorced?"

"Well," Addy said, bringing Gabriella's mind back to their conversation. "The answer to your first question is that by the time people get divorced they're too far gone, in love with someone else, or too hurt to see straight, as you know. And as far as the island goes, most of the people our age are gone, so you've got older couples or your cousins and brothers and others who aren't exposed to the disposable lifestyles we are."

"Oh, Addy. Is that it? Like everything else in this world, has love become selfish, too?" She drew in a deep breath. "Don't answer that. Of course it has. Look at us. We're selfish, too."

"Yeah, we want men who can give us multiple orgasms, let us work crazy hours without complaining about not having dinner on the table, and only speak when spoken to." Addy lifted a glass and held it up. "Here's to equal rights."

"You're such a freak." Gabriella laughed. Addy's forthright nature was one of the things Gabriella loved most about her. "I'll settle for a guy who sticks it out through thick and thin. Someone who takes his work as seriously as I do...*and* gives multiple orgasms."

They talked for a while longer, and by the time they ended the call, although Addy had tried her best to talk Gabriella *into* bed with Duke, the McGrady divorce and thoughts about her life back in New York brought reality home. Gabriella was determined to stop focusing so much on a certain tall, handsome man.

At least she was determined to try.

CHAPTER TEN

DELIGHTFUL SOUNDS OF music, laughter, and impassioned voices carried on the air as Duke walked toward the celebration at the big house. He was arriving later than he would have liked, but it had taken him forever to get a solid Internet connection, and he'd finally had to use his phone as a hot spot to download and read the documents Pierce had sent over.

Pierce had met with the land development team, and they were working through just how grand they'd have to go to get a solid return on their investment. Meanwhile, the descriptions alone of the elaborate casino, twenty-story hotel, and decked-out marina made Duke's nerves string tight. He debated skipping the celebration altogether, knowing how painful it would be to see Gabriella and think about the very things she was fighting against, but he knew he was just delaying the inevitable. Plus, the idea of not seeing Gabriella put him in an even worse mood.

Colorful lights hung from the trees. At least two dozen big round tables were set up around the lawn. Several buffet tables were lined up on the patio, every inch of the tablecloths covered with dishes overflowing with food. Children ran around in pretty dresses and shorts; some carried balloons, and others were kicking a ball around. Away from the group, teenagers gathered in clusters; the rectangular glare of a cell phone passed from one to the next. An orange cat nibbled on something beside an empty chair. Adults danced on the grass, gathered in groups, drinks in hand, or sat around enormous tables talking and eating. Just being around the festivities calmed his nerves. It probably shouldn't. After all, these were the people whose lives would change once the deal was done, but family events always calmed him.

Duke searched for Gabriella among the crowd.

He made his way to the table nearest him, where Gabriella's grandfather, father, brother Dimitri, and a handful of other men were sitting.

"Duke, join us." Dimitri stood and draped an arm over his shoulder, reminding Duke of his own brothers and how close they were. He wondered if Dimitri and the others would have greeted any investor the way they greeted him. Recalling the eldest Liakos man's words, *In my family, we greet as if you are part of our family*, he knew they would have. That made him feel a little competitive. He wanted to be the investor they chose.

"Thanks. I'm sorry I'm arriving so late," Duke said as the frizzy-haired blonde he'd seen earlier set a bottle of beer before him. "Thank you. I could have gotten that."

She patted his shoulder, then joined a group of women chatting by the buffet tables.

Dimitri leaned in closer and said, "They're plying you with alcohol. You better watch yourself. They'll have you married off before the week is over."

"Stronger people have tried." Duke was only half teasing. His family gave him hell all the time, urging him to settle down. His mind turned to Gabriella as the men at the table made small talk about the weather, the celebration, the food, which was suddenly filling the table, thanks to several of the women Duke had seen earlier in the day. The men filled their plates from platters of grilled meats, fried chicken, potpies and casseroles, and assorted vegetable dishes he didn't even try to name. The aroma of Southern and Mediterranean dishes mingled together, creating the very essence of the island he was falling in love with. It smelled welcoming and potent, warm and delicious.

He spotted Gabriella across the lawn, talking to a tall blond-haired man. She was wearing a flowing black spaghetti-strap top and the sexiest little skirt, which hugged her waist and flared at the hips, making her figure even more alluring. She was tanned from their day in the sun, and she looked happy and relaxed as she touched his arm and leaned in close, listening intently as he spoke. Duke's gut clenched at the intimate gesture. Her eyes drifted over the crowd, and then the blond guy touched the small of her back and guided her to the dance floor. Duke's muscles tensed. He forced himself to remain seated. She wasn't his to claim, no matter how much he'd read into their afternoon and their passionate kisses, but hell if he didn't want to go stake his claim anyway.

"You have been here two days. In my country that's a lifetime of getting to know a place," Gabriella's grandfather said.

"Yes, sir." Duke shifted his eyes away from Gabriella and focused on the man who should be getting one hundred percent of his attention. "It's a beautiful island, and I think it has a lot of potential."

Unable to resist, he glanced at Gabriella again. Katarina was dancing beside her, holding Mione, and when Gabriella reached for the little girl—instead of the man—Duke let out a breath he hadn't realized he'd been holding.

"How does this work?" Dimitri asked, drawing his attention back to the conversation again.

This was Duke's time to shine, and as always, he rose to the occasion. He turned his full attention to the sales pitch, even though he knew, as with most of his clients, they needed him more than he needed them. A while later, after outlining the process for the men and answering dozens of questions about his other investments, Duke searched for Gabriella again. He quickly found the blond man she'd been dancing with and was glad to see she wasn't with him. He spotted

Katarina and Mione, Gabriella's mother, and a handful of the women he'd seen that morning. Just when he was losing hope of finding her, the crowd parted, and her smiling face appeared like a shining light.

Their eyes connected, and he felt a jolt of electricity spike through his chest. *There you are, beautiful.* She lowered her eyes, then quickly lifted them again. Another spark of heat stroked through him.

Duke excused himself from the table and moved through the crowded lawn toward her. The women she was talking with watched him as he neared and covered their mouths, whispering to one another.

"Duke!" Vivi waved from the dance floor, where she and her girlfriends were swaying to the music.

He waved, undeterred from closing the distance between him and Gabriella. Every determined step shattered his resolve to treat her like anything but the woman whom he wanted to kiss again, and again, and again.

He noticed David sitting alone beneath a tree, watching a group of kids playing stickball. As badly as Duke wanted to get to Gabriella, there was no way he could ignore the dejected look in David's eyes. Duke walked around the crowd and knelt beside David.

"Hey there, buddy. How are you doing?"

David shrugged.

"Why aren't you playing with the other kids?" When

David shrugged again, he realized that the boy wasn't going to clue him in easily. "Mind if I join you, then?" Duke sat beside him on the ground.

He was met with another silent shrug.

"You don't like stickball?"

"I'm not very good," David said. "I can't catch the ball. That's why those other kids at school were giving me a hard time. We're on the same baseball team."

Duke recalled that when he'd met David at the welcome center the day he'd arrived, David had told another boy that he'd gotten in trouble at school for calling a kid names.

"They call me spider hands." David held up his hands and splayed his unusually long fingers.

"With hands like that they probably expect a lot from you, huh? You're lucky to have big hands." Duke leaned in closer and lowered his voice. "When you're older girls will want to hold those big hands."

David laughed.

"Has your dad worked with you, shown you how to hit and catch?"

"My dad works shifts on the mainland and comes home every couple days, but he's usually busy when he's home. It's okay. I don't really care if I play or not."

Duke's heart ached for the boy. He was sure it was hard being transported to the mainland for school and feeling like an outsider from the get-go. Being teased would only make him hate it even more.

"I have an idea," Duke said. "How about if I talk to your parents and see if they'd mind if I showed you a few things?"

"My uncle tried to show me once," David said. "I'm just not good at it."

"Well, sometimes it takes trying things a little differently. One of my younger brothers was the worst basketball player ever. Jake was tall, like me, but he couldn't get the ball in the net if he had a map."

David laughed. "Does he still suck?"

"Hey, I didn't say he sucked. That's probably not the language your mom wants you to use, so let's just say he stunk. Deal?"

He nodded.

"Good, and no. He doesn't stink. He's the best player in our family." Duke looked around the crowded yard. "Is your father here?"

He shook his head. "He's coming home in a few days."

"Where's your mom?" Duke asked.

"She's the one holding my brother." David pointed to one of the women standing with Gabriella. She had a young boy in her arms and another little girl running circles around her legs.

"If she says it's okay, do you want to spend an hour with me knocking the ball around tomorrow?"

David nodded vigorously.

"A'right, then. I'll talk to your mom, and we'll set something up." Duke rose to his feet and held out a hand to David. "Come on." He lifted the boy to his feet. "Men handle their own negotiations."

David followed Duke across the grass. "I'm not a man."

"Don't kid yourself. You're a man in the making. It all counts."

GABRIELLA FORCED HERSELF to remain still, to wait for Duke to reach her. She'd spotted him when he'd first arrived, looking insanely handsome in a pair of black slacks and a white button-down shirt. The man knew how to fill out his clothes. Every step outlined his powerful legs. The top buttons of his shirt were open, revealing just enough skin to cause her heartbeat to accelerate. The women she was standing with were some of the most proper women she knew, but even they lacked their usual decorum at the sight of him, whispering things that told her that by now the whole island must be trying to work their matchmaking magic. *So sexy. You have to kiss that man. Can I borrow him?*

"Good evening, ladies," he said as he joined them. His eyes never left Gabriella's, and despite herself, a thrill shot through her as he leaned in close, put a hand on her arm, and kissed her cheek. "You look stunning."

"Thank you." There was no way in hell she was going to keep from kissing him. She needed reinforcements. Armor. A tank. An entire army.

He placed a hand on David's shoulder and turned to Natalia, David's mother.

"Hi. You must be David's mother."

"Yes. Natalia."

"Natalia, it's a pleasure to meet you. I'm Duke. I met David yesterday on his way home from school, and tonight when I saw the kids playing ball, it reminded me of what fun it used to be. David was kind enough to say he'd play a little ball with me tomorrow, if it's okay with you." He lowered his voice and said, "To be honest, I could use a few pointers, and…" He shrugged, and David's eyes filled with pride.

Gabriella felt herself falling for him even more. Where the heck was her army?

Natalia took one look at her son's beaming expression and Gabriella saw a world of gratitude in her cousin's eyes. "Well, I'm not sure if you can keep up with my little man, Duke. But if you want to give it a try, I won't stand in your way."

Duke squeezed David's shoulder. "Tomorrow around two? Does that work for you?"

"Yes, sir." David nodded.

They made plans to meet on the field by the schoolhouse the next afternoon. When Natalia took the kids to get dessert,

Duke returned his attention to Gabriella.

"Would you like to dance?" he asked.

Dancing would bring their bodies close together, and then her mind would scramble and she'd be useless. She really did need reinforcements. She turned, but the other women she'd been standing with had gone their separate ways. There was no army, not even a single soldier.

Before she could answer, his hand was around her waist and he was leading her to the dance floor.

"Don't overthink this," he whispered against her cheek.

Well, okay then. He was a mind reader, too.

She was in his arms, their bodies moving together in a seductive dance, like two lovers with years of practice. Her arms wound around his neck. Somehow, in the space of a few hours apart, she must have forgotten how tall he was. They'd kissed so much during the afternoon that she imagined his mouth closer to the same height as hers.

"This is a nice celebration," he said.

"Mm-hm." She didn't *want* to overthink tonight, despite the pep talk she'd given herself. Maybe Addy was right. What's the worst that could happen? She could have a few great days before returning to the stress of tearing apart people's lives.

"Thank you for what you're doing with David. Natalia is so busy with her kids, and—"

"Gabriella, I did what my heart told me to do. Once I

understood what was wrong, how could I turn away? But I don't want to talk about David."

His gaze turned feral, possessive, and she couldn't have responded if her life had depended on it.

"I came here tonight with the intent of keeping my distance from you, despite our talk. I thought it might make things easier."

He searched her eyes, and she stifled the words *Me too*. How could she say them when she wouldn't mean them? When every time they were together she wanted more of him, not less.

"Okay," she finally said, but she didn't understand his comment, because she was right there in his arms and she could feel the effect she was having on him.

"I don't want to keep my distance. You know that. You can see it, feel it. Hell, baby, you can probably hear it in my voice."

He smiled, and she did, too, not just because his honesty was again beyond refreshing, but because he'd called her *baby* so naturally. Despite how often she told herself not to, she already felt like she was his.

"Maybe a little," she teased. "I came here with the same determination to keep things professional between us and focus on the future of the island."

"How's that going for you?" he asked, tightening his grip on her hips.

Every time he did that, visions of how his hands would feel on her naked body raced through her mind. He was so big. She could only imagine what it would feel like to have all that power holding her close as he sank into her.

"Not so well," she said with a shaky breath.

He leaned down and pressed his cheek to hers. "I want to kiss you so badly I ache, but I won't. Not here, in front of all these matchmakers. They'll have us married off in no time."

Her eyes widened. Her family. *Holy crap.* What was she doing, dancing like they were all alone, rocking her hips against him? She couldn't form a single word as she shifted her hips back to put a little space between them. Instantly missing the connection, she moved close again.

He lifted her chin and gazed into her eyes. "I don't want to hide what I feel for you. I'm trying to give you the space to decide what you want others to see."

"Thank you." She loved that he thought of her and her family ahead of his own desires, but she also longed for him to just take control and kiss her already. Having the power to make the decision made it even more difficult to decide.

"If we're going to kiss again, we need ground rules. And unless you tell me you don't want this, then we're going to do a hell of a lot more than kiss."

With her heart in her throat, she glanced around them, making sure no one else could hear that sexy promise. "Ground rules?"

"Yes, Gabriella. I want to invest in this island, and your family needs the right person to invest. You said that yourself. There are probably going to be—no. There will *definitely* be opposing opinions between us. If we move forward…"

His hand slid to her lower back and pressed, holding her against his arousal.

She. Couldn't. Breathe.

"Whatever this is between us has to have no effect on the deal. And the deal can have no effect on us."

"How are we supposed to do that?" She could say she'd try, but really, how could she separate the two most meaningful parts of her life?

"Trust."

"Trust?"

"Trust. It's the belief in the reliability, truth, or ability of someone or something. Surely you've heard of it?" His sense of humor, when their bodies were nearly combusting, only made her want him more.

"I need to trust that you'll think about and work toward what's best for your family and the other residents on the island, and you need to trust that my goal is to do the same."

CHAPTER ELEVEN

GABRIELLA NEVER THOUGHT she had trust issues. How could she, when she worked with people who didn't tell the truth? But as she listened to Duke talk about their relationship, the island, *and* trust like they were all sewn together, goose bumps raced up her arms. The music moved seamlessly from one song to the next, and couples crowded in around them. She'd never felt claustrophobic on the island before, but she needed air and space to deal with the emotions Duke was unearthing in her. And the concerned look in his eyes made her want to share her discovery with him.

"Can we take a walk?" she suggested.

He settled a hand on her back as they walked away from the crowd. "I'd like nothing more, but I hope I didn't upset you in some way."

He was so attentive to her, so in tune with everything she did and said, that he made it easy to forget they were on opposite sides of a negotiation table.

"You didn't upset me. It's been a long time since I really

thought about what it means to trust someone. I mean, beyond attorney-client trust, of course."

He held her close as they walked arm in arm. As they neared the lighthouse, the light and the din of the celebration faded, replaced with the sounds of waves crashing along the shore. The glow of the lighthouse cast a beam of light over the ocean.

"There was a time when trust came easily. As a kid, if my parents told me something, I never doubted it. If a friend or relative made a promise, it was always fulfilled."

"That's how it should be."

"Yes, I know. If what I say sounds strange, it's because I've never told anyone about it before, so it might come out convoluted."

Duke stopped walking and gazed deeply into her eyes. "You don't have to share anything you don't want to. I'm not going anywhere, and even though I think it's good that we talk about all these things now, you shouldn't feel pressured to."

"Thank you, but I want to share this with you."

He glanced back at the big house, and she knew he was checking to see if they could be seen.

"They can't see us," she assured him. "But thank you for worrying."

"I don't want to hide any part of what I feel for you. But that's your call." He pressed his lips to hers in a tender kiss.

"Thank you for trusting me enough to share whatever it is with me."

She hadn't realized she *was* trusting him, but that's exactly what she was doing. Wanting to share her innermost thoughts in and of itself meant that she trusted him. Funny how easily that happened.

"I spent my youth in this blissful wonderland, where everything was as it seemed," she explained as they began walking again. "Maybe it's like that for all kids. I don't know. But when my grandfather's thoughts on my future began changing, that trust diminished. Not because my grandfather had ever made promises to me that he didn't keep, but because *I* had read far too much into the words 'You can be whatever you want to be.'"

He kissed the top of her head but remained silent. She sensed that he was giving her the space she needed to work out what she wanted to say, and she appreciated that.

"I think he meant what he said, but he didn't believe that what I really wanted to be—the *only* thing I wanted to be— was an island girl. I wanted to live with the ocean breeze at my back, helping my family with the resort, the welcome center, the *taverna*." It felt so good to get this off her chest. She hadn't even admitted these things to Addy, but it felt right to share them with Duke.

"I wanted to raise babies alongside my cousins, with my family and all the other people I love so much there to love them up. I wanted my children to experience this." She inhaled deeply, filling her lungs with the cool sea air.

The ground was rockier near the shore. Duke kept her steady as they walked around the enormous gray lighthouse and sat on the grass overlooking the shore. Waves broke against the rocks, spraying them with droplets of water, making them both laugh.

"This, Duke. This is all I ever wanted. For my kids to grow up attending the two-room schoolhouse, then taking that long boat ride to the mainland, only to come back and experience the same sense of relief, the same sense of *home*, that I did."

"And instead you moved away and became a hell of a lawyer," Duke said. "But you come back often, which is probably more than most people."

She lay back on the grass and looked up at the starry sky. "Yes, I do. Every summer, every holiday."

Duke leaned on his elbow and came down over her, brushing a wayward lock of hair off her cheek. He pressed another soft kiss to her lips, then another to her cheek, and finally, her forehead, and she felt every kiss all the way to her toes.

"So when I asked you to trust me," he said, "you worried that I wouldn't fully understand, or maybe that I wouldn't really believe how desperately you want things to remain unchanged on the island?" He ran his finger along her side, bringing all her nerve endings to life. "You're worried that trusting me will leave you with an island that's full of everything you don't want, and you'll wake up one morning in a bewildered state of 'How the hell did we end up here?'"

"Something like that," she admitted. "I know you can't make promises, and I don't expect you to."

"Gabriella, doing what's best for the future of everyone here on the island won't be easy for anyone. Not for you, not for me or my staff, and certainly not for the residents who, like you, probably adore the simplicity of life here. Things have to change, and I know you understand that. I can't promise you exactly how it will all turn out, but what I can promise you is that I hear you."

He stroked his fingers over her cheek, and his tone turned even more serious. "I'm listening to everything you tell me. About your family's history, the reason there are no paved roads, no vehicles. I hear it all, and it means something to me because it means something to you. I will do my best to make this island a place where you would not only be proud to live, but that you will feel just as passionate about as you do now."

"You can't promise me that," she said breathlessly, hoping on all things good and holy that he could.

"I just did."

CHAPTER TWELVE

DUKE GAZED INTO Gabriella's beautiful, hopeful eyes and knew in that moment that he meant every word he said. Even if it meant going head-to-head with Pierce, this was one battle he was willing to fight. The urge to seal his promise with a kiss was so strong, so urgent, that he almost forgot to make sure she was as all in as he was. He needed that reassurance, needed it as badly as he needed the gorgeous woman gazing up at him.

"Do you trust me, Gabriella?"

Her lips parted, and when she said, "Yes, Duke. I trust you. I trust you and you know you can trust me," he heard the invitation in her voice, and only then did he slant his mouth over hers.

She tasted sweet and hot, willing and wanting. The kiss started slow and sensual, but every slick of their tongues, every press of her fingers on his back, made lust spike through his body. He deepened the kiss, devouring her mouth as she clawed at his back, and his control shattered. His hands moved over the curve of her hip, to her warm, bare thigh.

"So sweet. So sexy." She felt so good as she arched against his touch and kissed with the same desperation he felt coursing through him.

"Only you," he whispered against her mouth, "could make a kiss feel like so much more."

He moved over her, shielding her from the water spraying their legs as waves crashed along the shore. He slid a hand beneath her head, cradling her against him and angling her face just enough to allow him to consume even more of her. Their hips rocked to the silent beat of their hearts. Every sweet, sexy sound she made, every touch of his fingers on her heated flesh, brought more need. He gave her hair a gentle tug, and the sigh of surrender escaping her lips was the most erotic sound he'd ever heard. He needed to feel her flesh against his.

Raining kisses down her neck, he whispered, "I need to touch you." He sucked on her neck, and she fisted her hands in his hair.

"Yes," she said breathlessly. "Duke, touch me."

She tugged his shirt free from his pants, and he went up on his knees to unbutton his shirt, but the sight of Gabriella lying beneath him slowed him down. His eyes shot across the darkness. He knew no one could see them, but he didn't know if anyone would come over, and he didn't want to embarrass her.

"Duke." She fumbled with his buttons.

"Your family?" His heart beat a mile a minute, but between her nimble fingers and his urgent need, his shirt fell open. Her eyes widened as her hands roved over his muscles, stoking the inferno inside him.

"They won't"—she leaned up and licked his nipple, pulling a greedy groan from his lungs—"leave the party."

"Thank Christ."

He shrugged off his shirt, lifted hers over her head in one quick move, and laid her down as gently as he could, which wasn't gentle at all. He was too greedy, too lost in the sight of Gabriella in nothing more than a skirt bunched up around her waist and a black lace bra.

"You're beautiful," he said as he kissed the sweet swell of her breast. "So beautiful."

He licked and kissed and loved her mouth, her neck, the creamy path down the center of her chest. His fingers played over her nipple, which strained against the lace. He claimed her mouth in another demanding kiss, consuming, tasting everything he could. She sucked in a sharp breath as he unhooked her bra and lifted it off her chest, just long enough to drag one strap down her shoulder, following its path with his mouth. She arched her back as he dragged his tongue along her collarbone, laving it over the dip in the center, fighting the urge to strip her bare and bury himself deep.

"Duke, please."

"I want this to last. My first taste of you, the first time

you trusted me, the first time your hands played over my flesh." He pulled her other strap down her shoulder with his teeth, placing kisses along her arm. He slid her bra free and tossed it aside, taking a moment to drink her in.

"Holy Christ, Gabriella. Feel what you do to me."

He guided her hand between his legs and groaned when she palmed his hard length. He brushed his thumb over her nipple as she stroked him through his slacks. Lust rushed through his veins, simmering beneath every inch of his skin until it became too much to control. He moved her hand away.

"Need more," he gritted out as he captured her mouth again, trying to quell the ache as he rocked his eager erection against her core.

He pressed hard kisses down her neck, over her breastbone, and dragged his tongue over one taut nipple, earning another seductive moan.

"Mm, baby, you like that."

"Yes—"

She fisted her hand in his hair, holding his mouth to her breast as he sucked it in, teasing, taunting, taking his fill, while his other hand traveled up her thigh. Her hips bucked and he clutched her tightly, holding her to the ground.

"Jesus, every move you make…You're killing me," he said more desperately than he meant to. He sealed his lips over hers again as the spray of a wave rained down over them.

She kissed him hungrily, her whole body moving with him, groping, clawing, and driving him out of his blessed mind. He moved quickly, taking her other breast into his mouth, giving it the same attention as the first. Her skin was hot and sweet as he moved down her ribs to the swell of her hips. This was torture. He was barely holding it together as she pushed at his shoulders. Finesse went out to sea as he ripped her skirt and panties from her body and finally got his hands on her beautiful ass. He'd never been an ass man before, but damn, from the moment he'd seen her, her ass had turned him on. She arched back against his hands and moaned as he caressed her silky skin.

Holy hell, she was beyond gorgeous. Beyond stunning, with rounded hips, a slim waist, and full breasts. But it wasn't her pin-up girl body that had his heart thundering. It was the trusting look in her eyes that had him vowing never, *ever* to give her a reason not to trust him. He lowered his mouth to the damp curls between her legs, placing soft kisses there. She rocked her hips, pushed on his shoulders, and arched up to greet his greedy mouth as he slicked his tongue along her wetness.

"So damn sweet," he said before claiming all that wet heat with his open mouth. He plunged his tongue inside her, lapping up that sweet honey taste, then teased her with soft kisses and thrust his tongue in deep again. She fisted her hands in his hair as her thighs flexed.

"Duke. *God*…Duke."

He stroked his thumb over her swollen clit as he sealed his mouth over her center, and she shattered against him. He licked, sucked, loved her through her climax, and just as it started to ease, he brought his mouth to her overly sensitive nerves and took her over the edge again.

GABRIELLA LAY SPENT beneath Duke, trying to catch her breath. The man's mouth should come with a warning label. After two intense orgasms, she could barely move, but when Duke's fingers sought her most sensitive spot again and he took her in a kiss that was the perfect mix of rough and gentle, it took only seconds before she was coming apart for a third magnificent time.

"Baby," he whispered against her mouth. "I can't wait another second. I need to be inside you."

It was all she could do to reach for his pants and fumble with the button. He grabbed her hand and sucked two fingers into his mouth, swirling his tongue deliciously around them.

"Ohmygod…" The sight of him sucking her fingers made her want to suck *him*.

His eyes narrowed as he pulled them from his mouth and lowered them between her legs.

Holy. Shit.

He lowered his mouth to hers and kissed her again—hard—thrusting his tongue as if he were thrusting his shaft between her legs, and she nearly lost her mind.

"Touch yourself," he whispered.

Oh God. Could she? She'd never touched herself in front of a man before. But he was looking at her like nothing in the world could ever be as beautiful, and after the way he'd made her feel, she wanted to please him. And herself.

He settled his fingers over hers, pressing hers into her wet folds. "That's it, baby. Show me how you like it."

She didn't even try to tell him that he already knew exactly how to touch her. She could see the heat in his eyes as she touched herself, feel the need rolling off of him as he rose to strip off his pants. He pulled off his dark briefs, and her hand stilled. Holy Jesus. The man was hung.

"Don't stop, baby," he said as he stroked himself. Once, twice, three long delicious strokes that turned her on beyond anything she'd ever known. Her limbs trembled as she watched him remove a condom from his wallet and tear it open with his teeth. *So hot.*

He came down on his knees between her legs. Her eyes traveled over his broad shoulders, down his muscles, and lingered on the ink on his biceps. She didn't have more than a second to wonder about the tattoos, because her eyes were drawn to his hands. She could barely breathe, much less remember to move her hand as he sheathed his hard length with one hand and cupped his balls with the other. She'd taste him before he left this island, but right now she needed to feel him inside her. Every blessed inch of him.

He lowered his mouth and slicked his tongue over her fingers, spreading her juices and making her even wetter.

"Oh God…." It came out as a desperate whisper, and desperate she was. Just the sight of his tongue laving over her, the heat of his mouth as his tongue circled her clit, brought her right up to the edge again.

He lifted her fingers and pinned her to the ground with his heated stare as he dragged his tongue up the length of them, then sucked them into his mouth again.

She squeezed her thighs together, trying to stave off the need to come. She lifted her hips as he came down over her again, settling the head of his cock against her center. He kissed her hard and fast as he thrust in deep in a single stroke. She cried out, and he swallowed it down, the smile on his lips evident even as they kissed. He didn't screw like it was a race to the finish line, like the other men she'd been with. It took a moment for her body to adjust to his girth, and in that moment Duke slowed the kiss, moaning into her mouth and moving his hips in slow, sensual circles, each time stroking over the special spot that had her panting, clawing. One big hand cupped the back of her head and the other slid beneath her ass, lifting her slightly, until their bodies were aligned so perfectly, not even air could come between them.

"Feel that?" He pressed shivery kisses to the corner of her mouth.

"How can…" she panted out, "I not?"

"Tell me what you feel," he whispered. "Do you feel the way we fit together? The way you took all of me in, so tight, so perfect? Do you feel this?"

His penis jumped, and she nearly lost her mind with the sensation.

"Yes." She closed her eyes, and he kissed the lids.

"Open your eyes, baby. I want to see you as we come together for the first time."

Lord. His words. His stare. His talented mouth, hands, shaft. She'd died and gone to heaven, right there with the moonlight shining down on them and the ocean spraying over their heated flesh.

She rocked her hips as he began to move, and they found their rhythm. God, their glorious, perfect rhythm stroked over all the right places. He slanted his mouth over hers again, kissing, licking, sucking her tongue into his mouth in an erotic dance she never wanted to end. Her hands moved over his bunching, flexing muscles. He was the most confident, virile man she'd ever met. Forget overly mani-cured—the man could wax his entire body and he'd be more of a man than the men she knew.

"Can I lay your head down?" he whispered against her neck.

"Yes. Anything." He could turn her over and do her from behind and she'd be all in.

"Christ, baby. Don't say that to me when I've got you naked in my arms. You have no idea what I want to do to you, the places I want to take you."

Her thoughts fragmented as he guided her legs around his hips and clutched her ass with both hands. The intensity of his stare pierced through her, as if he could see right into her thoughts. She had never explored her darkest sexual fantasies, and she was sure they were nothing compared to what he probably had in mind. The thoughts excited her. His fingers slid between her ass cheeks as he lifted her hips and pounded into her, masterfully taking her right up to the edge.

"Du—"

Her words were lost in her pleasure. He buried his face in her neck and sealed his teeth over her skin, bringing a sting of exquisite pain that shot her over the edge with breakneck force. Her body thrust and bucked, and sweat pooled between their bodies as he eased his bite and sucked gently, pressing tender kisses to the sting as he drove harder with every rock of his hips.

His mouth disappeared from her neck.

"Gabriella, open your eyes." It was a command of pure possession.

Her eyes fluttered open as his powerful hips continued to pound into her. The look in his eyes was pure, hypnotizing seduction. She'd never forget the way he looked at her, the way he spoke to her, touched her. His body moved with the magnitude of a gale-force wind, pulling her under as passion raged through them, carrying them over the edge in a mass of tangled limbs, groans, and pants.

And when he whispered in her ear, "I can't hide. Can't hide my feelings."

She knew she couldn't—wouldn't want to—either.

CHaPTeR THIRTeeN

DUKE AND GABRIELLA lay beneath the stars as they came back down to earth. She felt so right in his arms, with the sweet cadence of her breath whispering over his skin and the warm press of her thigh lying atop his. Duke ran his fingers through her hair while his mind tiptoed over uncharted territory, trying to decipher the feelings coursing through him. He didn't want this night to end, couldn't imagine waking up without Gabriella in his arms.

When they finally decided to head back to their villas it was nearly two in the morning. The celebration had long ago ended.

Gabriella was tucked against Duke's side. One of her hands was splayed over his stomach, beneath his shirt, the other around his waist. He loved having her so close, feeling the warmth of their emotions binding them together.

"Baby?"

"Mm?"

"I want you to stay with me tonight."

She lifted sleepy eyes in his direction. "I don't know."

His stomach plummeted as reality crept back in. He'd been so swept up in them, he hadn't thought past his own desires.

"Because of your family?" he asked.

"Yes, but also…" She shifted her eyes away.

He curled a finger beneath her chin, lifting her face, and kissed her softly.

"Also what, baby? What more could keep you from me?"

"I haven't…I've never spent the whole night with a man before. I'm not sure how I'll feel when the sun comes up."

He breathed a sigh of relief as he gathered her in close. "I won't push you, but I'd be lying if I didn't say I'm disappointed."

After walking Gabriella home and checking out her villa, because she didn't lock the doors, he kissed her good night on the front porch.

"You're not upset?" she asked.

"Upset? How could I possibly be upset after how close we've become? After the night we shared?" He pressed his lips to hers again. "Gabriella, I respect you and want you to be comfortable and happy."

"Thank you."

"There's no thanks necessary, baby. I want to be your man, and being the first man you stay overnight with is now on the top of my to-do list. But what I failed to tell you, and what you really should know, is that I've never *asked* a woman to stay overnight with me before."

"Come on," she said with wide eyes. "A guy like you? You're all…passion and heart. I can't see you *not* asking a woman to spend the night."

"That's because you don't know me well enough yet. Risk versus reward. I've never wanted to risk any woman becoming too attached to me."

She wrapped her arms around him and kissed the center of his chest. "Then why me?"

"You really don't know how special you are, do you?" She lifted her eyes to his, and he kissed her again. "When I saw you on the front porch of the welcome center that first day, I was physically attracted to you. You're a gorgeous woman, and I'm sure you have tons of men vying for your attention. But when you spoke to me, assessing me with your sharp, inquisitive mind, I knew you weren't just another attractive woman. You were sassy and a little combative, but you were also warm and loving to your niece and to Katarina. And then you became playful, and I was a goner from that moment on."

Her cheeks flushed as he tried to explain why he wanted her to spend the night, and he knew he wasn't doing the depth of his feelings justice, but he had to try.

"After two days of learning about who you are, your fears, hopes, dreams…I'm *hoping* you become attached."

"Because you find me attractive and smart," she repeated

with a straight face that confused the hell out of him.

He looked up at the sky, and he realized that for the first time he had no valid reasons for what he felt. There was no data in his head to balance any type of risk versus reward scenario. What he felt came from his heart. When he met her gaze again, she was smiling.

"I'm not making fun of you." She pressed her finger to the center of his chest with a flirtatious smile. "I'm—"

"Weighing the validity of my answers. Christ, I can't imagine what it would be like to face you in the courtroom." He covered her hand with his, holding it against his chest. "There are no hard and fast answers. I don't know why you made my heart stutter, but you did, Gabriella. When I'm with you my focus is on *you*. Your thoughts, your hopes, your fears for the future of the island, which might not seem like much to you, but it's a world away from who I usually am. I'm usually ultra-focused on my work. Women have always come after work, after meetings, after my business. I've never let a woman who was in any way involved with any of my investments into my life, or into my bed."

Her cheeks flushed with the vehemence of his words, but he needed her to hear the truth. He paused long enough to calm himself down, and when he spoke again, it was with all the emotion he'd been trapping inside.

"Baby." He gazed into her trusting eyes. "Can't you feel it? I couldn't have resisted you if my life depended on it."

"Well, technically"—she smirked—"you haven't taken me to your *bed* yet."

"Not for lack of trying," he said as he sealed his lips over hers, turning her sassy smirk into a sensual moan that aroused him all over again.

CHAPTER FOURTEEN

THE NEXT MORNING Gabriella awoke wondering what in the hell was wrong with her. She'd set out last night intent on keeping her distance from Duke, and she'd not only fallen under Duke's spell, but she'd *slept* with him. *Outside*. This was out of the ordinary enough for her, but she'd also *believed* him when he'd made a promise there was no way in hell he could keep. Not that she thought now, even in the light of day, that Duke would intentionally lie. No, it was obvious that he was too thoughtful, too genuine in his statements and feelings to do that. But she was a lawyer. While he dealt with risk management of what *could* be, she dealt with the reality of what *was*.

And, she realized as she showered and dressed, that she didn't know what that reality was, exactly. Duke hadn't been specific about what his visions were for the island, only that they were changing.

She headed down to the beach to watch the sunrise. She needed some perspective, and the ocean always calmed her. Well, except last night when the sprays of the water had rained over them, cooling her heated skin so every breeze heightened her arousal.

The sun was just beginning to sneak over the horizon as she reached the main road. It was too early for shops to be open, another favorite time of day. On the island, it seemed every minute was her favorite time of day.

A cat strolled down the center of Main Street. She slowed to watch the cat and take a good look at the street she knew by heart. When she'd given Duke the tour, she'd veered away from the shops that had been closed for ages. Sometimes it was easy for her to ignore them, pretend they simply weren't there, but now she deliberately walked down to what used to be Milton's Hardware. She used to love visiting Mr. Milton at his store when she was young. He was such a Southern gentleman, and always smelled of Old Spice and mothballs. But she didn't mind; it was *his* smell. The glass doors were dirty with fingerprints and dust. She shielded her eyes and peered into the empty building. She could still make out the counter to the right, where he used to keep a bucket of lollipops to hand out to kids. Her favorites were the green ones. Rows of metal shelves, once full of tools and paints, stood bare in the middle of the store. But those were things growing communities needed, and not significant enough on an island where more people left each year than visited.

She walked a few doors down, to what was once the Elpitha Souvenir Shop. New York City tourists were so numerous that the shops not only remained busy throughout the year, but sales of souvenirs had spilled over to kiosks and tables on the sidewalks. Here they couldn't even keep a single shop open. The beauty parlor slash barbershop next door was still alive and kicking, although the shop was open only on Wednesdays and Saturdays.

Gabriella looked down at the chipped polish on her toes. Her sandals and feet were already dusty from her walk. As she headed toward the pier, her thoughts turned to Duke, and she sighed inwardly. It had been so tempting to go to his villa last night. The idea of waking up in his arms seemed luxurious in a way that she knew only he could make it feel. She wasn't by any means a prude, and certainly hadn't been a virgin, but somehow she'd always kept the morning after as her own, and today she was glad she had—even if part of her wondered if she'd have woken with the same conflicting thoughts if that wonderful man had been the first thing she'd seen. Somehow she doubted that her brain would have functioned that clearly.

The transition from the hard surface to the sandy beach felt like heaven, and her anxiety instantly calmed. The sun rose in the distance, bringing with it a renewed sense of hope that this would all work out. As she crossed the beach, stepping over driftwood and a pile of seashells and pebbles, she knew that there was no way she could keep her feelings for the island and her feelings for Duke separate. The island had owned a piece of her heart for so very long. Duke was quickly seeping past those boundaries, becoming as important as the island was to her. It seemed so fast, but it felt so right. How was she supposed to slow it down?

"*Gabrielaki mou.*"

She turned, smiling at her grandfather's voice. "I didn't hear you behind me." She hugged him, not surprised to see him out this early. They'd had many discussions while they'd watched the sun bloom in the sky.

"I'm quiet in my old age," he said in Greek. "May I join you?"

"I'd like that."

They walked to the dock, and Gabriella reveled in this time with him, taking comfort in his familiarity. He wore a maroon button-down shirt she'd seen a million times and leather sandals that looked as aged as his dusty feet.

The dock creaked as they made their way to the end. Gabriella helped her grandfather lower himself to a seated position on the edge, his feet dangling above the water. She remembered how he used to do the same for her when she was so little that he teased her about fish swallowing her whole. It saddened her that time was passing so quickly, and she was only sharing fits and spurts of time with him as her work schedule allowed. Family meant so much to her. She often longed to see the love in her mother's eyes as she spoke Greek with her Southern drawl, or to see amusement in her father's eyes when it was so conflicting to the words he'd spoken.

"How are things with the investor?" he asked. "Duke."

She sighed, thinking of all the things she could say: *He's wonderful, so honest and sweet. So strong and masculine. He makes my heart turn over every time he looks at me. But he promises things he can't possibly do, even if he wants to.*

She gazed into her grandfather's wise, caring eyes, wanting to confess all those feelings to him. But her love for her grandfather mingled with the hurt of being ushered off the island, and she realized there were things she needed to understand before she could move forward with any of this. Maybe even before she could move forward with the rest of her life. It was time for her to face the one person, the one issue that brought sadness to her memories.

Speaking Greek, she asked, "Why did you ask me to come home and show him around? Why not do it yourself, or have one of my many uncles, or *your* attorney, show him the island?"

Her grandfather took her hand in his. The feel of his thick palm, rough with age, brought a pang of guilt for questioning his decision, wrapped in love so thick it tightened her chest.

"Because, my sweet girl, you see what no one else sees." He looked out over the water, like he had just given her the answers she needed instead of leaving her with even more questions.

"What does that mean, exactly?"

He covered their joined hands with his other hand. "Tell me, my doll, sitting here, what do you see?"

Gabriella warmed all over at his use of the endearment that he'd used her whole life: *kukla mou*, my doll. He'd called her so many loving things, but *kukla* had practically been her first word because she'd heard it so often.

"I see the dock where you taught me to fish. The water where my father taught me to swim." She turned and scanned the sandy shoreline, the tips of the buildings off to the right and the beautiful trees to the left. "The town and the trees where I used to climb and read for hours. Remember when Niko hung a tire swing from the old oak by the bike shop?" As she turned around a little further, she continued on her nostalgic journey.

"I see the welcome center and the gardens my mother and I planted the summer I started high school. Mama and I ended up covered in dirt. I remember her chasing me down the dock, and we both jumped right in the water. Gosh, it was hot that summer."

He gave her hand a gentle squeeze and said, "What would my sons see?"

She thought over the question and realized that while she'd been answering him, she'd lost the thread of her initial question. With that thread reclaimed, she thought about her uncles and father and what they might see of the island.

Still speaking in their native tongue, she answered him easily. "I'm not sure what they'd see."

"Yes, my doll. That is why I chose you. My attorney? What would he see? Dollar signs maybe. Your heart is here, Gabriella. My sons' livelihood is here. They will most certainly see things differently than you do. Different views, different outcomes."

A spear of hurt set in with the need to understand why she was made to leave when others were allowed to stay. On a cognitive level she understood that he wanted her and those relatives who came after her, to have more, but her heart— her aching, lonely-for-the-island heart—needed to understand what else drove him to make such a life-altering decision. She understood that he wanted her to deal with Duke so the most precious parts of the island and their heritage weren't lost in the transition, but sending her away and bringing her back were so conflicting. She needed more answers.

"I know why you made me go, but to bring me back now, for something so important, to make me long for what I cannot have. Why would you do that?"

"My doll, you have always longed for what you cannot have. That is why I had to let you go. Are you not happy in New York?"

She didn't understand his answer. When had she longed

for more than the island had to offer?

"Happy?" Happiness was comprised of so many things, and after spending time with Duke, she realized how much happier she *could* be. Just the thought of seeing him, knowing he'd light up—and heat up—the minute he saw her, the same way she did, made her happy.

"Do you have friends?" he asked.

"Yes."

"A safe place to live?"

"Yes."

"A respectable career?" he asked with pride in his eyes.

Her stomach tightened. "I have a solid career, but I'm not sure it's respectable. Nothing is as it seems with law."

"Nothing is as it seems anywhere, my sweet girl. If you were here, what would you have?"

Her mind rushed to answer with the most important thing of all. "Family."

He laughed. "Family? You have family, my love. We are here. You have relatives all over the mainland."

"Yes, but all I ever wanted was to have a family of my own here on the island. Why can't anyone accept that?"

"We do. We always have. But you would not have found that here. There are no jobs for the men, no careers for the women beyond the family. You have always needed more than that, Gabrielaki. There was no chance at finding a husband here, and then you would have stayed on the island for…what?"

"A peaceful life."

He shook his head, and his gaze turned serious. "You would grow bored of a peaceful life."

"No, Grandfather, that's not so." She couldn't imagine ever being bored on the island.

"Do you remember what you did each summer while you were in college?" he asked.

"Yes. The first summer I helped the Eastmans negotiate with their suppliers to get more timely shipments, even though they needed fewer of them. And the second summer I helped Uncle George and Niko set up online inventory systems for their businesses. And that was the summer I worked at the library with Georgette and we got involved with all the online databases." As she recounted the things she'd done, she realized that she had spent that time moving them forward, not keeping them at a standstill.

"You see, sweet girl? You have always needed more. You're too smart to be limited to what's here."

She crossed her arms against the truth. "I disagree."

Her grandfather's smile widened. "Then make your dreams come true. I have given you the tools, but I cannot do the work."

Holy crap. That was why he'd put her in this position. She wrapped her arms around the man who had sent her away—and the man who had brought her back—and she filled with hope.

"I won't let you down, Grandfather. And I won't let myself down, either."

CHAPTER FIFTEEN

DUKE SPENT THE morning at the library going over the due-diligence reports he'd received from Pierce. He'd been over them several times, and he'd known what they contained before reading them, having had his team fill him in during the discovery process. But he needed to see the data, numbers, and issues in writing again to remind himself to keep a critical eye and not allow his professional views to become overshadowed by his heart.

He'd scheduled a meeting with the land development and finance team for Tuesday, which gave him only today and tomorrow on the island with Gabriella. It wasn't enough, but would any amount of time ever be? He'd looked into Gabriella's very successful practice. Having handled many high-profile divorce cases with people who were noted in the media as being rude, entitled assholes, she appeared to be exactly the shrewd businesswoman he'd assumed she was. He wondered about her desire to return to the island. Would she really want to give up everything she'd worked so hard to achieve?

He'd hoped to see her this morning, but when he'd gone to her villa, she was already gone. He'd left a note with his cell phone number and the flowers he'd picked from the woods along the path to her place. It was almost lunchtime and he hadn't heard from her. He worried that they'd moved too fast, even though he knew he didn't have a chance in hell of slowing them down. He'd wanted to carry her off to his villa last night and make love to her until she was too tired to go home. Instead he'd gone home and downloaded a book on the Greek language, studied that for an hour, then read half of *The Kitchen House*, the book Georgette had recommended. He'd been so engrossed in the novel, he'd gotten only two hours of sleep.

"Did you find everything you needed, Duke?" Georgette asked. She was a sweet woman with wide-set eyes the color of the sea and the type of friendly face that said, *Come in; have some tea and a piece of pie, and let's chat.*

"I did, thank you, Georgette. And I'm really enjoying the book you recommended."

She touched his shoulder and nodded. "I told you. She has a way with words, doesn't she? Why, I felt like I was right there on the plantation with Belle and Lavinia."

"Yes, she's quite a talented writer. Things have changed so much since then."

"Oh, yes, just look around you." She glanced around the nearly empty library. "There was a time when all the teenagers hung out in here, reading. Now only a few come in. The rest are on their phones, or they've moved to the mainland and are holed up playing video games."

"There is a lot of that these days, that's for sure."

"Yes." She sighed. "Kids no longer find joy in the quiet life, as my generation did." She lowered her voice. "I know we're not supposed to talk about Mr. Liakos selling his property, but if we don't do something, I worry what will happen to our sweet island."

Duke nodded. "I am hoping to help with that."

They talked for a while about her sons who had moved to Georgia a decade ago and how busy their lives were. She was obviously very proud of them, and while she missed her grandchildren, she said they were better off there, where they had the tools they'd need to make it in the changing world.

Duke had just enough time to grab lunch before meeting David. The sun was shining, and it seemed the whole town was hanging around the *taverna* patio. Children ran around giggling, while teenagers huddled together in groups and adults filled nearly every table. Red and white tablecloths were covered with bottles of wine, salads, colorful vegetables topped with large blocks of feta cheese, decorative baskets full of enormous loaves of bread, and plates overflowing with skewers of meats and French fries. Duke wondered if there was another celebration going on. Not wanting to interrupt, he walked past rather than stopping.

"Duke!" Dimitri motioned him over to a table where his brother, Niko, his parents, and his grandfather were sitting.

As he crossed the patio, he searched for Gabriella, hoping he might find her here with her family.

"Hi. I was just heading up to the resort to grab some lunch."

"The resort?" Dimitri said with surprise. "The resort has food, yes, but we're here. You're here. Eat with us." He grabbed a chair from another table and pushed Duke's shoulder, guiding him into it.

Gabriella's mother set a napkin in his hands while Niko filled a glass with wine and placed it in front of him. Dimitri handed him a plate, leaving Duke wondering how he'd pulled it out of thin air.

Gabriella's father lifted his glass. "To the future of the island."

Duke clinked glasses with the others. They filled their plates and dug into their meals. Conversation came easily, moving from food to Duke's family, then back to the island, and finally, back to the food. With a full stomach Duke checked his watch and realized he needed to leave to meet David.

"Thank you for the delicious lunch, but I'm afraid I have to meet someone in a few minutes." He rose to his feet, his pulse quickening when he spotted Gabriella walking up the street. He wondered if she'd found his flowers and the note he'd left on her porch. Her pretty yellow dress set off her olive skin, and her hair tumbled casually over her shoulders, conflicting with the serious expression she wore.

"How long will you be on the island, Duke?" Niko asked as Gabriella approached.

It took all of Duke's focus not to reach for her and ask her what was wrong. Holding her gaze and wondering about the strained look she was giving him, he answered Niko. "Unfortunately, I have to leave Monday, but I've greatly enjoyed my stay."

"*Gabrielaki mou*, join us?" Her father held a hand out to her.

Gabriella circled the table, kissing the cheek of each of her relatives. A spear of jealousy sliced through him. He wanted one of those kisses and the smile that came with it.

"Thank you, *Baba*, but I was hoping to speak with Duke for a few minutes."

"Ahh," Dimitri said with a wink.

"You two disappeared quite early last night, too," Niko said with a serious look in his eyes. "Do you need a chaperone?"

"Hush, boys," their mother said. "You two go talk, and ignore these cavemen. It was nice to see you again, Duke."

"And you as well." Duke settled a hand on Gabriella's back and felt her bristle. Though his insides were knotting, he realized he was touching her in a possessive way in front of her family and dropped his hand.

GABRIELLA'S HEART HURT as they left the *taverna*. Duke had looked so happy when he'd seen her approaching. She'd wanted to run into his arms, but she'd somehow managed to remain in control. And when he'd touched her back, she'd ached to turn into his arms, go up on her toes, and kiss his lips. But after spending the early morning with her grandfather, then spending time talking with her mother, aunts, and cousins, she'd gained perspective. Unable to separate her feelings for Duke from her feelings for the island, and knowing that her grandfather was counting on her to somehow make the best of both their simple lifestyles and whatever it was Duke could bring to the island, she was left with no choice but to put distance between them. *Again.*

As they left the jovial atmosphere of the *taverna* and were surrounded by sunshine and island sounds, she readied herself for what she knew she had to do.

"I missed you last night," Duke said as they left the main road and headed down a wooded path toward the school-house.

Afraid if she opened her mouth, *I missed you, too,* would tumble out, she swallowed her emotions and let silence fill the space between them. The space she hated with a passion, even after only a few seconds.

"Gabriella?" They were alone on the path, shaded by tall trees. He touched her arm and they both stopped walking. "What's wrong? Are you having second thoughts about us?"

No. She drew her shoulders back, needing every bit of strength she could muster, and lifted her chin. Meeting his gaze sent a spear of guilt through her.

"Not second thoughts about us, really, but about what we agreed to."

He looked sexy and distracting, in a soft gray T-shirt and low-slung jeans, and when he stepped closer, she wanted him there even though she knew she shouldn't.

"Which part of what we agreed to?" He used his index finger to move a lock of hair from in front of her eyes, and the edges of his lips curved up.

"The part where we agreed not to let our feelings for each other be affected by whatever happens to the island and vice versa."

He placed his big, warm hands on her hips and tugged her against him. God, she loved it there.

"I see." He licked his lips, searching her eyes. "And what should we do about that, Counselor?"

She'd loved it when he'd called her that last night, and now? She'd like to get her hands on his *briefs.*

That was *not* helping. Duke in his undercrackers was a sight to behold—and the thought sent her mind reeling back to him standing beside her, stroking his hard length. Heat pooled between her legs, and he must have sensed it, because he pressed his lips to hers.

His kisses were like crack, the way he wrapped his strong arms around her and made love to her mouth. She felt her brain cells melting away, and if that wasn't enough, he made a guttural sound deep in his throat and it vibrated through her. Her fingers slid into his hair as he found her ass, pressing their bodies as close together as they could get while fully clothed. Her knees weakened, and she surrendered to their kiss, taking as much as she was giving, soaking in every sweet swipe of his tongue, every beat of his heart against her own.

"I love kissing you," he said against her lips before taking her in another punishingly intense kiss.

You're my undoing.

My drug.

My…Ohmygod.

She forced her hands to his chest with the intent of pushing him away, but as her fingers played over his muscles, she wanted to climb beneath that shirt and lick him all over. Her eyes sprang open with the thought.

He smiled against her lips.

"Duke." She pushed away, breathing hard but somehow feeling like she wasn't breathing at all. "I can't do this. *We* can't do this."

He cradled her face between his hands and said in a surprisingly calm voice compared to his heated gaze, "Baby, I can definitely do this, and you might not know it yet, but you can, too."

Tears burned in her eyes. "No, Duke. I feel too much for you already."

"That's a good thing. Jesus, do you know how many years I've wondered if I'd ever feel for someone the way my parents feel about each other? I thought it was a farce, this whole, 'you'll know your soul mate when you meet her' thing. But, baby"—his gaze pierced straight to her heart—"I *know*. I'm falling for you, and I want more of you, not less."

"F-falling for me? No, Duke. You can't." But she knew he could, because she was, too. She took a step back on wobbly legs, and he gathered her close again.

"Too late," he said.

He felt so good. So right. "It's not that simple." She'd been falling for him since the first day, but she couldn't allow herself to have feelings for him. "I know myself too well. I can't do this. My family, my grandfather, the people on this island…They're counting on me to be smart."

"You can't help but be smart, baby. Why does that worry you?"

She pushed away again. "Because you and your seductive voice, your sexy words, and…" She raked her eyes down his incredibly hot body. "Your stupid, hot body, which looks like you were kissed by a sex god. It all makes me stupid."

His leer became wolfish. "You like my body?"

"Ugh!" She turned away, half laughing, half frustrated. "Duke, can't you see what you do to me?"

He spun her in his arms and his eyes rolled over her face, lingering on her lips so long she nearly took *him* in a kiss. "You mean the rosy flush on your skin?" He dropped his eyes. "Or the way your nipples are crying out for my mouth on them?"

She moaned, despite herself, and when he stepped even closer, she held her breath. She was *that* close to giving in. One whiff of him could shatter her resolve.

"Yeah, I see it," he whispered. "And I like it. A whole hell of a lot." He lifted her chin, forcing her to look into his serious eyes. "You're fighting the inevitable, baby. We're meant to be together. I feel it in my bones, and trust me, at closer to forty than thirty, I know the difference between infatuation and *this*."

"This…" She was tumbling like Jill, right down that big old hill. *Bump, bump, bump!*

"We don't have to name it, and you can try to fight it, but I won't let you walk away from us, Gabriella."

"I don't want to walk away from us. Just put us on hiatus."

He laughed, a wholehearted belly laugh. "Seriously? You think I can stay away from you? I'm so drunk on you, *kardia mou*, I hear your voice when you're not even there."

Ohmygod. "Wh-what did you just say?"

"I hear your voice—"

"No, the other part."

"I'm so drunk—"

"Duke!" She pressed her hand to his chest, reveling in the mischievous twinkle in his eyes. She went up on her toes, aching to be closer. "You called me 'your heart' in Greek."

"I might have studied up a little last night."

"Duke." His name came out drenched in emotions.

"I'm all in, Gabriella. There are risks for me, too, but I want this. I want you."

She couldn't say a word, because she wanted to be all in, too. He leaned in for a kiss, and with his hand on her back, they continued walking toward the school.

"I have a date with David, but I'm glad you came by to tell me your plans. While you're creating space between us, I'm going to just carry on with my life, okay?"

Her stomach sank. "What does that mean?" He was letting her go after all? Suddenly her idea seemed very, very bad.

"It means you do what you have to, and I'll do what I have to. I don't play games, baby. You'll learn that about me. Not that I think you're playing a game. You're just confused. Underestimating what you're capable of."

"No, I'm not confused." Okay, maybe that wasn't completely true. She *was* confused by the incredible rush of feelings she had for him, but not about what she was capable of handling. "I know what you do to me, and I know I need a clear head so that when you come to my grandfather with your plans for the island, I can help steer you back in the right direction."

He stopped walking again. "Excuse me?"

She thought about the responsibility her grandfather had entrusted in her and the sense of power she'd felt after talking with him. She needed to hold on to that resolve.

"That's right." She clenched her teeth to keep them from chattering. "And if you're too far off the mark, then we'll just have to find another investor."

His eyes turned serious. "You don't need to threaten me, baby. I don't break promises."

Apparently *unwavering confidence* had a name, and it was Duke Ryder. And she'd never seen anything so hot.

He placed his hand on her back and said, "I'll never underestimate you, baby. I have as much faith in you as I have in myself," before walking right past her and into the schoolyard.

She wanted to tell him she hadn't meant it, that she hoped it would never come to that, but she'd created this fissure for a reason. *She* needed it, even if he didn't.

CHAPTER SIXTEEN

THE WHITE CLAPBOARD schoolhouse was tinged with dirt, the siding cracked but holding strong. The stone foundation looked newly repointed, and the roof had patches marking recent repairs. Duke imagined that at one time the schoolhouse had been the pride of the community, the gathering place for kids and families. He tried to imagine Gabriella as a young girl, and he wished he'd known her then. Wished they'd grown up together so he would have been there for her when she left the island. He turned to ask her about what it had been like, but she was too far away, still standing by the edge of the path.

He tried to make sense of what she'd said. Obviously she knew herself better than he did, but did she really, if she didn't think she could handle separating their relationship from the investment process? He knew from her reputation as an attorney she was capable of handling anything she put her mind to. He didn't expect their relationship to be easy, especially once they got to the actual proposal negotiation, and he didn't want to force himself on her, but he wasn't about to let the best thing that had ever happened to him walk away. He'd just have to try harder to help her see that she could do this.

With that decided, he spotted David leaning against the far side of the building, and just beyond, a group of kids huddled together. David was a handsome kid, with big brown eyes and thick dark hair, but like most prepubescent boys, he was all knees and elbows in his T-shirt and shorts. Duke had always had a soft spot for the underdogs.

"Hey there, buddy," he said as he came to David's side. "How's it going?"

David shrugged. "A'right, I guess."

"You ready to toss a few balls?" He leaned down to grab the bat, glove, and ball lying on the ground.

David eyed the group of kids, who weren't paying any attention to them.

Duke motioned toward the other side of the field. "Come on. Let's go show them what we've got."

"Not much to see," David said as they crossed the field.

Duke glanced over his shoulder, searching for Gabriella, and found her sitting by the back of the school, watching them. She met his gaze, then looked away. His gut fisted, but he was there to help David, and he couldn't let his emotions get in the way of that.

"Okay, big guy," Duke said. "What position do you play?"

"Outfield."

"Outfield. Cool. The first thing you need to know—and this is a life lesson, so listen closely…Rule number one of any sport is to be confident. Act like you do things well, and everyone else will think you do. If everyone believes you're good, that's half the battle. The other half is making it real."

"Yeah, right. I'm not a kid," he said with all the arrogance a thirteen-year-old could muster. "I know making it real isn't going to happen."

"First, you *are* a kid, a very bright and capable kid. Second, it's the truth, so smile and tell me you'll try it."

"Fine. I'll try it."

He wasn't giving in on the smile, but Duke let that slide. "Good. Now let's throw this ball around and see if we can teach you to catch."

David's eyes shifted to the other kids again.

Duke touched his shoulder to get his attention. "Eyes on me. Concentration is key to doing well in any sport." He waited for David to put on his glove. Then he put some distance between them and called out, "Ready?"

David looked at the other kids again.

"David, focus, buddy. Pretend they don't exist." He waited until he had David's full attention; then he threw the ball to him.

David held his mitt out. The ball *plunked* off the edge of it and fell to the ground by his feet.

"That's okay. Toss it back here."

David threw the ball hard. It hit Duke's mittless hands so hard it stung. "Wow, you've got a good arm."

He shrugged one shoulder. "I guess."

Duke tossed him the ball again, and it landed in his mitt, then rolled out. "David, when the ball hits your mitt, close your fingers around it. Watch." He closed the distance between them and set the ball in David's mitt. "Close your hand." David did, trapping the ball. Duke turned his mitt upside down, and the ball remained in David's glove. "See? Anticipate the catch. Then the second it hits, you close the mitt."

"I told you I suck."

"First of all, you're breaking rule number one. What is rule number one?" He stole a glance at Gabriella, glad to see she was watching them again. She looked so beautiful with the afternoon sun shining down on her. He wished he could run over and try to smooth things out between them.

"Act confident."

David's voice brought Duke back to their conversation. "Right, and do you know what comes next? Rule number two?"

David shrugged.

"Believe rule number one. Rule number three?" Duke said. "Do everything within your power to make it happen. Got it?"

David laughed. "Got it."

Duke walked back to the mound and tossed the ball again. David caught it, and he threw it so hard that Duke cursed under his breath.

"Hey, buddy? Has anyone ever asked you about pitching instead of playing the field?"

"If I can't catch, how can I pitch?" David shifted his eyes to the other kids again.

"You're kidding, right? Plenty of pitchers can't catch very well. Your arm is on fire. Give me your glove." Duke slid David's glove onto his hand and handed the ball to David. "I want you to pitch this to me as hard and as fast as you can."

David walked out to the pitcher's mound and Duke crouched at home plate.

"Whenever you're ready, buddy." He could feel the heat of Gabriella's gaze, and as he shifted his eyes for a quick look, David burned a perfect fastball right over home plate.

"Damn, kid. You sure you're only thirteen?" Duke threw the ball back and tried to catch Gabriella's eye, but she seemed to look away every time he looked over. It took all his focus not to take a few minutes from David to try to talk to her, but he didn't want to do that to David when he was just beginning to gain confidence.

They practiced for another half hour. The kids who were talking by the school had moved in closer and were watching them.

"Have you ever thrown a curveball?" Duke asked as he approached the mound.

"No. I barely ever get to touch the ball."

"It's time for that to change. Your hands were made for pitching, and there are very few people in the world who can say that. The curveball is all about the topspin and the grip. With those incredible hands, you're going to kick some batter butt."

David smiled, and it warmed Duke's heart.

"The grip is fairly simple. See the stitching on the side of the ball? You hold the ball so the U shape is facing you, upside down, like this." He gripped the ball between his thumb and first two fingers. "Here, you try it."

David took the ball, turned it, and gripped it exactly as Duke had shown him.

"Good, how does it feel?"

"Good. Like a baseball." David laughed.

"Cocky, aren't you?" Duke teased. "That's good, actually. Keep it up. Now, the goal is for the ball to curve as it reaches the plate. To do that, you need to put topspin on the ball. Topspin generates wind resistance with the laces and causes the pitch to drop. Once you master this, you can learn the slider. We're going to make you your team's secret weapon."

"Cool," David said with another wide smile. "That would be awesome."

"Believe it?" Duke asked.

He nodded.

Duke held his hand up for a high five, and David returned it with a strong slap.

"Good, then let's make it happen. You already know how to throw a fastball. With a curveball, you're going to throw it just like a fastball to here." He went through the motions of throwing a fastball and stopped when his elbow and arm formed an L, his arm perpendicular to the ground. "Then you turn your hand inward."

David mimicked the motion perfectly. "Like that?"

"Dude, you've got this." Duke patted his shoulder. "But there are a few key elements to keep in your head at all times. Your middle finger is the key to this grip. You've got to find the place where the seam provides the most resistance against your middle finger."

"I can do that." David's eyes turned serious as he gripped the ball.

"And you know how I said your big hands were ideal for pitching? Well, the other key is that you keep the ball from resting on your palm. Most guys can't do that. Their fingers are too short." Duke stole another glance at Gabriella. He waved, and the half wave she gave back pierced his heart.

David held up his hand, a smile spreading across his lips as he showed Duke the gap between his palm and the ball. "Dude, I've got this."

"You sure do, buddy. Remember, when you release, it's

not like releasing a fastball. You're pulling down the front of the ball, trying to increase the rate of rotation and create as strong of a spin as you can."

"Like this?" David practiced the motion a few times.

Duke explained the proper angle of his elbow and arm at release, the hook of the wrist, the path of the ball and how it differs from that of a fastball, and finally, he explained how David's stride could affect the pitch.

He watched David practice the motion until he felt comfortable, and then David practiced pitching. He was a natural. After half a dozen tries, nearly every ball curved perfectly.

"This is awesome. Can we practice until dark?" David's increased confidence showed in his consistent eye contact, the excited inflection of his voice, and the way he stood up tall, owning his lanky body with pride.

The other kids were watching with interest, moving in closer. One of the boys, a blond-haired, serious-eyed kid who looked to be around David's age, crossed the field toward Duke and called out, "Hey, can you show me that?"

Duke didn't want to take any time or attention away from David, but he had an idea of how to help David even more.

"Actually, I can't hang out too much longer, but David here is a pro. I'd bet he can show you a thing or two, if he wants to."

The other kid turned hopeful eyes to David. "Would you mind?"

Duke took a step back, giving David space to take control, hoping like hell that his newfound confidence would remain.

"Sure," David said with a hint of nervousness.

Duke caught his eye and lifted his chin in a way that he knew David would translate to, *You've got this.*

David stood up a little taller and said, "We're throwing curveballs. Let me see your hands."

Two more boys joined them, holding up their hands to show David, too. David was smiling now, looking the others in the eyes. Duke listened to the smart boy tutor the others on what he'd just learned. Positively elated, he turned to share the moment with Gabriella—but she was gone.

Chapter Seventeen

GABRIELLA SAT ON the front porch of her villa reviewing the file for the McGrady case. The evening breeze carried the sweet scent of the flowers Duke had left for her. They were proving to be just as much of a distraction to her as Duke was. Watching the way Duke connected with David, with the perfect blend of confidence and care, had been too hard. She'd felt herself getting even more swoony over him, and she'd come home to take her mind off of him. But when she'd found the flowers on the porch, she'd stumbled over those emotions again.

She'd made arrangements to go back home to New York tomorrow. With the McGrady case looming, she needed to be on top of her game. At least that's what she'd told herself when she'd made the arrangements. If she stayed on the island with Duke, she'd never be able to resist him. She didn't want to resist him. But eventually that proposal that was hanging in the wind would come to fruition, and she didn't want to ever look at Duke and see the man who ruined the place she loved. It was better to table their relationship until that was over, wasn't it?

Her heart squeezed with the thought. She definitely need-ed space, and a few hundred miles should do the trick.

She picked up the note Duke had left with the flowers and read it for the millionth time.

Don't overthink us. Good things are going to happen. Can't wait to hold you in my arms again. Xo, Duke.

Even his handwriting was neat and commanding, like him. She traced his name with her finger, then did the same with the phone number he'd written below. She went inside to retrieve her cell phone and add his number to her contacts. At some point, the island negotiation would be over and maybe then they could spend more time together. If it went well. His promise came reeling back to her. *I will do my best to make this island a place where you would not only be proud to live, but that you will feel just as passionate about as you do now.*

"Hey, baby."

She lifted her eyes and her insides went soft at the sight of Duke on the other side of the screen door. He was there, even after she'd told him she needed space. She should probably be irritated, but it had the opposite effect on her. His dark eyes grazed over her, warming her like a caress. His voice was husky and low. She wished she could memorize his voice and play it over and over in the time between now and when the island transaction was done.

"May I come in?" he asked.

"Yes, of course." She set down her phone and the note and went to him as he opened the door. "Thank you for the lovely flowers. They were so unexpected."

"Just like you," he said as he leaned down to kiss her cheek. "You missed David's big finish."

She didn't resist when he touched his fingertips to hers. She wanted that connection. It calmed her anxiety over how cold she'd been to him earlier, threatening to bring in another investor. Oh, how she'd hated to say it, but she'd needed the barrier. The barrier he was apparently choosing to ignore.

"How did he do?" she asked.

"His catching needs work, but he'll get it. He's a really bright kid. Turns out he's also a talented pitcher. Picked up on curveballs right away." He cupped her cheek. "But I didn't come here to talk about David. He was teaching the other kids to throw when I left a while ago."

His eyes roamed over her face as she tried to picture the nervous boy teaching other kids to do anything.

"He was okay?"

"Better than okay. But how are you, baby? I was sad that you left. I think you would have gotten a kick out of seeing how confident David was by the end."

She dropped her eyes to his chest, feeling guilty for taking off but knowing she'd had to. Every second she'd watched him seeded him more deeply into her heart.

"I had work to do. I'm leaving tomorrow morning to

prepare for a case."

"Tomorrow? I don't have to be back until Tuesday. I was planning on trying to meet with your grandfather again tomorrow, and talking to a few more business owners, but I was also hoping we'd have most of the day together."

She fought the urge to tell him she'd delay her flight, which was really, really hard to do. "It's a big case. I'm leaving around eight so I have time to prepare."

"I understand." He lifted his eyes to the back patio, where her laptop and papers were spread out on the table. "I'm interrupting. I should let you go."

Her heart was beating fast. She didn't want him to leave. He was giving her the space she needed after all. He was so darn good! Screw work. She didn't want a distraction. She wanted Duke. She wrapped her fingers around his and held on tight, holding his gaze. "I've done enough for tonight. Do you want to stay? Have a glass of wine?"

His lips quirked up in a sexy, relieved smile. "There's nothing I'd rather do."

She didn't let the debate in her head dissuade her. How could she when her heart was telling her that she needed one more night with Duke? A few more hours to hear his voice, to feel the heat rolling off of him and her insides burn.

He helped her gather the wine and glasses from the kitchen, and on the way outside, Duke picked up two candles and a lighter that she kept on the mantel. He flicked off the outdoor light and her nerves went a little crazy.

She gathered her papers, feeling his presence behind her as he set the candles and wine down, then wrapped his arms around her from behind.

"I missed you so much today." His warm breath whispered over her neck, sending a shiver down her spine.

She closed her eyes, reveling in the heavy thumping of his heart against her back, the way his hands splayed across her stomach, sending heat through her core. When he pressed kisses to her shoulder, she leaned in to him, wanting more.

"God, how I missed you, baby." He pressed a kiss to the back of her head.

She turned in his arms and clutched his shirt, fighting the urgency inside her, the desire to tear his shirt right off. He gripped her hips tight, like he was never going to let her go— and God help her, because even after just a few short days, she wished he never would. One look at the smoldering flames in his eyes brought back the fantasies she'd had all afternoon of being crushed beneath him again.

"I missed you, too."

A silent war appeared in the twitch of his eyes. "You can do this, Gabriella. You can separate us from my upcoming negotiations."

"Can I?" *Oh, how I want to.*

"I have no doubt that you can do anything you put your beautiful mind to. The question is, do you want do?"

His fingers splayed over her hips as he lifted her easily onto the table, pushed her legs apart, and settled his powerful hips against her core. *Lord.* How was she supposed to think like this?

He pressed his lips to her forehead, her cheek, the edges of her mouth, setting every nerve on fire.

"It's your call," he whispered in her ear before trapping her lobe between his teeth and sucking it sensually.

She closed her eyes, not wanting to think. Not wanting to decide, because what her heart wanted and her grandfather had asked of her conflicted so badly. He dipped his tongue in her ear, rocking her body with heat. She fisted her hands in his shirt, arching against him as his talented tongue explored a path down her neck. He nibbled, then stroked his tongue over the sting, before returning his heated breath to her ear.

"I want to make love to you in a bed, Gabriella. In your bed. But I want so much more than tonight." He licked the shell of her ear, then tipped her chin up with his fingers, and holy cow, the passion in his eyes reeled her right in.

"I want mornings. I want to know everything about your life, not just the sexy…" He pressed his lips to hers. "Mind blowing…" He stroked his tongue over her lower lip. "Ravishing side."

"Yes…" It came in one long whisper. "I want you, Duke. I want you so bad."

He sealed his mouth over hers in a hard, hungry kiss as he

lifted her into his arms, and her legs wrapped around his hips. He carried her inside, never breaking their connection, and set her on the edge of the bed. He reached over his shoulder, tugging off his shirt, pulled his wallet from his back pocket, and tossed two condoms on the bed. *Two!* Her eyes zeroed in on the grooves between his abs. She leaned forward and dragged her tongue over them. She reached for him, and he led her hands to the button on his pants.

Thank God.

"Take them off," he said in a commanding, powerful voice that she wanted to obey.

Her fingers were shaking so badly. He covered her hand with one of his, then cupped her face with the other, leaned forward, and kissed her again, hard at first, smothering and demanding and so delicious she went damp. Just as quickly the kiss turned slow and loving, to a series of intoxicating, drugging kisses. When their lips parted he didn't move away. He was so close, his eyes nearly black with desire.

"If I'm too aggressive, tell me. I get carried away with you. I want all of you, Gabriella."

"You're not. I'm...I love this side of you." Her head was spinning, her body was humming, and she wanted more. More of his dirty talk, more of his touch, more of his heart.

He pressed another tender kiss to her mouth. "Okay, baby. You tell me if I cross a line. Don't worry. I don't have a secret dark side that wants you to submit to my every whim.

Only some of them." He searched her eyes again and said with a wicked grin, "You hold all the strings."

Ohmygod. She'd never heard anything sexier, never felt so desired.

"Take them off," he said in a steady voice as he released her hand, which he'd trapped at his button.

She tore open the button and ripped his zipper down, feeling empowered, emboldened by his desires. She tugged his pants down his thick thighs, leaving him in his black briefs, the tip of his erection peeking out over the waistband. She licked her lips, wanting to taste him, to pleasure him like he pleasured her. He toed off his shoes and took his pants the rest of the way off.

"Everything," he said.

She glanced up, and the sight of his predatory stare spurred her on. She was so hungry for him, to feel the weight of him on her tongue, the thickness stretching her lips. Her hands shook as she pulled his briefs down his legs and his erection sprang free. She didn't wait for direction—couldn't wait another second to taste him. The first slick of her tongue brought a guttural moan as his head tipped forward, his eyes glued to her. She licked him from base to tip in one slow stroke, wetting his shaft on the sides, then took him in her hand. She stroked him as she licked the bead glistening at the tip, and his essence burst in her mouth.

"Baby." He reached down and stroked her cheek, bringing her eyes up to him. "I love watching you."

She kept her eyes trained on him as she worked him with her hand and swirled her tongue over the swollen tip.

"Suck me, baby."

She gripped his hips and moved his cock to her lips, then glanced up at him, feeling in control and sexy as hell as she opened her mouth and guided him in. He groaned again as her lips circled his shaft, and she dug her fingers into his hips, moving him in and out of her mouth.

"That's it, baby. Take me deep."

She moved one hand to his shaft as she worked him with her mouth. He rocked his hips, though she could see restraint in his jaw, feel it in the tension rolling off his body. She knew he was holding back, and she didn't want him to. She wanted to know she could shatter his resolve as wildly as he shattered hers.

She rose to her feet and said in a commanding voice she didn't recognize, "Take my dress off."

"You have no idea how hot you are when you say that to me." He lifted her dress over her head and tore her bra right off, breaking the clasp. The sting of material as it tore against her skin amped up her arousal. She'd never done this before, never had anything but missionary, boring sex, and she didn't want to stop. Everything he did, from the feral look in his eyes to the way he was tearing her panties off, made her ache for more of him. More of his strength, his passion.

"You're so beautiful, baby." He reached for her, and she dropped back down to the bed, tugged his hips closer, and licked his balls. He fisted his hands in her hair and growled. *Holy hell, that noise!* She needed him, needed this. She licked his balls again, then lifted them and licked the tender skin beneath.

"Holy Christ. Gab—"

She sucked his balls into her mouth, laving them with her tongue as she worked his shaft. Every pleasure-filled moan told her she was touching him right. His jaw clenched, and he was barely breathing. She knew he was struggling to remain in control.

"Do it, Duke." She wanted to say the F-word, but she was having trouble getting up the nerve. Her whole body was shaking. She was so wet between her legs, so ready, and he hadn't even touched her yet. She threw caution to the wind. "Fuck my mouth. Let me taste you."

"Baby?" His hands stilled. "This is so much more than fucking."

She felt the truth in her entire being. Being with Duke was like an out-of-body experience, where she was watching herself fall for a man, touch a man, in new, exhilarating ways, and she didn't want to stop.

She guided him into her mouth, circling the base with one hand, while clutching his ass with the other. Her eyes were glued to his as he began thrusting into her mouth. Every thrust brought the tip to the back of her throat.

"So fucking sexy."

She pulled away. "Don't hold back. I want this, Duke. I want you."

"I don't want to hurt you," he said so carefully she wanted to thank him.

"You never will. I trust you."

"Relax your throat baby." He stroked her hair. "Close your eyes and relax, and if you need me to stop, tell me."

She closed her eyes, knowing he'd take care of her. He pushed in slowly, caressing the sides of her face as he began moving faster, harder. She gripped the backs of his thighs, wanting more, wanting to taste his seed.

"Baby, I'm not going to last."

She didn't want him to. She pressed on the backs of his thighs, letting him know, and then his hands fisted in her hair, and he thrust in hard, pistoned his hips again and again. His thighs went rigid, and the next thrust brought a hot stream of come to the back of her throat.

"Gabriella—"

She let him give everything he had, and she took, took, took. When the last of his release left his body, his hands brushed over her cheeks again. He lifted her up to her feet and sealed his mouth over hers. His pungent taste lingered on her tongue, in her throat, and the thrill of knowing he tasted himself made the kiss that much hotter. He clutched her ass, slipping one hand between her thighs. She was so ready, so sensitive, she nearly came apart.

DUKE LAID GABRIELLA on the bed and came down over her, still recovering from the intensity of his orgasm. Her body was flushed, her eyes hazy with desire, and as his chest brushed over her sensitive nipples, she gasped.

"So sexy," he said, unable to keep the sentiment locked away. He brushed her hair from her forehead and whispered, "Are you okay?"

She nodded. "More than okay."

"Don't ever feel like you have to do anything you don't want to with me, okay? I want to experience everything with you, but not at the expense of your enjoyment." It had taken a Herculean effort not to thrust into her mouth as hard as his body craved, but he didn't want to take a chance of hurting her.

"I never knew it could feel this good. Just being with you brings a new level of pleasure." His hand slid over her ribs, up her breast. He rolled her nipple between his finger and thumb. He was hard again, ready to feel her heat surrounding him.

"Oh God, that feels good." Her eyes fluttered closed, and she trapped her lower lip between her teeth.

Duke sucked that lip into his mouth, and seeing her so close to the edge stoked the fire within him. He claimed her mouth in another demanding kiss, pulling a series of sexy moans from her lungs. He kissed a path straight down her body, unable to curb his desire to taste her for another second. Splaying his hands over her inner thighs, he spread them wide and brought her knees up so her feet were flat on the bed. He licked and kissed one inner thigh, dragging his teeth across her sensitive skin. She fisted her hands in the mattress, and he moved to the other thigh, enjoying the view of her glistening promised land.

"You're so wet, baby, so beautiful and ready."

She moaned, and he sucked her inner thigh into his mouth, laving her skin with his tongue, as if he were kissing her mouth.

"Duke." She breathed hard, reaching for his head. "I need you."

"Oh, baby, you'll get me. Don't you worry."

He slicked his tongue over her wet, swollen sex. She tasted sweet, so damn sweet. He pressed his tongue to her clit and sank two fingers inside her. She gasped and her thighs trembled, but he kept them trapped as he devoured her center. She arched against him as he loved her with his fingers and mouth. Her head thrashed from side to side as her hot channel tightened around his fingers.

"That's it, baby. Let go."

"Duke," she cried out as he continued moving his fingers in and out at a quick pace, while his mouth kept her at the peak.

"Ohgodohgod. So good," she cried.

Duke moved up her body, sealing his mouth over one of her nipples, while rubbing his hard length over her sensitive nerves. He pinched her other nipple just hard enough to make her hips buck and her breathing hitch. Her fingernails dug into his back as he ground his shaft against her in slow, sensual circles. The friction was almost too much for him to bear, and when she arched back, he knew she was close. He used his teeth to tease her nipple, and she cried out in long, indiscernible noises that nearly pulled him over the edge, too. He lifted his hips, pressing the head of his shaft against her swollen, hot center. He had to feel her, even if just for a second. Had to be inside her unsheathed and feel all that warmth, tight and wet surrounding him.

He stayed there as she came down from her climax, the head of his shaft drenched at her opening. She gazed up at him with trusting eyes. He knew he shouldn't ask, not when she'd told him she needed space. Not when she'd made arrangements to leave the island, which was a huge fucking signal about that space. But just as he couldn't stay away from her tonight—he'd had to see her, had to kiss her, had to touch her—he was powerless to keep his greedy thoughts to himself.

"Baby." He touched his forehead to hers and gazed into her eyes. "I feel so much for you. I can't get close enough to you. I cannot wait to feel all of you, with nothing between us."

"Yes. God, yes."

Her answer slayed him. Silence hung between them for a beat as he debated. He shouldn't have asked, because now that he had her consent, he knew it wasn't enough. He needed more.

He reached for the condom, and confusion filled her beautiful eyes. He cradled her face in his hand. "When you trust me completely, when you no longer need space and a clear head, because you trust that my head will be clear enough for the both of us, when you realize I never break a promise, especially to you, then we'll indulge. Then you'll really be mine."

She groaned with frustration. "But—"

He shook his head. "I shouldn't have asked. I'm sorry. We both know you'll wake up tomorrow and overthink us again. I don't ever want to be the guy you wish you hadn't done something with. When you're sure, we'll know, and until then the anticipation will only make us that much closer."

"God," she whispered. "You do know how to make a girl crazy."

He sheathed his erection and settled his hips over hers.

"Baby, you're the only woman I ever want to drive crazy. And just the thought of feeling your heat wrapped around me without protection has me so fucking hard."

"You have such a naughty mouth. I like it." She leaned up and licked his lips.

"I love that dirty mouth of yours. When you were sucking me…"

He gripped her ass, lifted her hips, and pushed just the head of his shaft inside her.

"Seeing my cock go in and out of your swollen lips, baby. That was unfuckingbelievable. I can't wait to feel you come around me, to feel your body pulsing with need as I—"

Overwhelmed, he sealed his mouth over hers and thrust in deep, and he didn't slow down. Gabriella clawed at his back, tearing through his skin and leaving a scintillating burn. He slid his fingers between her legs from behind, coating them in her wetness, before bringing them to the tight pucker of skin and teasing her tightest opening.

"Duke," she panted out. "God, that feels good."

He sealed his mouth over her neck and sucked as she gasped and panted, pressing her ass down against his finger. He took the hint and pushed just the tip of his finger in, capturing her cries of passion with his mouth. Her tongue stroked his as her body trembled, climbing the peak toward release. He lifted her hip with his other hand and drove in deep again, stroking over the spot that stole her last shred of control. Seeing her come undone for him, feeling her inner muscles pulse so tight around him, was too much, and he followed her over the edge in his own mind-blowing release.

Gabriella lay beneath him, her eyes closed, her body glistening with a sheen of perspiration. Duke took care of the condom and then tucked her body against his. She felt so good in his arms, so right, and though he'd come there tonight wanting to take a walk or just spend time with Gabriella, somehow he knew they'd never be able to resist each other. The connection between them was too strong, too real. He could control most everything in his life, but he was quickly learning that where his heart was concerned, he was merely the vessel that carried out its plan.

"One day," he whispered against her cheek while she slept, "you'll realize we can't escape what's between us. You're already mine, baby, and I'm definitely already yours."

CHAPTER EIGHTEEN

GABRIELLA TOUCHED THE empty bed beside her as the sun crept into her room. She must have fallen asleep in Duke's arms. She listened to the silence of her villa and knew she was alone. Longing washed through her. He knew her feelings on staying together overnight, and she was sure that was why he'd left. But she couldn't help wishing he'd stayed.

Stepping naked from the bed, she saw her dress and lingerie folded neatly in a pile on the chair by the window. Her heart warmed at Duke's thoughtfulness. She showered and dressed, wondering how she'd slept through him leaving. He must have really worn her out. *In the most exquisite way.*

It was an incredible feeling, being in his arms last night. She'd felt loved. She knew that was skipping way ahead, but there was no other way to explain the way he'd made her feel safe and cherished, and so much more. She felt a deeper connection to him than she'd ever thought possible.

She was leaving today, and she had to pack her bags, but packing made her think about leaving Duke, and that made her sad. She could put it off for a few minutes. It was only seven. She padded into the living room and found the flowers, candles, lighter, and her computer and papers on the counter. Duke had cleaned up, closed and locked the back door, and without looking she knew he'd locked the front door, too.

She turned on the coffeemaker, and her heart leaped at the sight of a note from Duke.

Good morning, beautiful,

I didn't plan on making love to you last night. I wanted so much more, especially since you're leaving today. But I'm glad we had one more night to be close. Please trust yourself, and please trust me to keep my promise. I plan on running the proposal by you before any deals are made, and I know how tough you can be. I expect you to be a harsh critic. Besides, you're hot when you're aggressive. And right about now you're turning that pretty shade of pink I love so much.

She covered her mouth, embarrassed that he'd anticipated her reaction so accurately.

I wanted to stay with you last night. God, Gabriella, did I ever want to stay. Leaving was torture, but I know it's what you wanted, even if I don't think it's what you needed. One day you'll see.

Love, Duke

She reread the note as she retrieved her phone and sank down to the couch. He was so confident about them, and she was sending him mixed messages on a daily basis. Heck, she was sending herself mixed messages hour by hour. Landing in bed with him—and doing things she'd never let anyone else do to her—only solidified how much she wanted and trusted him. Obviously it wasn't her connection with Duke that was the problem. It was her inability to create distance between them. Maybe she didn't really need *that much* space after all.

She typed a text to Duke. *It was nice being close again last night. I guess we'll catch up when you're ready to negotiate.*

She stared at it for a long time. It wasn't at all what she wanted to say, and it felt cold, but didn't she need that right now? Just a little bit of a cooldown?

Her finger hovered over the send button. She thought about how close they were last night, the things they'd done, the look in his eyes when he told her that he'd wait to make love to her without protection until she was really his. Her heart ached at the thought of leaving him. She didn't even know when she'd see him again, and there he was, talking as if they'd made lifelong plans.

When would this darn negotiation happen, anyway? How long would it be until she knew if he was going to kill her dreams or not?

She deleted the message and typed a new one. *Last night was incredible. Thanks for picking up. You didn't have to.* She sent the text and set the phone down. There. It was done. Why did she feel guilty? Like she was letting her grandfather down? And maybe letting herself down, too?

Ugh! Being with Duke was like being a kid let loose in a candy store. Everything she could *ever* want was right there in front of her—too enticing to pass up. But if she didn't pay attention, all that sweetness had the potential to rot her teeth. And Duke? He had the potential to ruin the place she loved most. No dentist in the world could undo that type of damage.

AS SOON AS the text from Gabriella came through, Duke was out the door of his villa and heading down the path toward hers. Leaving her last night had been hell, but he'd known that staying would cause her to freak out in the morning. Hell, he assumed she'd overthink things this morning anyway, the same way she had after the first time they'd made love. But *Last night was incredible* didn't exactly translate to overthinking, did it? That sounded pretty damn reassuring to him.

He knocked on her door, nervous for the first time in forever, and praying she was just as ravenous to be in his arms as he was to have her there.

She pulled the door open and the second their eyes connected he tried to read her emotions, but his own were too close to the surface. He couldn't slow them from pouring out as she joined him on the porch.

"Hi, baby. I couldn't wait another second to see you." He leaned in for a kiss, and when their lips met, gone was the tenderness and warmth, replaced with tension. He pulled back and searched her eyes again.

"You regret last night?" he asked, readying himself for whatever storm was brewing inside her.

"No." She pressed her lips in a tight line, holding his gaze.

"Then what is it? Did something happen?" He glanced over her shoulder, into her house.

"No, I just…" She paced, and he knew she had no idea that she was even sexier when she was upset. She put her hands on her hips and then faced him again. "I'm mad at myself."

"At yourself? Why?" He stepped closer, and she held up a hand to stop him.

"Because I should know better than to eat so much candy." Her eyes were narrow and serious, and her hands on her hips made her look even more adamant, but she was making no sense.

"What did I miss? Did a candy fairy come in the wee hours of the morning?"

"Something like that," she snapped. And just as quickly

her shoulders dropped. "God, this is impossible. I'm falling for you, Duke, and I can't. Not yet. We need to put our relationship on hold, just until you get this negotiation over with. What's taking so long, anyway? Can't you just offer money to my grandfather, sign the deal, and move on?"

Now he was beginning to understand. She was so sensitive and felt such a sense of duty to her family—and to herself—that she was tied in knots over all of it. Duke stepped closer and reached for her hands.

"Gabriella, there's more to it than that. I don't invest without a clear vision, and as I said early on, my initial vision is changing."

"How, Duke? I feel like I'm playing a waiting game. What exactly do you have planned?" She crossed her arms, and he told her the truth.

"I still don't have a definitive answer. I'm going head-to-head with my partner on a number of things at the moment. I spent two hours this morning on the phone with him. I have meetings set up this week to try to make those decisions, but we can't let that interfere with us."

She paced again. "You keep saying that, and I want to believe you. I tried again last night. And I *believed* you. But in the light of day it's really hard to see a clear path to divide my emotions. I should just step out of the middle of whatever it is that's going on with the investment. Because really, it's all talk right now anyway. There's no offer. No architectural plans, nothing concrete to deal with. So it's like this cloud of doom hanging over me. I'm just waiting for the storm to hit. And it's not like I have the power to change a single thing."

"I made you a promise, Gabriella, and I meant it," Duke reminded her, reeling in his frustration over her inability to believe him. "Every single thing you've said to me is being given strong consideration with regard to development here."

"Right. I know. I hear you, Duke. And the crazy thing is that I believe you, but I also know how business works." She looked up at him with tears in her eyes. "How long will it take for you to get a deal together?"

"Gabriella." He gathered her in close. "Don't do this. Don't make yourself choose between us and the island."

"How long?"

He could see by her trembling lower lip that she was barely holding it together, and that pained him. He hated knowing he was causing her any heartache. "I'll have a much better idea of how things will play out after this week's meetings."

Sadness filled her eyes.

"Seems like forever, doesn't it?" He pressed his lips to her forehead. "Don't you see, baby? That's how you know what's between us is real."

"I've never felt this way before," she said quietly. "I have never felt like I needed someone else in order to breathe, and the thought of not seeing you for even a few days is…"

"Torture."

Her gaze warmed and she nodded.

"Then don't go without seeing me. I'm not the bad guy, Gabriella. I'm on your side, and I will not let my girl be tortured." He pressed his lips to hers, and her body melted against him.

"How do you always do this to me? You make me feel so much, like everything will be okay." She rested her cheek against his chest.

"Because it will be, and I couldn't stop it if I tried," he said honestly.

"I think this only further proves that I can't be in the middle. Even though I know you're not the bad guy, you have the power to ruin everything I love. It's just too hard to be in this wait-and-see mode."

"You belong in the middle, Gabriella. Everything in life happens for a reason. There's a reason your grandfather asked you to show me around, don't you think?" He held her tighter. "If you feel torn between me and what's going to happen with the island, then you can have your space. Your family's legacy is important, your comfort is primary, but don't think for a second that I'm letting you go completely."

CHAPTER NINETEEN

GABRIELLA SAT IN the back of the cab, trying to ignore the ache of longing that had settled into her stomach the moment she'd left the island. Every time she returned to New York she experienced the same uncomfortable feelings. Leaving the white sandy beaches and her family behind and returning to the busy city, where grass and trees were oddities and people pushed and scowled, barely slowing down enough to eat a meal, made her feel like Dorothy in Oz. And today was even worse. Not only had she left the place she loved, she'd left the man who owned her heart.

Feeling trapped, she rolled down the window and was assaulted by the rancid smell of the city. She looked up, searching for something bright and cheery to remind her that she wasn't a world away from Elpitha. They were still connected in so many ways, sharing the same beautiful blue sky. She knew the sky was a beautiful shade of blue today because she'd seen it on the way into the city, but now the sky was blocked by tall buildings, and all she saw was the one place she didn't want to be.

She would be back on the island for her parents' anniversary celebration in two weeks, but it seemed so far away. And it was only May, so her summer vacation was still months away. She checked her cell phone to see if she'd missed any texts from Duke, but there was only one text from Addy. Why would there be texts from him? Every time they got close she pushed him away. Why couldn't she be like other people who left their hometowns and never wanted to go back? Why did she care about the island so much?

Because she'd left a piece of her heart in Elpitha all those years ago.

And now she'd left another piece of her heart behind, in Duke's strong, capable hands.

She needed a distraction before diving into the work she had to do to prepare for her case. She needed to see a smiling face, and Addy's text provided the perfect opportunity. *Meet for a drink when you arrive?*

She returned Addy's text and twenty minutes later she was standing in front of NightCaps, tugging her suitcase behind her. She should have gone home first to drop off her luggage, but she had a feeling that her empty apartment would just make her lonelier.

She tugged open the heavy wooden door, and a group of guys at the bar yelled "Thrive!"

"Excuse us, please." A tall, handsome man guided a pretty dark-haired woman toward the bar. A bearded guy and a rail-thin woman with tattoos on her arms both got up to hug the couple.

Addy appeared at Gabriella's side, looking cute in a pair of skinny jeans and a white sleeveless blouse. She was as petite as she was bossy.

"Welcome back, sweetie. Do you know who that is?" She grabbed Gabriella's bag and pushed through the crowd to the table she'd taken over with shopping bags.

"Some guy who likes the word 'thrive'?" Gabriella said as she slid into the booth across from Addy.

"Obviously!" Addy rolled her eyes. "It's Dex Remington. He's that video game developer that the Waring kids talked about every time their mom was in our office, remember?"

Gabriella had handled the Waring child custody and visitation negotiations a few months earlier.

"Huh. I remember. Well, they all look happy, which only makes me want to drink. A lot."

"Uh-oh. I've got you covered." Addy waved to the bartender. "I ordered a pitcher of margaritas to be brought over when you arrived. I want all the juicy details about our man Duke. And just so you know, I spent no less than the last twelve hours stalking his brother Jake. I'm going to start mountain climbing."

The bartender brought the pitcher and Gabriella poured them each a drink. The music was loud and the bar was crowded for an afternoon on a weekday. Addy leaned over the table with an excited look in her eyes. Gabriella held her glass up in a toast.

"At five one with arms like twigs, you should do really well mountain climbing. Didn't you once tell me that camping meant staying in a regular hotel room instead of a suite?" Gabriella laughed and sipped her margarita.

"Yeah, well, that was before reading about Jake." She tucked her hair behind her ear and dug into one of her shopping bags. "Look. I'm ready." She pulled out a cute pair of pink hiking boots and a flannel top.

"Ready for…? This is very unlike you to be so stalkerish."

Addy stuffed her boots and top back in the bag. "I'm kidding about Jake. Sort of." She took a swig of her drink. "I mean, I wouldn't kick him out of my bed or anything, but that's not why I have this stuff. I was reading about all this cool stuff he does with search and rescue, and it reminded me of how I've never *done* anything."

"You have done *everything*. You've been practically all around the world." Addison's father was a big-time fashion designer to the stars, and she'd lived a charmed life. She had more money than any ten people Gabriella knew, but Addy had wanted to prove to herself she could be something other than a famous fashion designer's daughter, that she could make it on her own. Gabriella was lucky to have her as an assistant, and she rued the day Addy would wake up and decide she wanted to take advantage of the glitter and glitz of her family's life.

"Yeah, but that's just traveling, not really roughing it. I've never actually camped. I've never climbed a single hill, much less a mountain. I've never even seen the Grand Canyon. That's, like, a staple of life."

Gabriella rolled her eyes. "You've been to top fashion shows all over the country. We went together to Greece for my cousin's wedding. You've sailed on more yachts, been to more celebrity events than half the state ever will."

"Exactly. I've lived the life of money. It's time to see what I'm really made of."

"Ohmygod. Are you quitting? Please tell me you're not quitting. At least not today."

Addy sipped her drink and waved a dismissive hand. "Don't worry. I'm not leaving work for good, just thinking about a vacation. And not yet. I don't know when. You're stuck with me until the day you decide to run back to your beloved Elpitha to raise babies and eat souvlaki and fried chicken. How's your family, by the way? I miss your mom's fried chicken and macaroni and cheese. All that feta cheese and heavy cream, Greek spices…mm-mm." She licked her lips. "Only your mom could find a way to make a Southern dish taste so Greek."

"My mom and every woman on the island. I miss her already."

"I know. That invisible umbilical cord always returns for

the first day or two after you come back to the city. Tell me about the person you really miss. What's happening with Duke? Did he come back with you?"

Gabriella shifted her eyes away and shook her head.

"Gabriella Persephone Liakos, what did you do?"

"I might have told him I needed space." She slumped back in her seat. "I have the McGrady case to concentrate on, and he has the proposal to put together. By the time my case is over, he should have a better idea of where he's headed."

"And then?" Addy asked flatly. "What if you don't like what he proposes? You're going to dump a guy because of what he does for a living?"

"I don't know. I just know that every time I'm in his arms, all I see, all I think about is him." She sighed. "And it's wonderful. Magical. I've never felt anything like it, Ad. He promised he'd keep all of my concerns in mind when making his decisions, but you know what that island means to me. How will I feel if he ruins it?"

"I think you mean if he *saves* the island. You'll feel like you're with a great guy who did what was best for the people there." Addy reached across the table and covered Gabriella's hand with her own. "I know we work among snakes and cheaters, and we both hope we don't end up with that type of relationship, but life is all about taking risks and enjoying the ride."

"Says the girl who's never camped." Gabriella rolled her

eyes with the tease and guzzled her drink, then refilled their glasses.

"Oh, please. Going against my father's wishes was a huge risk and you know it."

"I do know it, and I'm reaping the benefits of your rebellion. You're the best assistant, and the best friend, a person could ask for."

"Then you should listen to me. Call that beefcake and tell him to get his ass on a plane and come see you."

"That's the problem, Ad. I want to do that so badly. I want to be in his arms every second. But every time I put Duke together with the island, I see big, huge question marks."

"That's the attorney in you. I think it's time to let the woman in you win a case for once, don't you?"

They talked for a while longer, and the conversation moved from Duke and the island to Addy's father's newest fashion line, to work and their upcoming cases, bringing her mind back to all the ugliness of her job. They left the bar a few hours later, as the sun dipped behind the buildings and the sidewalks became even more crowded.

"Call me if you need me later, okay?" Addy said as they hugged goodbye. "No staying up all night worrying. I'm happy to come over and bore you to sleep."

"Thanks, Ad." Gabriella watched Addy flag down a cab.

She walked home, tugging her suitcase behind her, and

mentally slid into her thicker skin. She had to in order to ignore the shoulder bumps of people rushing past, too busy to apologize for the intrusion. When she reached her apartment building she felt a modicum of relief and headed inside.

The elevator landed in the lobby just as she arrived, and she hurried inside, tugging her suitcase beside her. She dug her keys from her purse and watched the numbered buttons light up as the elevator passed each floor.

She'd lived in this building for five years, and as far as apartment life went, she liked it. The halls were kept clean, the neighbors were pleasant enough, though she rarely saw them, and she felt safe there. The elevator stopped on her floor, and she dragged her suitcase into the hall, stopping cold when she found Duke sitting on the floor beside her door. He rose to his feet, unfolding all those glorious muscles, and a panty-melting smile appeared—and did its job perfectly. Gabriella dropped her suitcase and leaped into his arms.

DUKE HADN'T BEEN sure how Gabriella would react to his showing up at her apartment, and as she kissed his lips, his cheeks, his chin, and ran her fingers through his hair— *God, how he loved her touch*—he was glad he'd taken the chance.

"You're here!" She pressed her hands to his cheeks, and Duke couldn't remember ever seeing her so happy.

"Have been for a few hours. You're here, baby. Where else would I be?"

"Hours? Here? Like at my door?"

"Just since three." Every hour had felt like a lifetime.

"Ohmygod. I'm sorry. I had a drink with Addy."

"Don't be sorry. I would have waited days."

Her eyes dampened at that. "But I thought you had to stay on the island for meetings."

He kissed her again as she slid from his arms.

"You were so upset when you left. I wanted to make sure you got home safely."

"You came hundreds of miles to make sure I got home safely?"

"Of course. I rearranged my meetings and called my buddy Jack, who picked me up in one of his planes. You should have seen the kids' faces when he landed on the water. It was the highlight of Vivi's and David's morning." He set her on her feet and kissed her again. "By the way, David's spending the afternoon practicing his curveball with the other kids, and he's excited to show his father when he returns home tomorrow."

She pressed her hand to his chest, and he covered it with his hand.

"Duke, what you did for him was so sweet. And you're

214

here. That's just…" She pressed her forehead to his chest. "You suck at giving me space."

He heard the tease in her voice but knew that she was probably still wrestling with the looming proposal. He cupped her face in his hands and gazed into her eyes. They were full of emotions that he knew were scaring her.

"Hey, I'm going to give you space. I just wanted to see you. I brought you a little something to cheer you up." He reached behind them, then handed her a bucketful of sand and shells from the island.

"Oh my goodness. You brought the island to me?" She ran her fingers through the sand, her eyes damp again. "Duke…"

"I'd have brought the whole island if I could have." He pressed his lips to hers again and swept his arms around her as she cradled the bucket between them. He deepened the kiss and smiled against her lips as she went up on her toes.

"I've got your back, baby. I always will if you let me."

CHAPTER TWENTY

AFTER EATING DINNER at a café, Duke and Gabriella took a cab to Carl Schurz Park.

"I still can't believe you rearranged your schedule to see me, or that you brought me such a thoughtful gift," she said. "And now, taking me here. It's like you knew exactly what I needed. I would have sat inside and worked all night."

Duke stopped walking beneath a beautiful flowering tree and gathered her in close. "I had the sense that you were feeling ripped away from the island again, even though it was you who was doing the ripping this time."

"I had to come back to prepare for my case."

"I know you did, but I also know you were trying to protect your heart." He pressed his lips to hers, and when their tongues touched, she melted against him. He loved when she surrendered to her feelings, even though she was still so conflicted.

"I love kissing you," she whispered.

He recaptured her lips, his hunger for her taking over as he took the kiss deeper. Her moan vibrated in their mouths, heating the far reaches of his core. Duke forced himself to pull away before he was unable.

"God, baby…" He touched his forehead to hers, trying to regain control. Her fingers clutched his shirt so tight, he knew she was fighting the same flames.

"I can barely breathe. How do you do this to me?" She wrapped her arms tightly around him and pressed her cheek to his chest. "The closer we get, the more it's going to hurt if it all goes to hell."

"That's why you left the island." He gazed down into her eyes. "Because there, every kiss we shared, every touch, every blessed, glorious moment that brought us closer together haunted you the next day." He saw the confirmation in her eyes. "I'm hoping that here, miles away from the island, we can see if that feeling goes away."

"Don't you get it, Duke? I'm scared to death that if you turn the island into a concrete playground I'll never be able to look at you or feel the same way about you again."

"Baby, you're full of threats. It's your job. You threaten, and I'm sure it gets you what you want. I get that. But you never need to threaten me. I'm on your side. Always."

"I'm not threatening," she said softly.

He kissed her again, slow and loving, driving his point home. "I made you a promise. I wish you'd trust that." He pulled her closer despite the way she tensed against him. "I haven't let you down yet, have I?"

"No, but—"

"Let's set aside the worries and just enjoy our time together." Duke kissed her hard, hoping to silence her worries. The kiss was messy and hot, and he felt her letting go again, her body succumbing to their connection.

"I'll never hurt you," he said as he gazed into her eyes.

"Okay," she said with a confident nod, but Duke had a feeling she was trying hard to fake that confidence. "No more worries."

They continued on their walk, marveling at the beauty of the gardens and how it felt a world away from the city, when it was, in fact, in it. Gabriella told him about how much she missed the island on her way home and how hard it had been to leave him. With every minute that passed, he felt her confidence in him growing, and he hoped it was truly sinking in that she could count on him.

They made their way to the statue of Peter Pan in the center of the plaza. It stood in the center of a beautiful garden, surrounded by flowering bushes and lush greenery. A couple sat on the steps by the stone wall that circled the plaza, holding hands and talking.

"I think Peter Pan had it right," Gabriella said as they admired the statue. "Growing up is highly overrated. It would be so much easier to be young and carefree forever."

Duke draped an arm over her shoulder and thought about what she'd said. "I had a great childhood, but I don't think I'd want to be a kid forever. I remember being anxious to grow up and get on with my life."

She was so beautiful, with the moonlight reflecting in her serious eyes.

"I wouldn't want to change a thing," Duke said as he brushed his thumb over her cheek. "Everything that happened before now brought me to this exact moment, and it's the best moment ever."

"That's quite possibly the sweetest, most romantic thing anyone has ever said to me." Her eyes were warm, but there was a spark of fierceness in them that he recognized from when they'd first met, and that made Duke wonder what was coming next.

"It's embarrassing for me to admit this," she said as she pressed her hands to his stomach and dug the tips of her fingers into his muscles. "But I've been so jaded by my job that the first thing that popped into my head when you said that was 'How many of my clients probably said that to their significant others when they were first dating?'"

Duke wanted to take her in his arms and shield her from the destruction that those thoughts could cause.

"You are not very good at setting worries aside." He softened the tease with a chaste kiss. "How about if I'd said it to you on the island? What do you think you would have thought of it then?"

Gabriella stepped in closer, her arms circling his waist.

"Probably just that it was the sweetest and most romantic thing I'd ever heard. My mind isn't on work when I'm there."

"Baby, that beautiful, brilliant mind of yours sounds like a pretty serious battleground of thoughts." He pressed his hand to her lower back, bringing her body flush with his, not because he wanted the sexual contact—although just being near Gabriella made him hot all over. But because he wanted her to feel safe, to know she wasn't alone and that he wasn't going to walk away, no matter how much she pushed.

"First and foremost," he said with a serious tone, "I'm not one of your clients, so please don't compare me to them. As I've told you, I've never felt this way before, and my feelings for you are so consuming, so much a part of who I am now, that I have to believe they won't change. And lastly, baby, you've just given me another reason to make the island someplace that you will love as much as you love it now. I'd never take that joy away from you."

He kissed her again, slow and sweet, letting his love pour into her.

"One day you'll trust me. You've got too big of a heart to have it iced over with worries that will never come true as long as you're with me."

DUKE SMELLED SO good, felt so strong and safe, and the things he said, the sincerity in his voice, the honesty in his eyes, stole Gabriella's worries away once again. She felt like she'd been home from the island for a month and that Duke had been by her side the whole time, which made being home feel better. How could he possibly, continually, know exactly what she needed? They'd kissed throughout the evening, quick, shivery kisses and long, passionate kisses. Kisses that made her knees weak and her pulse sprint. And now, as they neared her apartment building, their lips barely parted long enough to make it inside the door.

Waiting for the elevator, he pulled her around the corner, into a hallway that was out of sight of the lobby, and lowered his mouth to hers. He traced the swell of her lips with his tongue, rocking his hips against hers and driving her out of her mind. His arousal pressed against her belly, and his big hands—God, she loved his hands—blazed down her hips to the curve of her ass, reminding her of what he'd done the last time his hand had been there. Heat pooled between her legs.

"I want you so badly." His gravelly voice sent a thrum of excitement rippling through her.

Before she could say a word, the elevator dinged, and he practically carried her around the corner and into the dimly lit, confined space. He pressed the button for her floor, and as the doors closed, his mouth captured hers again. Their tongues crashed and tangled as he cupped her breast and squeezed her sensitive, taut nipple between his fingers. Her leg climbed his hip, hitching at his waist as their cores ground together.

"I wish I could take you right here. Just fuck you right against this wall."

She groaned—*groaned!*—with need. His naughty words, the roughness of his touch, made her wish he *would* take her right there.

The elevator stopped on her floor, and he lifted her into his arms and kissed her as he carried her down the hall. She loved that he could carry her so easily. One hand splayed beneath her ass, the other fisted in her hair. His fingers teased between her legs, tearing another needy moan from her lungs.

"Keys," he panted out between kisses.

"Purse."

He pressed her back up against the door, nibbling and kissing her neck as she dug in her purse for the keys. She gripped them in her fist and rested her head back against the door. She felt him chuckle against her neck.

"You going to unlock the door, or do you want me to strip you bare and have my way with you right here and now?"

"I'm debating." She giggled, and he squeezed her ass.

"Bullshit. I am not letting your neighbors get an eyeful of my girl."

My girl. She loved that! She dangled the keys in her hand,

and when he reached for them, she pulled them away with a smirk. "What do I get in return?"

"My face buried between your luscious thighs."

She couldn't unlock the door fast enough.

Duke kicked the door closed and her back met it with a *thump* as he lifted her higher—*how the hell did he do that?*—positioning her thighs over his shoulders. He tore her panties to the side and, *Lord have mercy*, he buried his talented mouth there. His tongue stroked and teased with tantalizing perfection, then plunged deep inside her as he brought his hand to her clit, and—*fuuuuuuuck*. He knew just how to touch her, how to lick and suck until all she could feel was him. His hands, his mouth, his breath filling her. Her head lolled back and she fisted her hands in his hair, needing to hold on to something as she lost all control and cried out as pleasure radiated out from her core.

Before she could catch her breath she was in his arms again, and his mouth was on hers. He tasted of sex and lust and *him*. He carried her through the small living room directly into her bedroom and lowered her to the bed. He stripped his clothes off quicker than she could register a single thought. Her brain was still foggy from the intensity of her orgasm, but she registered the condom landing beside her. He crawled up the bed, powerful and graceful at once, like a panther on the prowl. *Come get me, baby*. His hands slid up her thighs, and he dragged her panties off and tossed them to the floor. He lifted her to a sitting position, and without a word, his hungry stare holding hers, he pulled her dress over her head and tossed that away, then made swift work of stripping her of her bra.

"You're so damn pretty." He lowered her back down to the bed and kissed her again, making her emotions whirl and her brain short-circuit.

"Baby, how did I get lucky enough to meet you?"

"After what you just did to me, I think I'm the lucky one." She reached up and brought his mouth to hers again, taking what she so desperately wanted.

She couldn't get enough of him. She wanted that hot, sexy mouth of his on every inch of her skin. His hands roved over her waist, her hips, her thighs. He lifted her legs and wrapped them around his waist. *Yes, yes.* She needed him inside her. *Now.* Their mouths came together again in a painfully tender kiss.

"More," she pleaded.

His tongue slid over her teeth, then thrust inside. She clawed at his skin, tugged his hair, couldn't get close enough to him.

"Duke, please," she begged.

His hands masterfully groped, squeezed, one on her breast, the other on her ass, sending tides of need rushing through her. The base of his erection crushed against her, creating the perfect amount of friction and taking her up, up, up.

"Let go, baby," he urged.

He lowered his mouth to her breast, sucking her sensitive nipple. Heat shot south, coiling, burning, churning low in her belly. Her thighs tightened around his waist, and in the next breath his teeth grazed her nipple and the world spun away.

"Gotta have you, baby," he said between gritted teeth as he reached for the condom.

She grabbed his wrist. "Just you."

His eyes narrowed, restraint written in the tightening of his jaw. "Baby."

"Just us. I want to feel you, Duke. I'm ready. I'm *so, so* ready."

"Baby, you're physically ready, but you still don't fully trust me. You're my careful, smart girl. You'll overthink us in the morning, and I don't ever want you to regret our closeness."

He grabbed the condom and ripped it open with his teeth, and her heart cracked just a little. She *did* trust him, so much more than she'd ever trusted anyone in her life. But she knew he was right. Even though the worry wasn't front and center in her mind, it lingered. Sheathed and positioned at her entrance, Duke must have read her thoughts, because he kissed her tenderly, lovingly stroking her cheek.

"We'll get there, baby. We're moving so fast, and I feel it, too. God, how I feel it." His eyes went serious. "I'm falling so hard for you. I want to be the first and only man to make love to you without anything between us, and I want to be the *only* man you ever wake up with in the morning."

"I want that, too," she said honestly. "Duke, you're unlike any man I've ever known. Thank you for caring enough about me to make me wait. Even though I kind of hate you for it."

He grinned and grabbed her waist as he kissed all around her mouth, driving her out of her mind.

"Hate me?" The tease in his eyes made her giggle. "I'll change that, baby. I'll chase that hate so far away you won't remember the word."

Their mouths and bodies came together at once. The sensations of his hard shaft stroking her, filling her, while he kissed her and loved her with his hands, mouth, and entire being, was pure and explosive.

"You're mine, baby." His breath stroked over her skin. "You own me."

Ripples of emotion seared through her with his words. Their bodies moved in perfect sync, gasps of pleasure mingled with cries of passion. Her skin sizzled with his touch, and when he looked deeply into her eyes, holding her at the brink of ecstasy, she was sure she'd pass out from sensation overload. His hands skimmed down her sides to her hips, and he held on tight.

"Duke…" She arched toward him.

"I'm right here with you, baby."

He captured her mouth with his at the same time he thrust in deep, and they tumbled over the edge together.

chapter twenty-one

THE SUN STREAKED in through Gabriella's living room windows, cutting across the table where she'd been working since five o'clock in the morning. By the time Duke left last night it was after midnight, and she'd been too worn out to prepare for work today. Now it was almost seven thirty and the noises of the city played like a symphony outside her window. It wasn't the sounds of the sea or the whimsical chirping of birds that she loved so much, but the sounds of cars on pavement, horns blasting, and the energy of people passing by were more comforting than the silence of her four walls, and that was something she needed. Especially this morning.

Her thoughts were so tangled up in Duke that she felt like she could barely think straight. When he'd left last night he'd kissed her like he might never see her again. When their lips parted, he'd made only one promise. It wasn't a promise to call, or a promise of another date. No, Duke Ryder's confidence went well beyond the here and now. While her lips were still stinging from their passionate kiss, he'd said,

One day I will *wake up with you in my arms.* She'd wanted to beg him to stay, to tell him that she wanted this morning to be that day, but even if she had, he would've explained again that he didn't want to be her regret. He continually put her best interests first, and doing so showed her who he really was. She admired that quality—*and disliked it*—in equal measure. Weren't guys supposed to cave about things like sex and spending the night? Wasn't the allure of sex without a condom, the feel of their most intimate parts coming together without any separation, as exciting to them as it was to a woman?

She pushed her fingers into the sandy bucket he'd given her and closed her eyes. If she tried hard enough, she could feel the sand beneath her feet, see Duke walking beside her that first day she showed him the island. His easy ways filled her thoughts. He'd never said a word about the hem of his expensive pants getting dirty, or having to walk for hours in the blazing heat. Despite her efforts to turn him off to the island, he'd connected with the people and fallen in love with it one minute at a time. He was unlike any businessman she'd ever known. He wore his heart on his sleeve, and not just for her; she'd seen it with everyone he spoke to, in everything he did.

As she gathered her papers and slid her feet into her heels, she took one last look at her apartment, remembering how they'd burst through the doors last night, unable to keep their hands off each other. The air had pulsed with their passion. It filled every room, seeped into every crevice of the apartment and her heart. Now the air felt stagnant. Even the sounds of the city didn't bring the energy she craved. How could it when there was only one person on earth who could?

As she put her documents and her purse into her leather messenger bag and slung it over her shoulder, she realized that even after just a few short hours, she was missing Duke in the same way she missed the island—deeply and achingly, as if he, too, had already become a part of her.

She pulled the apartment door closed behind her and checked the lock, remembering Duke checking out her villa the first night he'd walked her home.

The elevator was nearly full. Staring straight ahead as the doors closed, Gabriella wondered why the first day back to work after being away always felt like it was narrated in her head as, *Another day in the crazy, mixed-up life of Gabriella Liakos. Out with the happy-island persona; in with the steel-skinned lawyer.*

If she were on the island, she'd be watching birds land on the sand, getting ready to go help her mother, or walking the kids to the bus, or whatever else anyone needed help with, instead of pushing through these glass doors and waiting for a break in the sea of people so she could step onto the sidewalk without being pushed or trampled.

She pushed away thoughts of the island and tried to get

comfortable in her steel-skinned facade.

DUKE STOOD BESIDE the black sedan parked outside of Gabriella's building, where he'd been for the past twenty minutes, as she pushed through the doors and scanned the throngs of people passing by. She looked so beautiful, so professional in her dark suit, peach blouse, and high heels. He stepped through the crowd, and when their eyes met, confusion flashed in hers only seconds before her smile reached them.

"Good morning, beautiful."

"Duke?" She wrapped her arms around his neck as he leaned in for a kiss.

Her lips were soft and warm, the perfect remedy to a morning of missing her.

"I couldn't go all day without seeing you." He waved to the car. "I'll give you a ride to work."

"It's only a few blocks. I usually walk." Her eyes dragged down his chest, bringing the heat that had been simmering inside him all night to the surface. "Wow, you do clean up nice."

"So do you, babe. I'll walk with you. Just give me a second." He brought her hand to his lips and kissed the back of her knuckles, hating to leave her even just to cross the sidewalk. He opened the back door, pulled out the papers he wanted to show her, and told his driver to meet him at her office in twenty minutes.

Settling a possessive hand on her lower back, he kissed her again. "Shall we?"

"Don't you have to go to work?" She glanced at the papers in his hand.

"I've been at work for the last two hours." He leaned in close again, wrapping his hand firmly around her waist, and said, "I missed you last night. I hope you slept well."

They moved with the crowds to the corner and waited for the light to change.

"Not well, but…"

"One day you'll go to sleep in my arms. Then you'll sleep well." He lifted the papers he wanted to show her. "I did some research this morning and looked into islands that don't allow cars." He flipped through the pictures. "This is Hydra. It's one of the—"

"I know Hydra," she said with a look of awe in her eyes. "It's one of the Saronic Islands of Greece. A short trip from Athens."

The light changed and they followed the crowd across the street. Holding the pictures in one hand, Duke kept an arm around Gabriella.

"I figured you might. This is Bald Head Island, which I'm sure you know of. They don't allow cars, but they do have roads."

Her brows knitted in that adorable, confused way she had. "Why are you showing me these?"

"Research, baby. I'm putting together ideas for our proposal, and I wanted you to weigh in."

"Me to…? Really?" She took the pictures of the two islands from his hands and looked them over. "What do you mean, weigh in?"

They were walking quickly to keep pace with the pedestrian traffic, too quickly for Duke. He wished he could stretch the morning out into the afternoon, then the evening, all the way to the next morning.

"Give me your two cents. You don't want streets on Elpitha, but roads allow rescue vehicles to reach their destinations quicker than dirt roads would. And there are other things to consider—"

"I don't know what you want from me, Duke. I understand that roads help rescue vehicles move quicker, but they also cause habitat fragmentation for animals. Some animals won't cross the open space that roads create because of the threat of predators. Did you know that?"

He hadn't thought of that.

"Disturbing the natural environment of plants and animals will definitely have an impact on both. Besides, once there are roads, cars aren't far behind." Gabriella stopped in front of her office building. Gone was the smile that reached her eyes, replaced with the serious face of a competent attorney making her case.

He admired her ability to remain steadfast in her beliefs, but he also had a partner to appease and returns on investments to consider. He wasn't a quitter. He had the will, and he'd find a way to fulfill his promise to Gabriella without failing Pierce.

"There can still be rules and regulations for the island that prohibit cars."

She shook her head. "Until the investment begins losing money and you sell out. Then the next investor will take it to the next level. I don't know, Duke. I don't think I should be involved with this because it's only upsetting me."

He gathered her in close, hating that he'd upset her, and kissed her forehead.

"I'm sorry. I'm not trying to upset you. I'm just trying to involve you in the process, to get your insight."

She pushed the pictures against his chest and took a step back. "Well, now you have it. I have to get inside for an eight o'clock meeting."

"Gabriella." He closed the distance between them. "Baby, I honestly wasn't trying to upset you."

She went up on her toes and gave him a quick kiss. "I know you weren't. I'm still glad I got to see you this morning."

He tugged her in closer. "Baby, I—"

"Well, hello, Mr. Ryder."

Duke turned toward the pretty, petite brunette holding a to-go cup in each hand. She had a scrutinizing look in her dark eyes. He had no idea who she was, but the smirk on her painted lips and the quick shift of her eyes to Gabriella told him that Gabriella did.

"Hi, Addy," Gabriella said in a much kinder tone than he'd received only moments earlier. "Duke, this is my friend and assistant, Addison Dahl."

"Ah, Addison, the woman who's like a sister to my Gabriella. She speaks very highly of you. I'm glad we have a chance to meet." Duke was trying to concentrate on Addy, but Gabriella's response to his earlier efforts to include her in his planning left him a little worried, and her momentary bristle at his possessive words did nothing to ease his concern.

Addison handed a coffee cup to Gabriella and said, "Gab's full of lies, lies, lies." She winked at Gabriella and added, "I'm ten times greater than she's led you to believe."

"You'd have to be to keep up with her," Duke said without missing a beat.

Addison's eyes ran between the two of them. "True, and I've got her back in all regards, so be good to her."

Gabriella rolled her eyes.

"She's lucky to have a friend like you, Addy," Duke said, undeterred by the hint of tension in Gabriella's eyes. "It's a good thing my only plan is to be better than good to her."

"Good to hear." Addy leaned in close to Gabriella as she walked past, and he heard her whisper, "Hot, hot, hot."

"Ohmygod. I'm sorry. She's…" She laughed. "She's Addy."

"She's awesome. A little spitfire. I like her, and she obviously thinks the world of you, which makes me like her even more." He lifted the flap on her messenger bag and slid the pictures inside. "Baby, I'm sorry I upset you. Hold on to these. Maybe at some point you'll feel differently."

Her gaze softened, and when she touched her hand to his waist, he breathed a sigh of relief.

"I know. I have a hell of a day ahead of me, and…I'm sorry. I'm glad I got to see you this morning. It's crazy how much I missed you in just a few hours."

His car pulled up at the curb and his driver stepped out to open the door.

"I've got to run to a meeting." He gave her a quick kiss. "If missing each other is crazy, then someone better get a straitjacket made for two."

CHAPTER TWENTY-TWO

AFTER HIS MEETING with his legal team, Duke spent the afternoon researching alternative ideas for the island and trying to figure out a compromise that would appease both Pierce and Gabriella. When his cell phone rang with a call from his brother Cash, he was glad for the distraction.

"Hey, Cash. How's it going?" Duke and Cash made a point of getting together fairly often, since they both lived in New York.

"Well, big brother, that depends. Are you free tonight?" Cash's deep voice rang with excitement.

"I'm seeing Gabriella. What do you have in mind?"

"Gabriella?"

She'd already become such a big part of his life, he'd forgotten that he had yet to tell his family about her. "My girlfriend. I met her last week."

"Damn. Seriously?"

Cash had been on Duke about settling down ever since he'd met his wife, Siena. "Yes, *seriously*. What's up?"

"Whoa, feisty, aren't you?" Cash laughed. "Trish is coming into town for a few days. She decided not to take time off as she'd planned. She's got some new role and has a meeting tomorrow, and Jake is coming with her. Apparently he was out in Cali for a search and rescue mission and the timing happened to work out. We're all having dinner tonight. Mom and Dad are meeting us. Bring Gabriella. I'm curious about the woman who's got you tied up in knots."

Of course his brother would sense how much Gabriella meant to him. "Who says I'm tied in knots?"

"You said her name—that was my first clue. Usually you say you have a date, or an appointment, and then you follow it up by saying you'll reschedule it and blow them off for the chance to get together with family. And you went with 'girlfriend.' Bro? For you, that says it all."

He laughed. "Dude, she's got a lasso around my heart and she doesn't even realize it."

"It's about time," Cash said with his own deep laugh.

They talked a while longer and made plans to meet for dinner. After ending the call, Duke texted Gabriella.

Would you do me the honor of joining me at dinner with a few of my siblings and my parents?

Gabriella's answer came a few seconds later. *Meeting the family? That's a big deal.* He frowned, wondering if this was another push for space. Her reaction to their discussion that morning had concerned him, but she'd been so sweet by the time he'd left that he'd thought they were over it.

His phone vibrated with another text from Gabriella. *Ha-ha! I'm in!*

"You tease, you," he said as he typed another text— *Thanks, baby. I'll call when I finish up here. And I'll be in you tonight. Xox.*

With a self-satisfied smirk on his lips and his cock twitching with just the idea of being buried deep inside the woman he adored, he set to work figuring out a way to make the island investment work.

Gabriella's response came in a moment later. *Blushing…*

An hour later he and Pierce were going head-to-head over the phone.

"Duke, we had a plan," Pierce said with his typical all-business self-confidence. "A solid investment plan. Now you're changing the game midstream."

Duke knew he was in the wrong. He and Pierce were close buddies beyond being investment partners. They'd known each other for years, and Pierce was right. But Duke wasn't about to screw with Pierce's trust. He had to lay out all the cards.

"You're right, and I'm sorry, Pierce. But I've fallen for Gabriella, and honestly, she means too much to me to go against her wishes."

"Well, hell, Duke. Why didn't you say so from the get-go? That's a whole different animal than simply changing shit based on a bug you've got up your ass." He heard the joy in

Pierce's tone. "I know just how quickly love can consume a person. Look at me and Rebecca. I'd have given up an investment for her in a heartbeat." Pierce had been a major player before meeting Rebecca, and she'd stolen his heart as quickly as Gabriella had captivated Duke's.

"I'm not giving up on the investment. Now I have even more of a reason to make Elpitha something spectacular," Duke explained. "Only I want to do it with her thoughts in mind."

He and Pierce agreed to try to move forward in a way that would ensure a strong return on investment without creating a mini Las Vegas on Elpitha Island. They conferenced in Pierce's cousin Emily, an expert in passive houses and green building, and two hours later their plan was set in motion.

GABRIELLA HUNG UP the phone with Mary McGrady and groaned. Mr. McGrady's attorney had pulled major strings, but even he hadn't been able to pull off a court date this week. They weren't scheduled to appear in court until next week, which meant another week of stress for Gabriella.

The case should have been open and shut in mediation. Divide the property, put together a fair custody agreement, child support, all the usual garbage that goes along with breaking up eighteen years of marriage. Now Mary was having second thoughts about the divorce altogether. And her dickhead husband, who kept a lover in an East Side apartment, was leading her right down the path to hell, making promises he'd never keep, like saying he'd break it off with the girlfriend he'd been sleeping with for fourteen months. Gabriella had seen spouses make this mistake too many times to count, but she had to be careful with her advice. She'd wanted to remind Mary that she shouldn't have to threaten divorce in order to win her husband out of someone else's arms. But like most of her clients, Mary already knew that. Instead, Gabriella told her what she told all of her divorcing clients who had children: Their decision would affect their entire family and they should make it with great care to remember that their actions—no matter which way they decided to proceed—were lasting messages to their children. What she didn't ask was if she'd want her daughter to remain with a man who cheated on her. It still amazed her, even after years of dealing with divorcing families, that parents seemed to think they were living in a bubble and that their children saw only what they wanted them to see.

Addy knocked as she pushed open the door and peered into Gabriella's office. It was six o'clock, and Addy could have left half an hour ago, but she never left when Gabriella was talking with a client, just in case she needed her to find a file. Gabriella had told her a million times that she didn't need to hang around, but telling Addy anything was futile. The girl did what *she* thought was best. Always.

"Hey there," she said sweetly. "I thought I heard you groan, and since Duke is nowhere in sight, I knew it wasn't a sexually frustrated groan and thought you might need saving."

Gabriella shook her head. "You're a freak. You know that, right?"

"The best kind of freak." She winked as she sat on the edge of Gabriella's desk. "In case I didn't mention this earlier, if I had a man like Duke and he met me before work to show me he'd been up since dawn trying to come up with a compromise for the island I adored, I'd have stripped naked in the street and taken him right there."

"You did mention that, about a dozen times. Isn't there some rule about scamming on your best friend—and boss's—boyfriend?"

Addy laughed. "I don't know, since your boyfriends never last more than a week, and they're kinda few and far between. You don't really give me much to play with." She narrowed her eyes and pointed at Gabriella. "Very selfish of you, by the way. We should fix that. Stat."

"Whatever." She crossed her arms over her desk and laid her head down on them.

"Jesus, what is going on with you?" Addy tapped Gabriella's head.

She rose to her feet and paced. "My clients are selfish and not very smart when it comes to taking care of themselves, but really selfish when it comes to their children, and I'm falling for Duke."

"We'll get back to the client thing, and define 'falling for'?"

"One hundred percent, head over heels, pit of my stomach fluttering falling for him. The kind of falling that makes rational thought impossible." She gazed out the window at the busy streets below and wondered what Duke was doing. Was he upset over her reaction? She hadn't even thought about how long he might have been waiting outside her apartment this morning. Guilt washed through her.

She glanced at Addy and said, "The kind of falling that turns my brain to mush every time I hear his voice. It scares the shit out of me. Why couldn't I meet him a year from now? After whatever is going to happen to Elpitha happens?"

"So break up with him." Addy picked up a Hershey's Kiss from a glass bowl on Gabriella's desk, unwrapped it, and popped it into her mouth.

"Seriously? That's your wonderful advice?" She dropped her chin and shook her head, feeling completely and totally at a loss.

"Of course not, silly. You'd have to be an idiot to break up with a man whose sole goal in life is to make you happy." She unwrapped another Hershey's Kiss and brought it to

Gabriella. "He left last night when you know damn well he wanted to stay. He waited outside your apartment for you. Who does that?"

Gabriella shoved the chocolate into her mouth. "Why can't men be like chocolate? There when you want them to bring you sweet pleasures, and…Shit. I can't even think of a smart way to end that sentence because I don't want him to go away. I just want the island stuff over with."

"That will happen, you know. Eventually. And he's trying, Gab."

"I *know* this is all my issue. He's…God, Addy. He's everything I could ever want in a man. He says and does the sweetest things. Did I tell you that he brought me sand and shells from the island?"

"Yes. Sand. Shells. Dinner. Orgasms. Walked you to work like a schoolboy carrying your books. A man whose greatest fault is that he's fallen in love with the same island you have. We should shoot the motherfucker."

Gabriella grabbed another chocolate. "I want to be *all in* with him, you know? Like he is with me. But then I think about Mary McGrady and I wonder about the things her husband did for her when they first started dating. I don't want to end up as a statistic."

"I see where we're coming from now. See? Ply you with chocolate and the truth comes out. Tell me what Mary said that's got your panties in a bunch."

She shrugged. "Same stuff, different client. She's thinking about going back to him, and he's promising her the world. You know if they don't divorce now she'll be back in three months, like all the other clients before her. Why did I even go into family law? I should have been a day care provider, or a teacher, or…"

"Our job isn't very good for promoting romance, is it?" Addy grabbed the bowl of chocolate, then pulled Gabriella down on the couch beside her.

"I just don't think people know anything about commitment anymore. Maybe it's a generation thing. You have to admit, we rarely have clients who are in their sixties."

Addy's eyes turned serious. "Duke knows about commitment."

"Yeah," she said with a sigh. "He's proven that time and time again, hasn't he?" How many times could she push him away and expect him to come back? She wasn't just hurting him. She was hurting herself with five simple letters. S-P-A-C-E. *The hell with space.* She didn't want space. She wanted D-U-K-E.

"If there's one thing I've learned from working here, it's that there are no safety nets in marriage. If couples aren't all in, all the time, they're going to end up on different sides of the playing field." Addy unwrapped another chocolate. "But then there are the couples who figure out how to make it work, like your parents, right?"

"Yeah, but my parents aren't dealing with the real world. The island isn't the real world—you know that." Gabriella grabbed a chocolate and unwrapped it, then offered it to Addy.

"The island is *their* real world, Gab. They might not deal with as many people flirting with them, trying to get them to cheat. I swear single people think anyone is fair game these days. The harder the challenge, the more fun, or something like that. But I'm on a tangent. Where were we? Oh, right, your parents. They don't deal with crowds and city stress, but they deal with their own stresses. Like life on an island where they're not sure if they'll make enough money to live from year to year."

"That's the truth." Gabriella thought about Duke, and she felt guilty for negating his ideas so quickly that morning. He *was* trying to compromise, and she'd acted like a spoiled child. It was time for her to get her shit together before she ruined the best relationship she'd ever had—and the only one she wanted. Yes, she was definitely going to pull her shit together. Starting this very second. She handed Addy another chocolate as she tried to will herself into a calmer place.

"And then there are parents like yours, Ad. The couples that maintain a fake persona for the public, when they really have no love left. I'm sorry, but I don't want to end up like that."

"You won't. We won't. Why do you think I got out from

under their thumb?"

"Because you thought working for a girl who wanted to help children but ended up lost in a sea of unhappy marriages would be more fun?"

"Yeah, something like that." Addy rested her head on Gabriella's shoulder. "We could turn lesbian, give each other orgasms, go live on your parents' island, and eat fried chicken and souvlaki and get fat. I promise to always hit your G-spot and never, ever to make you swallow."

Gabriella laughed, although just thinking about tasting Duke made her skin hot. "And I'll never pull your legs so far over your head that you get that fat bulge in your stomach."

"That is never pretty. Why do guys do that?"

"I don't know. Why do they do anything?"

"Because we get lost in lust," Duke said as he walked into Gabriella's office.

"Ohmygod." Gabriella covered her face.

"Holy crap." Addy grabbed more chocolate.

"I knocked, but you were lost in chocolate and sex talk." His eyes roved over Gabriella's face, hovered around her lips, then dropped to her chest.

Her nipples pebbled beneath his heated gaze.

He leaned down to kiss her cheek. "Missed you, baby," he whispered, then louder, "Guys are pretty simple. That fat bulge you spoke of? Guys don't notice it or care. If they're in that deep, they're too far gone to notice anything."

He reached for a chocolate and casually leaned against the desk as he unwrapped it. "Don't worry, baby. I'd never do anything you didn't want to do."

Gabriella's heart was beating a mile a minute, and Addy's eyes had gone wide. And Duke—*holy fricking moly, Duke*—had already set her heart on fire.

"I'm sorry for interrupting. I probably should have called, but I couldn't wait to see you." He set the chocolate on his tongue, and Gabriella swore she melted right along with the sweet treat. The man was seduction personified, but more than that, he was full of so much goodness in so many ways that Gabriella could no longer fight her feelings for him.

"I'm glad you're here. I missed you, too." The dreamy sound of her voice gave away her most intimate emotions, but she didn't care. She loved this man. She felt it to her very core, and she didn't want to try to deny it or let her worries over the island or her stressful job come between them anymore. He had so much faith in their relationship, in her. Wasn't it time that she did, too?

AFTER ADDY LEFT, Duke gathered Gabriella in close. He'd had a hell of a day, and having Gabriella in his arms was exactly what he needed. He gazed into her trusting eyes, felt her lush curves conforming to his solid frame, and he knew he'd made the right decision with Pierce. He'd do whatever it took to make sure Gabriella's dreams not only remained alive but came true.

"You look incredibly sexy at the end of the workday." He kissed her, and her bewitching taste drew him in deeper. His hands moved over the dip at her waist and the delicious roundness of her hips. He loved the way they filled his large palms. He felt her body shudder against him, and it took every ounce of restraint not to lift her onto her desk and love her right there. But they had a dinner engagement to get to, and once he got started with Gabriella, he'd never want their intimacy to end.

When their lips parted, she reached up and stroked his cheek. "Duke, I'm sorry about earlier. I acted childishly. I do appreciate you wanting my thoughts on the island."

He pressed his lips to her forehead, then to her mouth again. "Baby, you were right. You can't be expected to be in the middle. It causes too much stress. I'm sorry I put you in that position and I took care of things today, so that won't happen again."

"Took care of things? What…?"

"Let's not go into details. Do you trust me to have your back? To make sure you aren't in the middle of this and to make sure your beloved island isn't overrun with all the things you hate?"

He searched her eyes, and in them he saw about a hundred questions. She swallowed hard, but she didn't move away. She didn't bristle against him as she had that morning, or gasp in horror at the idea of letting him do his job.

She pressed her body against his and said, "I do trust you, Duke. And I want this. I want everything that's happening between us. I'm *all in*, and I want you to stay with me tonight, and I promise not to overthink us tomorrow. Or at least I'll try not to."

The surprise of her words brought a rush of emotion that burned behind his eyes. "Baby—"

Their mouths crashed together in a fast, hard kiss.

"I'll never let you down, Gabriella."

She had tears in her eyes, and he brushed one away with the pad of his thumb.

"What is it?"

"I just…" She trapped her lower lip between her teeth, and then her lip sprang free in the most heartwarming smile Duke had ever witnessed. "I just feel so much for you. It's a little overwhelming."

"For me, too." He hugged her close, soaking up her confession. "Do you want to skip dinner with my family?"

"No. I want to meet them. All of them." She went up on her toes and kissed his chin. "And then I want to go back home and spend the entire night wrapped in your arms."

CHAPTER TWENTY-THREE

THERE WAS A nest of bees swarming in Gabriella's stomach as she and Duke followed the hostess toward a corner table in the restaurant. They were meeting Duke's family, and she'd never been so nervous to meet anyone in her life. As they approached a table where three pretty women and three handsome men were chatting, the men rose to their feet.

"Bro," the darker-haired man said as he pulled Duke into a warm embrace and whispered something Gabriella couldn't hear.

"Behave, Jake. Man, I've missed you." Duke pulled back to arm's length as he looked him over. "You look great." He turned to Gabriella. "This is my girlfriend, Gabriella. Gabriella, this is my younger brother Jake."

Girlfriend! Gabriella's heart skipped a beat.

Jake's gaze turned sinful, and Duke punched him in the arm.

"Sorry," Jake said with a chuckle that told Gabriella he was having fun teasing his brother.

She immediately liked his playful nature and thought about how much Addy would have loved meeting him. He and the other man were Duke's height, which made Gabriella feel small and feminine. "Hi, Jake. It's nice to meet you."

Duke moved to embrace the other man as Jake embraced Gabriella and whispered, "He's a great guy, but don't tell him I said that."

"Jake's all talk, Gabriella," one of the women said as she rose from the table. "I'm Siena, Cash's wife." She was tall and lanky, with auburn hair and the bluest eyes Gabriella had ever seen.

"And I'm Cash." The other man, whose hair was the same sandy blond as Duke's, wrapped Gabriella in a tight embrace.

"Pop, so good to see you." Duke hugged his father, then leaned down and hugged his mother. "Pop, Mom, this is Gabriella. Baby, these are my parents, Ned and Andrea."

She warmed at his use of *baby* in front of his family. Each of the men were tall like their father. Both of their parents wore glasses. His father's salt-and-pepper hair was thick, and though she was surprised to see a silver soul patch beneath his lower lip, it somehow fit him.

"Nice to meet you, Gabriella." Ned embraced her, holding her as long as her relatives would, and it slayed that nest of bees instantly.

Their mother rose to her feet. Duke shared her warm

brown eyes and sandy blond hair. "Hi, honey. So glad you could make it."

Gabriella was pleased his family was as huggy as hers was. She already felt at ease.

"I'm glad, too. I can't wait to get to know everyone."

Duke placed his hand on her lower back as Siena hugged her, and the others sat down. Cash draped an arm over the back of Siena's seat, and the third woman rose to her feet.

"Baby, this is my sister, Trish." Duke's hand slid from her back as Trish reached for her.

"I figured I'd let everyone else maul you first," Trish said as they parted. Her hazel eyes danced with delight as they moved between Gabriella and Duke. "We Ryders can be a little overwhelming, even without Blue and Gage. I'm sure you'll meet them at some point, so this is a good way to ease into our craziness. I'm so happy you guys made it out with us tonight."

"So am I. Thanks for letting me tag along."

Duke pulled out a chair for Gabriella, then sat beside her and covered her hand with his while it rested on her lap.

"Tag along?" Trish said, sharing a knowing, sisterly look with Siena, even though Gabriella knew they were sisters-in-law. "Duke hasn't introduced us to a woman, like, ever."

"Christ, Trish," Duke said. "You have to tell her all my secrets?"

"Dude. You're not fooling anyone." Jake's lips quirked

up. "You're here, Gabriella. That means Duke has already told you all his secrets. Hell, he couldn't keep you a secret, could he? That says everything right there."

Duke squeezed her hand, and a thrill rushed through her. His family was as fun as hers.

"Let's give poor Gabby room to breathe," Siena said. "Is it okay if I call you Gabby?"

"Sure. No one ever does, but I like it."

"No one?" Trish asked. "I was just about to call you Gabby, too."

Gabriella shrugged. "In my family everyone has a bunch of nicknames. They call me Ella or Lala, and about half a dozen Greek endearments, but Gabby was never one of them. I guess I always introduce myself as Gabriella, so people just call me that." She thought of Duke calling her *kardio mou*, my heart, but that was such an intimate thing that she didn't share it with them.

"My family just calls me *nosy*," Trish said with a laugh.

"I want to know everything there is to know about your family," Andrea said.

"Let's see," Gabriella said. "Duke and I are going back to the island next weekend for my parents' thirty-third wedding anniversary."

His parents exchanged a loving glance, and Andrea said, "Our forty-first is next year."

They fell into an easy conversation about Gabriella's

family and the blending of Southern and Greek traditions she'd grown up with. Andrea, Siena, and Trish were easy to talk to, and the guys didn't seem to mind, as they were on to deep conversations about a rescue Jake had just completed and a new fireman at Cash's firehouse. Duke talked very little about his investing in the island, and Gabriella was thankful for that. She didn't want to get pulled into a conversation about what she did or didn't want to happen.

"Do you like being a divorce attorney?" Siena asked.

"Yes and no. I handle more than divorces. I love the adoption and surrogacy aspects, most of the time. But divorces are a major part of my practice, and I really dislike the way kids are used like currency. There's so much unhappiness that I'm really thinking of stopping the divorce end of my practice and just handling other aspects of family law."

"You are?" Duke asked. "I didn't realize…"

"Just thinking about it."

He leaned in closer and kissed her softly on the lips. "Whatever makes you happy, I think you should do. And if I can help in any way, let me know."

"Wow, Gabby." Trish shook her head with a serious look in her eyes. "What have you done to my brother? He's all sappy eyed and mushy."

"He's really great, isn't he?"

Jake shook his head. "Gage and I are going to be the only

two Ryder bachelors left, aren't we?"

They all laughed, and that started the men bantering about settling down. Duke held Gabriella's gaze before joining in on their conversation, and she felt a feather of hope tickle her heart. It was so easy to get lost in Duke and his family. They were so warm and welcoming, so funny, and so openly loving with one another. Cash hadn't stopped touching Siena for one second, and their father had kept his arm around their mother since they sat down. She could see herself blending in easily with Siena and Trish, enjoying girls' nights and chats on the phone. And she knew his family would get along just fine with hers.

She needed to distract herself or she'd get carried away. She'd only just been able to let go of her worries.

"When is your next film starting?" Gabriella asked Trish. She'd misjudged Duke's sister the same way she'd misjudged him the first day they'd met. Trish was a beautiful actress, but she wasn't the least bit stuck-up or entitled. None of them were.

"We're in preproduction mode, so we're months away from starting," Trish explained. "Lots of boring meetings, paperwork, PR work. My PR rep splits her time between LA and New York. Shea Steele, do you know of her?"

"Actually, the ex-husband of one of my clients used her. He was in the entertainment industry, and, well, let's just say that Shea had a lot of damage control to do after his tawdry messes." Gabriella sipped her wine and added, "But my client took great pleasure in exposing them."

"Yeah, I bet she did." Siena leaned closer to Cash, and he kissed her cheek. "One thing you never have to worry about with the Ryders is cheating. They're loyal, possessive, and honest as the sun is hot. I'm sure you already know that from being with Duke."

"You have the most possessive of the Ryders, sweetie." Trish pointed to Siena. "Cash doesn't know the meaning of smothering."

"Sure he does," Siena said. "And he does it so well." She cupped Cash's face between her hands and kissed him.

Seeing the love between Duke's parents, and Cash and Siena, gave Gabriella a little more faith in the strength of lasting love away from the island. It was so easy to forget that love could be real and present here, too, when she dealt with the tearing up of marriages day in and day out. She squeezed Duke's hand, so thankful that she'd stopped trying to keep space between them. She wanted to be closer to Duke. As close as they could possibly be.

The service was fast and efficient, and by the time they'd finished their meals, Gabriella and the girls had already made plans to meet tomorrow afternoon to go shopping, and after she told them about how close she and Addy were, they'd invited her along, too.

As they hugged and said goodbye outside the restaurant,

the girls exchanged cell phone numbers and confirmed their plans for tomorrow.

"Sweetheart, it's easy to see why Duke is so taken with you." His mother embraced her. "I hope you and Duke will come by the house sometime. We'd love to spend more time with you."

"Thank you. I'm so happy to have met the people who raised Duke to be the amazing, loving, intelligent man he is."

"You don't have to suck up to her," Duke teased as he kissed her cheek. "We'll come by, Mom. I love you." He hugged her before moving on to Jake. "I love you, man. So good to see you."

"Yeah, you too. I'll be in touch." Jake embraced Gabriella. "Take care of my brother."

"Always," she said softly.

Duke caught her eye and her pulse quickened. He said goodbye to the others, each with a warm embrace followed by those three little words that she hadn't realized she'd longed to hear from him until just now. Her feelings for Duke had grown so fast, but those three little words were perched on the tip of her tongue, ready to take the leap.

CHAPTER TWENTY-FOUR

IT WAS LATE when Duke and Gabriella left the restaurant, and since they'd need to drive out to Duke's house, which was close to an hour away, depending on traffic, to pick up his clothes for tomorrow, they decided to stay at his house instead. Duke called his driver and arranged to have a car dropped off at Gabriella's apartment. They stopped at Gabriella's apartment to pick up a few things, and as she hurried through the bedroom, packing clothes and toiletries, Duke leaned casually against the doorframe watching her. He loved her more with every moment they spent together, but seeing her with his family, introducing her as his girlfriend, had driven that love even deeper. And now, as she packed her things, he wanted to scoop her into his arms and tell her just how much. But he held back. She'd only just begun to trust him, and he didn't want to smother her.

Okay, maybe he did, but he'd refrain.

For a while.

Maybe.

"Thank you for spending time with my family tonight."

She grabbed an outfit from her closet and zipped up her bag. "I really loved meeting them. The way you guys tease each other reminded me of my family. It's obvious how much you care about one another. And Trish and Siena are so funny. I adored them. I'm excited to go shopping with them after work tomorrow."

He came to her side and turned her in his arms. "We're all very close. There's nothing I wouldn't do for any of them, and I hope you know there's nothing I wouldn't do for you, either."

She melted against him, and it was torture holding back what he really wanted to say.

"Bring more clothes," he suggested. "Enough for a few days, at least, in case you want to stay there at another time." He felt himself getting lost in the well of emotions in her eyes. "I'd tell you to bring all your clothes, but I know that's asking too much."

"Duke…?"

He kissed her again, deep and sweet. "One day." He wanted *one day* very badly.

They finished gathering her things. An hour later they were turning onto his street and Duke was telling her about his childhood.

"No way. You cook?" she asked with wide eyes.

"Cook, do laundry. My parents believed we needed to be able to take care of ourselves. And Trish learned to do all the things we boys did, like fish and mow the yard."

"The more I learn about your family, the more I want to meet the rest of them," she said as he pulled down a long, dark driveway.

He brought her hand to his lips and kissed it. "Thank you. I think they'd love to meet you, too."

"You drive a long way into the city."

Duke parked in the circular driveway and cut the engine. He'd bought the three-story stone home a few years ago. It was bigger than he needed, but having too much house was worth it to have the Long Island Sound in his backyard.

"I need to be in the city for business, but I wouldn't want to live there full time. I value my privacy, and I love the water too much."

"The water? How did I not know that you lived on the water? Mr. Ryder, what other surprises do you have in store for me?"

He leaned across the console and slid a hand on to the nape of her neck, drawing her closer. "Lots and lots of surprises, for many years to come, baby." He touched his forehead to hers and inhaled. "You smell so delicious. You smell like home."

He pressed his lips to hers, loving the soft sigh that left her lungs as he took the kiss deeper, held on tighter.

"Your lips...I love your lips." He kissed her again, and she pushed her fingers into his hair. "God, babe. Your hands.

I swear you have the most sensual fingers."

"That's a relief, because something happened when I realized that *I* was standing in our way, building walls where they didn't belong. I thought I could make sure that all the right things happen for the island, but that's not my job, and nothing is worth losing what I feel when I'm with you. When I finally let go of the whole island thing, it was like my feelings had been trapped behind a dam and now they're completely, totally, flooding me."

His heart swelled at her confession. "Let it flow, baby. You'll never be disappointed." He sealed his promise with a kiss, and if he weren't so big, he'd have climbed over the console and made love to her right there.

He came around to her side of the car and helped her out. Gabriella clutched his shirt and went up on her toes, and he met her halfway for another passionate kiss.

"I want everything with you, baby."

"Yes—everything. *Now,*" she said, going up on her toes.

SUDDENLY GABRIELLA WAS in Duke's arms and he was carrying her up the front steps. They kissed and laughed and kissed some more as he unlocked the door and kicked it shut behind them, all without breaking their connection. His strong legs carried her up a set of stairs, but she was too swept up in the need coursing between them to open her eyes and check things out. For the first time since they'd been together, she finally felt completely free to feel all of the wicked, wonderful emotions that had been brewing inside her.

Duke stopped walking, and as their lips parted, her eyes fluttered open.

"Bedroom." He nipped at her lower lip.

The raw need in his eyes rivaled the lust pooling between her thighs. "Why'd we stop?"

"Trying to gain control. I want to last and, baby, if I sink into you now it's going to be rough, and fast, and...*Fuck*...I'm sorry."

The naughtiness of his words turned her on even more. "Rough and fast and fuck sounds perfect."

A guttural sound rumbled through his chest as he crossed the threshold and they tumbled down on the bed in a mass of tangled limbs and desperate sounds. She kicked off her heels as he stripped her clothing away. She grabbed his collar and tore it open, sending buttons bouncing across the hardwood floors.

"Stores are going to love us," he teased.

He pushed up on his knees and peeled off the remaining fabric. Then he was on his feet, and she followed him off the bed, craving his touch as he stripped naked.

"Holy shit. One day you're going to do a striptease for

me."

"I am, am I?" he asked. "That sounds hot."

"Thank Addy." She giggled as she sealed her mouth over his nipple, loving the feel of it pebbling against her tongue as his hands slid over her hips and beneath her ass.

"Christ, baby. That feels so good." His low voice slithered over her skin as his fingers found the heat between her thighs.

She brought her mouth to his other nipple and gave it the same attention as the first, sucking and grazing her teeth over the tip. She bent over to take his hard length in her mouth, and he kept stroking between her legs, dipping his finger inside her, taking her higher and higher as he made love to her mouth.

"You've got the greatest ass," he said through gritted teeth as he gave it a little slap.

Her eyes widened—from the titillating thrill of it and the shock of need it sent to her core as much as from surprise.

He rubbed his hand soothingly over the sting, then dipped his finger inside her again as she worked his shaft with her hand and mouth.

"Baby, you're driving me insane," he ground out.

His wet fingers stroked up between her cheeks, then back down, teasing over her tight hole.

"God, Duke." She panted, trying to control the sensations racing through her, stroking him with her hand as her head tilted back. He lowered his mouth to hers, taking her in a demanding kiss as he slid his finger past the rim of muscles, and she groaned from the pressure—and the eroticism of it—as he sucked her tongue into his mouth, using the same rhythm as his finger in her ass. She gripped his hips and tore her lips from his with the need to drive him just as crazy as he was driving her. She buried his cock in her mouth, sucking hard, and he fisted his hand in her hair and held her in place. His movements were rough and greedy, loving and tender in equal measure, and she was right there with him, wanting everything and anything. Wanting him to consume every inch of her. When he yanked her head back, his shaft slapped against his stomach, and he captured her mouth with his again. His finger probed her ass as his tongue probed her mouth, taking her to the edge of sanity.

"On the bed," he said tenderly, but somehow commanding, too. "On your knees, baby."

She scrambled onto the bed, knowing without a doubt that Duke wouldn't do anything that would hurt her, but still a little nervous about what he *was* going to do.

"I don't know what it is, baby, but your gorgeous ass turns me on."

She gazed over her shoulder as he pulled her back to the edge of the bed, spread her cheeks, and ran his tongue all the way down to where his finger had been.

Mother of God. Her eyes rolled back in her head, and her head fell between her shoulders. She never knew that could feel so good, and he didn't stop there. He moved lower, teasing her swollen sex, then moving between the two while he massaged her cheeks. Every swipe of his tongue drove her further toward oblivion. She fisted her hands in the sheets to stabilize her trembling arms. When his mouth claimed her core again and he buried his tongue deep inside her heat, she surrendered to the overwhelming sensations as she came apart against his tongue.

"Duke," she begged.

"Want me to stop, baby?" He kissed the base of her spine.

"God, no." Her body was shaking so badly she went down on her elbows. "I want you inside me. Please. No condom. Just you, baby. Please."

He ran his tongue over her wetness again, and her whole body shuddered. God, how she loved his tongue. The head of his cock pressed against her entrance, and she moved her hips back in desperation. He slid the head of his cock in, and she went up on her palms again, pushing her hips back, trying— *aching*—for more.

"Duke. Please, I need more. This is torture."

"You're sure, baby? There's no going back once I'm inside you without a condom."

She hung her head between her shoulders. "You have the willpower of a god. Yes, I'm sure. If you don't take me now, Duke, I swear I'll tackle you to the ground and do it my way!"

"Holy hell, you're the hottest, baby. I'll let you do me any way you want."

He thrust in deep, and she cried out his name, arching her back with the exquisite sensation of his thickness stretching her. He began to move in long, strong thrusts, pulling out almost completely, then driving back in until he was buried to the root, pressed so tightly against her she could feel every delicious inch of him as he ground his hips. Then he started the whole scintillating rhythm again, all while his finger circled and teased her hole.

She pushed back, wanting more, needing more. He wrapped her hair around his fingers and tugged gently, angling her head so he could see her eyes as he leaned over her back. He stared at her for a long time, buried to the hilt. She couldn't read his expression. It was full of lust and restraint and something much bigger. He sealed his lips over hers in a languid, sensual kiss that turned her entire being to liquid heat.

"I am so in love with you, baby," he said so sweetly she sighed. "If you keep pushing that pretty little ass of yours back at me, I'm going to stop teasing and take it."

Her eyes widened. *Take it?*

"Don't worry, baby. I'd never do anything you didn't want." He kissed her shoulder, then dragged his tongue all the way across it to her mouth—sending ripples of heat stroking through her—and claimed her in another slow, drugging kiss. "Unless you want more."

More? Oh God, this was already more than she'd ever done. *Ever.* And God help her, she loved it all, craved him, wanted to overdose on Duke, but she wasn't ready for *that* kind of more.

"Duke," she said eagerly. "Not *more*…but…" She couldn't tell him she wanted him to do it, to take her with his finger. It was too naughty to say.

"I love you, baby, so damn much. I know what you need. I always know what you need."

He released her hair and stroked his hands down her back, rained kisses down her spine. She'd never felt so loved, and even though she was giving herself over to him in ways she never had, she felt in control. Her heart was so full of Duke, so full of his love. She was barely holding it together, trying to process his words as he teased her most intimate spots and thrust in and out of her center with impeccable precision.

He sank his teeth into her shoulder just hard enough to sting at the same time he slid his finger past the tight rim of muscles in her backside. Fireworks sparked through her body. Electricity seemed to arc through the air as her eyes slammed shut and heat consumed her from the inside out, pulsing through her veins, tightening her inner muscles around his shaft.

"Duke!"

He continued thrusting, loving, taking her to the edge of delirium with the exquisite pleasure of being so full of him. Right as she was coming down from her climax, he removed his finger and clutched her hips, taking her right back up again. Grinding out her name from behind clenched teeth, he surrendered to their passion. She felt his warm seed filling her, his hands holding her, his body engulfing her, and in that moment, Gabriella truly became his.

BREATHING HARD FROM the most intense orgasm he'd ever experienced, Duke collapsed against Gabriella's back. His arm curved around her belly as he pressed his lips to her back and said, "Love you, baby."

With her tucked tightly against his chest, he rolled onto his side. Her body fit perfectly against him. He hadn't planned on professing his love for her, but his emotions were too big to contain.

Her fingers trailed along his, so soft and feminine. "Love you, too."

He turned her in his arms, needing to look into her beautiful eyes. She smiled as their bodies met, and he pressed his lips to hers.

"I meant every word, baby. I thought I was falling for you, but I've fallen. I'm there. I love you."

"Me too, Duke. I didn't realize how much I was bottling up inside of me, but…" She blinked up at him, looking sweeter than life itself. "I can't run from what I feel for you."

He kissed her again. "I'll never give you a reason to run. Did I embarrass you or make you feel uncomfortable by the way I touched or spoke to you? I was just overwhelmed with emotions. I wanted to be as close as we possibly could, and I wanted to give you as much pleasure as I could."

She bit her lower lip and her cheeks flushed pink. "No. I mean, I've never done that before, but I liked it. I like everything with you."

"Me too, baby. Me too."

CHAPTER TWENTY-FIVE

DUKE AWOKE TO Gabriella's hot mouth on his chest and her delicate hands playing softly over his nipples, down his ribs, and over his abs. She kissed her way back up his body, and he groaned. She slicked her tongue over his lower lip. She had the sexiest mouth. God how he loved her mouth and every word that came out of it.

"'Morning, handsome." Her eyes were dark with desire, her voice husky and so seductive he was already hard as steel.

"Miss me?" He wrapped his arms around her waist and swept her beneath him. She laughed, and it was the sweetest sound. It cut straight to his heart.

"Maybe a little. I liked sleeping in your arms. Your body is like a furnace at night."

"So you're heat seeking? Is that what you're doing?" He nudged her legs apart with his knees. "Because I've got a heat-seeking missile you might like."

She giggled. "No. Yes. God, that's not what I meant." She wiggled beneath him, positioning his shaft to enter her. "I meant *during* the night."

"Oh, baby, I'm always up for fooling around *during* the night. During the day, in the morning, in the shower. You name it, and I'm yours." They'd dozed for a few minutes after making love last night. Then they'd showered together, and Duke had taken his time washing her body before they made love in the shower with all the tenderness that the first time had lacked.

He rocked his hips, pushing his cock into her as he sealed his mouth over hers. He sank in deeper, and they both moaned with pleasure.

"God, you feel so good," she whispered.

"*We* feel so good."

Their bodies moved in perfect harmony. She met every thrust with a lift of her hips. Duke reveled in the feel of her heat surrounding him as they kissed, and she ran her hands up and down his back, sending shivers of heat through his limbs.

He lifted her leg at the knee and brought it up beside her chest, driving in harder. Her eyes fluttered closed, and she dug her nails into his skin.

"You're so beautiful. Come for me, Gabriella."

Seeing her skin flushed with heat, feeling her muscles tightening around him, and hearing the sexy noises coming from her luscious lips brought him right up to the edge.

"Duke. OhgodDuke..."

He had a burning desire, an aching need, for more of her.

He captured her mouth and kissed her with reckless abandon. His tongue took, his lungs gave, and his emotions whirled. Holy hell, his body, his heart, all of him was a slave to her. Duke couldn't think past the woman beneath him, the pleasure she deserved, the pleasure she gave. Her sexy moans filled the room as their passion claimed them, and the world spun away.

They were covered in a fine sheen of sweat, their breathing erratic.

"Wow, waking up to you is *really* nice," Gabriella said with a sated look in her eyes. "I'm glad you were my first."

Hopefully your only. "Me too."

Duke kissed her lips, the edges of her mouth, her cheeks, then her lips again.

"Baby, I have businesses all over the world. I own a company jet, a yacht that I rarely ever use, and five houses." He kissed her again. "I never realized how little those things meant. Everything I need is right here in this bedroom—and we could lose the bedroom tomorrow and pitch a tent on Elpitha, and I'd still have everything I'd ever need, as long as you were in my arms."

GABRIELLA PLAYED DUKE'S words over and over in her mind all day, which was exactly what she needed as she returned phone calls and reviewed case files that were full of unhappiness. She was mystified by love, which she'd never spent much time thinking about until she met Duke. How had she made it through her whole life without ever feeling a need for a man? Without feeling like she was missing out on something because she'd never been in love? All it had taken was an afternoon with Duke to know she'd wanted more of him. The heart, she decided, was a strange and wonderful thing.

"Are you going to have that 'I've had the best sex of my life' look on your face all day?" Addy asked, with one hand on her hip and a smirk on her lips. "Because if you are, I might just back out of our little shopping adventure and go in search of a penis instead. I'm feeling a little jealous."

Gabriella laughed. "I have a feeling that this smile is here to stay. You know how I always worried that it would feel awkward to wake up with a guy?"

"Yeah, and you call *me* a freak?" Addy sighed. "God, morning-after sex is the best."

"It wasn't just that. Although that *was* utterly amazing." She gazed out the window, thinking about when Duke had dropped her off at her office that morning. He'd insisted on opening her car door and had taken his time saying goodbye, despite the fact that he had an early-morning conference call to attend to.

"Are you going to follow that up with something meaningful, or did you lose your train of thought?"

Gabriella pointed at her friend. "You are a smart-ass. Addy, the way he doted over me this morning, tenderly washing me when we showered…" She pointed at Addy again. "Don't look at me like that."

Addy held her hands up in surrender. "Hey, I'm cheering you on, baby. Continue."

"He was so…*loving*. He asked my opinion as he dressed for work and complimented me as often as he teased me as I dressed. I swear his arms circled my waist a million times, and that talented mouth of his…Never mind about that." She paused to push the dirty thoughts away. "He made me feel more than comfortable. He made me feel wanted."

"Aw, Gab. You so deserve this. You're a tireless advocate for all things right, and I'm happy for you. But seriously, you could have told me you loved him before you told him."

Gabriella gave her a deadpan stare, making Addy laugh.

"I do want to talk to you about something before we meet the girls." She came around the desk and leaned against it. "I've been thinking a lot about what you said last night. About our jobs not being conducive to believing in romance. After finally releasing all that negative energy about the island and feeling the effects of it, I felt so free. I think it's time to take control of the things that impact my life in a negative way."

"You're firing me because I eat all your chocolate and

made lewd comments about your man, aren't you?" Addy was trying her hardest to stifle a grin, and failing miserably.

"Yes, right after we discuss changing the direction of my practice."

Addy's eyes widened. "Oh my God. You're going to actually do it? After two years of all talk and no action, you're actually taking action? That man must have a hell of a dick, filled with smart jizz or something."

Gabriella swatted her arm. "You're a pig. Some guy is going to totally dig that nasty mouth of yours."

"No shit. I can tie a cherry stem into a knot with my tongue."

Gabriella couldn't help but laugh, then she thought about what Addy'd said.

"Seriously? That's kinda cool."

"Yes, seriously." Addy rolled her eyes.

"I bet that equates to doing something fun with your tongue and a guy's…you know…but I have no clue what."

"You're so cute, Gab. But as far as my *tongular* talents go, blow jobs are like ice cream, so they don't help much. Lick, suck, add a little teeth, a little hand action, give a little tug on his sac right before he comes, and *voilà*. Happy man!"

"Teeth? Ouch." She was not about to let Addy know she was mentally taking notes. *Teeth and tug. Got it.*

"Sweetie, you need to watch a little porn, or maybe we should visit an adult toy store."

"I never knew how much I *didn't* know," Gabriella admitted. "I think I'll have to ask Duke for a few pointers."

"We need to talk." Addy pulled her down onto the couch and whipped out her phone. "Do you really want to ask your man, or do you want to surprise your man?"

Gabriella spent the next hour glued to Addy's phone. The woman knew more about sex than Gabriella knew about law. She was a sex goddess, the queen of all things sexual and kinky, and Gabriella was taking mental notes like her life depended on it. By the time they left to meet the girls, Gabriella felt armed and dangerous in the sexed-up department. Of course, given who she was in love with, she had a feeling she'd pale in comparison to his idea of sexed up. But she was an eager student, and Duke was an excellent teacher.

TRISH AND SIENA were as close as Addy and Gabriella, and the four of them instantly hit it off. They spent two hours shopping and chatting, and when they stopped for a drink afterward before going their separate ways, Gabriella felt like she'd known them forever.

NightCaps was bustling, as always. They claimed a booth and settled in. Gabriella's phone vibrated with a text from Duke. *Miss you like crazy. Take your time. Have fun. Xox.*

She felt guilty that he had to wait for her instead of going home. She sent off a quick reply. *You can go home if you want. I can stay at my place.*

His response came quickly. *Home isn't home without you there. I'm happy to wait. Besides, I'm studying Greek so I can sweet-talk you in your own language.* His words wrapped around her like an embrace. She felt so lucky, so happy, so…in love.

"Was that from my brother?" Trish was wearing a short-sleeved blouse that revealed a tattoo of a butterfly just above her elbow. It was big and colorful and fit her outgoing personality perfectly.

"Yes. I was telling him he didn't have to wait for me."

Trish and Siena exchanged a glance and said in unison, "Yeah, right."

"Ryder men never leave their women behind," Siena explained. "Besides, he's going to want to see all that sexy lingerie we made you buy."

Gabriella hadn't needed much coaxing to buy the silk and lace. Just the idea of seeing Duke all hot and bothered over her made her want some for every night of the week.

"I have never seen my brother so head over heels for a woman before," Trish said. "Not that I've seen him with a woman, uh, ever. He's always kept his personal life separate from his family. Until you."

Siena reached over and patted her hand. "No need to blush. It's a good thing. Love is always good."

Gabriella loved knowing that they not only accepted her but that they seemed genuinely happy for her and Duke.

"Now, if someone could just order up some love for me, we'd be all set." Addy eyed the men in the bar.

"Me too," Trish said. "I'll be acting in a film with Boone Stryker in a few months, and I thought…"

Addy choked on her drink and pounded on her chest, eyes wide. "You're acting with Boone Stryker? The rock star?"

"He's super cute," Gabriella said. "And I love his music."

"Yup, but don't get too excited. He didn't even show up for the meeting today, and that tells me more about the guy than his looks ever could. Can you say 'diva'?"

"I hate those kinds of guys," Siena said. "As a model, I have to work with way too many of them. They're prissier than the girls." She looked around the bar and giggled.

"What?" Trish looked around.

"I was just remembering when Cash and I first met. He gave me my first screaming orgasm here." Siena sipped her drink.

Gabriella's head whipped in her direction. "Here?"

"Under the table?" Addy said playfully.

Was Gabriella the only one who thought that was a little risqué?

"Yes, here," Siena said with a glint of amusement in her eyes. "It's a drink. Oh, you thought…"

"You are wicked," Trish teased.

Siena leaned across the table and whispered, "But I'd have totally done that with him here, under the table, in the bathroom, behind the bar."

"Please! He is my brother!" Trish teased.

"You and me, Gabby. We're going to be very close," Siena said. "Because I can't share juicy details with Sis over here. But you and me? We can compare notes."

"Sounds fun to me." *More notes. Yay!*

They talked for a while longer, and as they gathered their things to leave, Cash, Duke, and Jake came through the doors. Duke's piercing gaze was locked on Gabriella. Her pulse quickened as she imagined kneeling beneath the table between Duke's legs and putting her newfound talents to good use.

"Hey, baby." He swept one arm around her back and kissed her, a little more deeply than was probably appropriate, and she loved it.

"How did you know we were ready to go?" Gabriella asked.

"My beautiful wife texted me," Cash said, as he draped an arm around Siena.

"He's trained me well," Siena said, gazing up at him. "He worries about me at night. Can you imagine what he'll be like when we have a baby?"

"Oh my God, are you…?" Trish asked.

"No, but we're talking about it." Siena wrapped her arms

around Cash. "Soon, we think."

"Really?" Duke's eyes warmed. "That's great, you guys. You'll be incredible parents."

"Baby talk. I'm outta here." Jake's eyes filled with wickedness as he ran them down Addy's body.

Duke leaned in close to Gabriella and whispered, "*Baby talk*. Why does that make me want to get inside you?"

Gabriella didn't know what excited her more, the idea of making love with Duke or one day having a family with him.

CHAPTER TWENTY-SIX

WHEN DUKE AND Gabriella arrived at his house, the moon hovered over the water, casting a long orange shadow like a red carpet waiting to greet them. They walked along the stone path that ran along the side yard, to the patio overlooking the water.

"You really do have your own little paradise out here." Gabriella stood before the waist-high stone wall surrounding the patio and sighed. "No wonder you were drawn to the island."

Duke gathered her hair over one shoulder and kissed her neck. "It feels like paradise when you're here with me."

"You're such a sweet talker." She leaned back against his chest and sighed. For the first time since she'd moved away from the island, she was truly happy. She wasn't waiting to return or wishing her life was different. She felt like she was right where she was supposed to be. Maybe Duke was right and everything in life really did happen for a reason.

"Have you ever thought about making free-form gardens down by the water? Or maybe creating little sitting areas defined by flower beds and a few flowering trees?"

"I'm thinking about it now." He kissed her neck. "When I bought this place, I thought I'd spend a lot of time out here but never have. I'd like nothing more than to spend time out here with you."

She turned in his arms. "Me too."

"I was thinking, when I was dealing with *the investment that we're not talking about*, you mentioned not taking on more divorce cases. Were you serious? That's a really big decision. Let's sit down. Do you want to talk about it?"

Her gaze softened, which was the opposite of what he'd expected. He thought she'd feel stressed over such a major decision. They toed off their shoes, and Duke lay on his back on a lounge chair. Gabriella stretched out beside him, resting her head against his chest.

"This is nice." She began unbuttoning his shirt as she spoke. "I've been thinking about changing up my practice for a long time, but I never realized how much the day-to-day negativity was dragging me down until you and I became close. I have a great practice. And a big part of that is handling divorces, but I also work with adoptions, surroga-cies, and smaller family issues, which I really enjoy." She ran her finger nervously along the waist of his slacks. "It'll mean less money, but money has never meant much to me. I need it to live, of course, but I would rather be happy than have tons of money."

"That's one of the things I admire about you."

"Thank you. But it's just who I am."

She parted his shirt and ran her fingers ever so lightly just above his waistband. Heat spread straight to his groin. "That feels incredible, baby."

"Close your eyes," she whispered.

He closed his eyes. "Mm, sexy time." Even without his eyes open he knew she'd blush at that, given what he'd walked in on her and Addy talking about. Hell, he'd thought about it ever since.

Her tongue stroked over his nipple. "I might have watched a little porn with Addy."

His eyes flew open. "With Addy?" *Holy Christ.*

"Get that grin off your face. There's no chance of a ménage in your future."

"Baby, you're the only woman I want. But if you—"

She smacked him, and he laughed. "I'm kidding!"

Gabriella shifted her body between his legs. Her eyes darkened as she ran her fingers along his jaw, then brushed her lips over his and said, with a shy and intensely sexy look in her eyes, "I was doing research. For you."

"I love you just as you are, baby, but that is the sexiest thing I've ever heard." He slipped a hand to the nape of her neck and captured her luscious mouth with his, kissing her deeply as she rocked seductively against his eager erection.

She drew back and licked her lips. "Close your eyes." Her

voice was a little shaky.

Duke closed his eyes and gripped her hips as she dragged her teeth along his jaw, then kissed her way to his ear and dipped her tongue inside as she palmed his erection over his slacks. His hips rose, and she moaned into his ear. With his eyes closed, the sensations intensified. Her sweet scent surrounded him. He felt each one of her shallow breaths as if they were his own. She kissed his pecs, down the middle of his stomach, still working him with her hand, and when her lips reached the sensitive skin below his belly button, he couldn't stifle the greedy groan that escaped from his lungs. She ran her tongue around his belly button, then dipped inside. His hips bucked with the feel of her hot, wet mouth.

He gripped the sides of her hair, sucking in air between gritted teeth as she ran her mouth over his slacks, along his rigid length, pressing with her teeth just hard enough to make him want to explode.

"Baby—" He rocked his hips, and she pushed them back down, as he'd done to her countless times.

"I'm in control this time." Gone was the tentative shakiness in her voice, replaced with confidence and seduction.

Christ Almighty, I've died and gone to heaven.

She unbuttoned his slacks and unzipped them painfully slowly. He fought the urge to rip them off and gave in to her sensual fantasy. With his slacks open and his cock still covered with his briefs, she dragged her tongue along his hard length. The heat of her tongue worked its magic through the fabric, and he groaned again, needing so much more. He curled his fingers around the edge of the lounge chair to keep from taking control. She cupped his balls over his briefs, sending shocks of lust searing into his core. He ground his teeth together as she licked and sucked his belly, just above the head of his cock.

"Fuck. *Fuck*, Gabriella. You're torturing me."

"You haven't seen torture yet." She moved off of the chair, and he opened his eyes. The moon shone behind her, illuminating her sexy-as-hell curves, as she swayed her hips and began unbuttoning her blouse.

Duke pushed up from the chair, and she set her foot on his chest, shoving him onto his back, and shook her head.

"Just enjoy. Next time you strip for me."

"Baby, I'll fulfill your every fantasy."

One by one those buttons opened, and flashes of lace and skin stole his brain cells a handful at a time. When her blouse was completely unbuttoned, she grabbed the two sides and gyrated her hips as she pulled the shirt free from her skirt, then stripped it off and tossed it away. Her foot was still on Duke's chest, and he gripped her calf, stroking, squeezing, needing the connection as she unhooked the front clasp of her lace bra and it sprang open, hitching against her nipples. She left it like that as she removed her foot from his chest, leaving Duke panting for more, and she turned around. With her back to him, she gazed over her shoulder. Her hair fell in front of one eye as she dropped one bra strap, then the other, and shook it off. It floated to the ground and landed at her feet. She unzipped her skirt, giving him another seductive dance. Duke palmed his cock, unable to wait any longer for relief. Her eyes widened, spurring him on. She was so sexy as she wiggled out of her little black skirt and it puddled at her feet, leaving her in only a pair of black panties. He pushed his pants and briefs down his thighs and licked his palm, then gave himself one long stroke after another.

She crossed her arms over her breasts and turned to face him. Her hair hung loose over her shoulders, covering the swell of her breasts. Her panties rode high on her hips, and the way her arms were crossed against her full breasts made them plump out to the sides. He licked his lips, wanting to run his tongue over that creamy skin and get his mouth on the hidden rosy buds he loved so much.

She eyed his hand, now stroking his cock faster, and she stripped him from his slacks. Then she shimmied from her panties, swirled them around on her finger, and tossed them aside.

"So fucking sexy." Lust pooled at the base of his spine. He was close to coming.

She made a come-hither motion with her finger. As Duke sat up, she positioned herself between his legs. He shrugged off his shirt so they were both naked, and he ran his hands up her thighs. She moved his hands around to her ass and pressed her hips forward. Her damp curls brushed over his chin.

"Kiss me," she said in the commanding voice she'd used earlier.

There was no command necessary. He was ready to eat her, fuck her, love her, whatever she wanted. He kissed her silky skin above her curls, then moved lower, pressing his lips into those damp, sexy curls, and kissed her there. He slid his hand over one hip and between her legs, and she gripped his wrist and forcefully moved it back to her ass.

He glanced up at her, smiling as he kissed her where she'd told him to, loving this new side of her. She fisted her hands in his hair and guided his mouth to her inner thigh, to the crease beside her sex, over her damp curls, and then to her other thigh. He groaned with the tease. Her scent was driving him crazy. He pressed his fingers into her flesh, holding her still as he kissed, licked, and sucked the areas she allowed.

"That's it," she purred. "Oh, so good. Touch yourself with one hand."

"Baby, you're killing me." He wasn't sure how much longer he'd last before he'd give in to his need and sweep her beneath him.

"I never..." She tugged him up to his feet by the hair, stopping him at her breast, and steered his mouth to her ripe, swollen nipple. "Oh yes. Oh God. That's so good. I've never done this, but watching those movies…"

He sucked her nipple against the roof of his mouth and released his cock, gripping her hips again. He needed the friction, needed to feel her soft curves surrounding him. She yanked his head back and crashed her mouth over his, kissing him deep and wild. Their tongues battled as she clung to his hair. She suddenly tugged his mouth away and steered him to her other breast.

"Fuck, baby," he said around her nipple. Then he sucked and licked, unable to resist nipping the tip. She cried out, but continued holding his head in place.

"I like you watching those movies." He narrowed his eyes. "Next time you watch with *me*."

WHAT STARTED OUT as a *let me see if I can be bold* moment, turned into a full-on exploration of Gabriella's sexual confidence—and she loved it. The more she guided Duke, the more turned on she became, and now having him in her control was like a drug. She wanted more. More control, more time to figure out what she liked. But she was fighting the urge to straddle him and quell the aching need between her legs during every second of this incredibly pleasurable exploration.

"I will watch them with you. Back…back on the chair."

She heard her strength failing with every flick of his tongue on her tender nipple.

He sank back down on the chair, and she motioned for him to lie down as she feasted on all those planes of hard flesh on display just for her. His long, thick shaft reached beyond his belly button, and his sac lay atop the junction of his powerful thighs. *Teeth and tug.* "God, Duke, those porn guys have nothing on you."

A cocky grin spread across his handsome face. "Good to know, baby."

Her nerves felt like they were on the outside of her skin. She set a hand by his hip, closed her eyes—*If my eyes are closed I won't be embarrassed*—and straddled his chest. She couldn't overthink this or she'd chicken out. As she wrapped her fingers around his shaft, she inched her legs back and lowered her swollen sex over his mouth.

"Lick me." She said it so quietly she wasn't sure he'd heard her, but seconds later his hands gripped her hips and he devoured her with his talented mouth.

It took all her focus to remember that she was supposed to be pleasuring him, and she lowered her mouth and licked the glistening bead at the tip of his cock. She loved the taste of his arousal, knowing he was hers. She felt empowered and sexier than she ever had as she worked him with her hand and swallowed him deep, relaxing her throat as Addy had told her to. She grazed her teeth along his shaft, and his hips shot up.

"Did I hurt you?" she asked quickly.

"No. You're driving me out of my mind."

With a satisfied smirk, she did it again, earning another strong shift of his hips. She fondled his sac, squeezing a little, and when he spread her thighs further and sucked her clit into his mouth, she moaned around his rigid length. His shaft swelled impossibly larger against the vibration, and she did it again, pleased with the same erotic response.

His fingers plunged inside her, and she arched back, holding tightly to his erection as he brought her right up to the edge. She wanted to give him the same pleasure and tried to push past the haze of desire that was making her head spin. She licked the length of his shaft, tickling his sac, as she focused on the swollen head, sucking, stroking, and licking until he was moaning into her. She had learned something else in those videos, and she wanted to try it all, but… When his finger teased her other hole, she groaned and licked her fingers, then gave him a little ass play, too. On the advice of Addy, she didn't venture too far, just teased and touched.

"So fucking good, baby." His husky voice was all the approval she needed.

"Make me come." Her words came without thought as she took him in deep, moving one hand between his ass and his sac.

Just as she felt her insides quiver and burn, he plunged his fingers inside her, sending her spiraling over the edge. She tugged gently on his sac, and hot jets of come filled her throat. Their bodies shook and thrust. She'd never felt anything as intense as she shattered against his hand and mouth as he was coming in hers. She swallowed his salty seed, circled the head, licking off every sweet drop. Her thoughts blurred together as she collapsed on top of him. Her whole body was numb as he gathered her in his arms and cradled her on his lap.

"I love you so much, baby." He brushed her hair from her face and kissed her softly. "You okay?"

"That was…intense," she said against his neck. "I never knew it could be such a whole-body experience. I feel like I can't move."

"You don't have to." He sat with her in his arms, his legs trembling beneath her, until his body settled from his own release. Then he rose with her in his arms and carried her inside. "I'll get our things after I run you a warm bath."

"I learned other stuff, too." She nuzzled against his chest, marveling at what they'd just done and the fact that he was carrying her, buck naked, through his house. It occurred to her that she hadn't worried about being naked on his patio. There were no neighbors to worry about, and it was pitch-dark outside. The house was light, and Duke could see every curve, every ripple caused by the chocolates she kept on her desk. But she wasn't self-conscious. Duke made her feel desirable, and the way he'd reacted to her outside gave her even more confidence.

He stopped at the foot of the stairs and gazed into her eyes. "Do you know how much it means to me that you wanted to do more for me? For us?" He paused, and his eyes went serious and his lips pressed together, as if he were trying to gain control of his emotions.

"You only need to be yourself to make me feel good, baby. I don't want you to feel pressure when it comes to our intimacy. It's who you're with, not what you do, that makes it special." He kissed her again, and then his lips curved up in a devilish grin. "But I do love this aggressive side of you."

Chapter Twenty-Seven

DUKE AND GABRIELLA spent the rest of the week sleeping at Duke's house, driving to and from work together, and making love into the wee hours of the morning. When the weekend came, they spent most of Saturday in bed, exploring each other's bodies, trying out all of the positions Gabriella had seen in the videos she'd watched with Addy. Watching Gabriella explore her sensual side was like watching a flower bloom. She moved from tentative and shy to in control in the blink of an eye, and it made her all the more alluring.

Sunday morning promised to be sunny and warm, and after showering together, which had become their habit, they had breakfast on the patio, and then Gabriella settled in with her case files to prepare for her impending court case.

Duke had purposely been shielding her from his work on the island deal, but he'd received an email from his team, and they'd put together a final briefing to go over details before preparing the proposal. Duke had to leave town tomorrow, and he wasn't looking forward to going away without

Gabriella. But with her case being tried on Tuesday, he knew there was no way she could get away.

He watched her now, lying on the lounge chair with her documents in her lap. Her pencil moved quickly across the paper, and a serious look lingered in her eyes. He imagined her with a rounded belly carrying their child. He took that thought even further, to a child in her arms, another one in her belly, and him by her side, holding the hands of their other two children. He pictured them on the island with her parents and relatives, dancing up by the lighthouse. His mind skipped ahead further, as their bodies aged and their hair became streaked with silver. When wrinkles would define her gorgeous eyes and those lovely children of theirs would have children of their own. Duke knew with his entire being, he wanted all of that with her.

She looked up and caught him daydreaming. "Why are you looking at me like that?"

He set down his files and went to sit beside her. He spread his hand out over her belly, swallowing what he really wanted to say. *I was just thinking about how beautiful you'd look carrying our babies.* They had a giant hurdle to get through before they were ready for that. The first step was owning up to his meeting, regardless of whether it broke the spell they'd been under while ignoring the looming proposal.

"I was just thinking about how I don't want to leave you, but I have to go out of town tomorrow."

"You're going out of town?" She set down her papers, and he noticed she hadn't been taking notes. She'd been drawing.

"What's this?" He picked up the paper and recognized his backyard, the stone wall around the patio, the water at the edge of the picture. She'd drawn gardens down by the water, around the patio, and throughout his yard in free-formed clusters.

"Nothing." She reached for the paper.

"You don't want to share that with me?" He hoped she would.

"Not yet. I'm just messing around. Where are you going?"

"Pierce and I have a meeting with our team in Reno, where he lives. I shouldn't be gone more than a day or two, I hope."

"Oh, for the Elpitha proposal?" She dropped her eyes.

He leaned in for a kiss. "Yes. Would you like to talk about it?"

"No." She picked up her papers and flipped over the design she'd been working on, turning her attention to the files below.

"Gabriella, I'll share anything you'd like to know."

"It's just…" She met his gaze. "We've gotten so close, and—"

"Why don't you come with me, so you can be in on it? Then you won't worry."

"No. I can't. I have court, and besides, this is your business, not mine." She smiled, but it never reached her eyes, and Duke's chest constricted.

He wrapped his arms around her and pulled her in close. "Baby, I've got nothing to hide. I promised that you'd be happy with the outcome, and I intend to keep that promise."

THROUGHOUT THE AFTERNOON Gabriella did her best to hide her mounting anxiety about the island. She'd kept it under control all week, and *bam*! Just like that the mention of it sent her mind into a flurry of worry. Her mother used to tell her that worrying made no sense unless she could control the outcome, and since she couldn't in this case, worrying *truly* made no sense. But that didn't stop her mind from playing tricks on her well into the evening. She imagined Duke telling her one evening that the deal was done and then finding out that he was moving ahead with everything she didn't want to happen: sky-high hotels, casinos, massive roads, big cruise ships. Could she really blame him? This was his business, after all. It wasn't even her island to worry about. She was holding on to childhood memories and dreams of an island that, if something wasn't done to bring in tourism, would surely be nearly vacant in the next decade.

She packed her bags that evening in preparation of staying at her own place Monday night while he was out of town. She couldn't stop thinking about how close she and Duke had become and how their lives had blended together so seamlessly.

"Hey, babe? Let's take a walk." Duke reached for her hand and pulled her in close.

He did that every time they were in the same room, kept her close, like he needed the contact as much as she did. How had she become so attached? The thought of a night without him made her feel lonely, and he wasn't even gone yet.

"Come on. We'll walk off all that angst brewing inside you. Besides, I want to show you something."

"Is this a ploy to have kinky sex on the lawn, or…?" She felt playful despite her newly returned worries.

"Somehow I doubt I need a ploy with you, but no. This is me wanting to take a moonlight stroll with my girl." He kissed her, and her entire body lit up inside.

Especially her heart.

They walked hand in hand down by the water. The moon cut through the clouds like a beacon, casting a gray-blue haze over the dark water.

"I know you've been stressing over this meeting, and I'm sure it's bringing up all your childhood dreams that you felt were torn apart when you moved to New York. And how you were worried about trusting me because you felt your grandfather had broken your trust by not believing what you'd told him." Duke draped his arm around her shoulder and pulled her in close.

He remembered what she'd shared that night at the lighthouse? He really was paying attention to everything she said.

"But I'm glad he asked you to go build a life off the island. We might never have met otherwise. Your grandfather might have allowed someone else to give me the tour."

"Maybe so." With one arm around his waist, she put her other flat against his stomach as they walked. "Don't worry about me, Duke. I've got this. Today was a momentary slip into nostalgia."

"That's just it, baby. Your nostalgia is important to me. I don't want you to try to ignore it. I want you to feel it, talk to me about it. I've heard everything you've shared with me, and I've thought about every concern, every hope, every hurtful confession. I will not let you down. We can't be afraid to tell each other things, or our relationship will never make it."

"Thank you, but I'm not afraid. I just do better when I lock those thoughts away."

He stopped walking and took her hands in his. "We don't have to talk about it, but I don't want you locking anything away. I want you, Gabriella. All of you. Not just the sexy parts or the parts that you want me to see."

She stepped in closer and pressed her lips to his chest. "Why are you so *good*?"

He laughed. "I have clients who would argue that I'm a shrewd bastard, hardly *good*. I care about you, and I hate to see you struggling over this."

"Duke, I can handle whatever happens. Seriously, I can." Could she? The doubts she'd had before were weaker now. They were lingering doubts at best, and the moment she looked into Duke's loving eyes, everything became crystal clear. She couldn't wait to go back to the island with him this weekend and let her family know they were a couple.

"Whatever happens won't change my feelings for you. I thought they might, but I love you, Duke, and I know there's no way anything will change that. Nothing ever will."

CHAPTER TWENTY-EIGHT

DUKE SPENT MONDAY with Pierce and his fiancée, Rebecca Rivera, who worked in his acquisitions department, and Pierce's cousin Emily and her fiancé, Dae Bray, along with Pierce and Duke's land development teams and financial advisers. The conference room was full, and tensions ran high. They went head-to-head all afternoon and into the early evening, trying to come up with an acceptable compromise. When they finally hit upon an amicable solution and called it a day, with plans for the financial teams to knock heads in the morning and present their calculations late tomorrow afternoon, it was after sundown.

"That was fun, huh?" Pierce rose to his feet and stretched. "Nothing like a strong negotiation to work up an appetite. Are we still on for dinner?"

He reached for Rebecca as she gathered her papers. As she took Pierce's hand, she blew him a kiss. "Give him a minute, Pierce. He probably wants to call the woman he's making all these changes for."

"Gabriella," Duke said, loving the feel of her name on his

tongue and wishing she were right beside him so he could taste her sweet lips.

Emily's eyes filled with mischief. Tucking her long dark hair behind her ear, she reached for her cell phone. "I want to call my boyfriend, too." Her words dripped with sarcasm.

"My ass." Dae spun her into his arms and kissed her as she laughed. "Rebecca, do you give Pierce as hard of a time as Em gives me?"

"My Rebecca?" Pierce said. "She's the perfect woman."

Rebecca rolled her eyes. "Just wait until you see how riled up he gets when the waiter talks to me at the restaurant. I swear it's fun to watch his claws come out over the littlest things."

They joked as they gathered their things, and watching them made Duke long to hear Gabriella's voice. He stepped outside the conference room and called her.

"Hey there. I miss you already."

He could hear the happiness in her voice.

"Hi, babe. I miss you, too. How was your day?"

"Good. We're still on for court tomorrow with the McGradys, at least as of right now. Mary hasn't backed out yet."

"So she's not going back to her cheating husband?"

"Not at the moment, I guess. Sometimes I'm the last to know. How was your meeting?"

"Long and loud." He glanced back at the conference

room. "I wish you were here with me. I'm getting ready to go to dinner with Pierce and Rebecca and Emily and Dae. You'd really like them. I'd give anything to have you here by my side."

"I'm sorry. But as it is I'll be up all night preparing and going over notes. Oh, your sister called me today, which was really nice. She said that she heard you were out of town and asked if I wanted to meet her, Cash, and Siena for dinner."

That didn't surprise him since he'd told both Cash and Trish that he was heading out to Reno. He was glad they'd called. He didn't like the idea of Gabriella being left alone. "You didn't go?" It was already ten in New York.

"I wish I could have, but with court tomorrow and two client meetings Wednesday, if I didn't prepare tonight, I'd never have time to review their cases. But I told her we'd catch up another time."

"Great. I'm glad she called. She really likes you."

"I like her, too."

"How long are you going to be at the office?" He didn't like the idea of her walking home alone in the dark.

"I don't know. Another hour or so. I need to try to catch up on some sleep before court tomorrow, so I won't stay past eleven."

"Why don't I send my driver to wait for you?"

"Duke, it's only a few blocks. I think I can handle it."

He closed his eyes for a second, reminding himself that

she'd made it on her own in New York for years before meeting him. Why should that change now? Even so, he still worried.

"It would make me feel better, especially if you're going to be there that much longer."

"I can get a cab," she offered. "Will that make you feel better?"

"Moderately. I'll call Ted and have him come by and wait."

"You're impossible." He heard the tease in her voice and was glad she wasn't upset. "But I guess I was forewarned. Siena told me that you Ryder boys were an overprotective bunch. Fine. If he doesn't mind, please tell him eleven. That'll ensure I don't stay too late."

"Thank you." Pierce and the others filed out of the conference room. "I've got to run, babe. You'll probably be asleep when we get back to Pierce and Rebecca's. Talk in the morning?"

"Aw, and I was so hoping to try phone sex. Addy says it's super fun."

A grin split his lips. "Baby, leave your phone on. I love you."

GABRIELLA HAD THOUGHT that Duke was being

overprotective, but when she left her office, she was glad she wasn't walking home alone. As she walked from the building to the car she realized that when she'd previously walked home alone at night, she'd walked with her shoulders hunkered in close to her body and her senses on high alert. It was so different from her life on the island, where she never even locked her doors.

Duke's driver, Ted, opened her car door.

"Thank you for the ride. I really appreciate it."

"My pleasure," he said. He waited until Gabriella was inside her apartment building before getting back into the car and driving away.

Other than this morning, when she and Duke had dropped off her bags, she hadn't spent any time at home for several days. It felt strange to be there instead of at Duke's house, and to be without Duke after work felt even stranger. She didn't know when Duke was going to call, but she took a warm shower to wash off the bad vibes of the impending divorce case and put on a silk cami and matching panties she'd bought with the girls when they went shopping. Then she settled into bed with her phone and her iPad.

She Googled Elpitha Island images, smiling when her favorite place appeared before her. Most of the pictures looked like they'd been taken in the last few years. She tried to picture the shoreline speckled with hotels and the island itself mapped with paved roads. Her heartbeat quickened, and she told herself that she was being silly. This was what needed to happen in order for the island not to fail, and that was best for her family and all the people there whom she loved. As she clicked through images of the bank and the library and the plantation-style homes, she felt warm all over. She thought back to Duke touring the island in his suit and forced herself to see beyond Duke. She had to wonder how many people wouldn't mind their shoes and clothes being covered in dust by the end of the day. That alone might be a deterrent for tourists. The very thing she loved might be killing the island. She thought about what Duke had said about emergency vehicles. When she was in second grade, her friend's house had burned down. No one was hurt, but they'd had to rebuild. She hadn't thought of that in years. Had the lack of roads played a part in that tragedy?

Her thoughts turned to Katarina and her children, her new baby, and sweet Vivi, who she knew wanted to get off the island. Would Vivi still want to leave if there were more people, more jobs, more chances to meet her one true love while she was there with her family? Would anyone?

How could she have been so shortsighted? How could it have taken her this long to see it?

And how could Duke have agreed to what he did? He *had* to do what was best for the island and the people there, regardless of what she wanted.

CHAPTER TWENTY-NINE

DUKE STRETCHED OUT on the king-sized bed in Pierce and Rebecca's guest room, wearing his boxer briefs and a hungry smile. He'd thought about Gabriella and her taunt of wanting to try phone sex that evening. Could she be any more adorable? Any sexier? He pressed her speed-dial number, already keyed up just thinking about hearing her voice.

She answered on the first ring, and before he could say a word, she said, "You have to do what's best for the island."

He was momentarily knocked off-kilter. "Okay."

"I mean it. I know I vacillate, and I'm a big pain in the ass when we talk about it, but you really must do what's best for it. I couldn't live with myself if you didn't. I've been so selfish—"

He wasn't sure what had driven her to this line of thinking, but he wished he were there to hold her, to look into her eyes when he responded. "Sweetheart, we'll do what's best for everyone. I promise you that, and I don't break promises. Especially not to the people I love, so please, don't worry. I've got this."

A relived sigh filled the airwaves. "Really?"

"Yes, baby. *Really*. I wish I was there with you to reassure you. It was nice spending time with everyone, but they're all so in love. It made me miss you even more."

"Aw, Duke. I wish I was there, too. It's weird being in bed without you."

His cock twitched at the thought of his girl in bed. "You're in bed?"

"Mm-hm. And I'm *so* lonely. If only there were a willing, sexy man to keep me company. Someone, maybe, six three or four, with hands that feel so good when they move over my skin and a mouth that should be patented for all the pleasure it gives."

"Someone's been watching porn again," he teased.

"No." She laughed, but he could hear embarrassment in the way she sighed at the end.

He'd memorized her laughs. There was the sexy, deep, teasing laugh that said she wanted to fool around and was usually accompanied by a sensual gaze. Then she had the real *ha-ha that's funny* laugh that was higher pitched and reached all the way to her eyes. And then she had this sweet, feminine, embarrassed laugh that always ended in the most seductive sigh. God, he loved that sigh.

"Porn was a onetime thing. Those were *my* words, *my* thoughts."

"You know how much I love touching you." His voice was as thick with desire as his heart was with love. "Is your light on, baby?"

"Yes."

"Why don't you turn it off for me, and lie down, get comfortable." He pictured her getting up to flick the light switch by the door, and as he heard her soft breathing, he pictured her settling back on the bed.

"Are you in bed, too?" she asked.

"Yes. The guest room is very masculine, with heavy wood furniture and thick dark curtains. It needs your femininity, Gabriella. I need you."

She sighed, and he imagined her luscious lips parted, her eyes heavy with desire.

"The lights are out, and I'm lying in the middle of the bed, wearing my black Calvin briefs. I can see the moon high in the sky through the crack in the curtains. I wish you were here, baby. I'd love to see you lying naked in the center of this big bed." She was breathing harder. "With your legs spread and me nestled in between them. Would you like that, baby?"

"Yes," she said in a needy whisper.

"What are you wearing, Gabriella?" He closed his eyes, picturing her in his mind.

"A silk camisole."

"Give me more, baby. What color is it? Does it have those

thin straps I love to take off with my teeth? Do you have on panties?"

She was silent for a beat, and he knew he'd embarrassed her.

"No pressure, sweetheart. We can just talk, or say good night. Whatever you want."

"No," she said quickly. "I just never knew this could be such a turn-on."

"Everything between us is a turn-on, baby. That's what love does. It makes you care so deeply that you never get enough of the other person." He heard the words coming from his mouth, so different from anything he'd ever felt, and the truth of them brought another flood of emotions.

"Relax, baby. It's just you and me. No one else can hear or see us. You're always safe with me."

"I know." She paused for a moment. "I'm wearing black silk panties that match my cami. I bought them for you when I was out with the girls and specifically looked for the thin straps, the kind that you could tear off if you pulled too hard. I love when you do that, when you take control and yank my clothes off."

"I wish I could do that right now." He palmed his erection over his briefs. "If I were there, I'd tear those silk panties right off your gorgeous body, bind your wrists above your head, and tease you until you came so hard your body went limp."

"Jesus."

"Would you like that, baby? For me to lick your thighs, to tease you with my hands, my mouth, my hard cock?"

"Yes—" Her voice trembled.

"Take your panties off for me and tell me if you're wet." He pushed his briefs off and kicked them to the floor, listening to her breathing quicken as she moved. "It's okay, baby. I'm right here, hard as steel for you. So fucking hard I ache."

"I took off everything, and, Duke?"

"Yes, baby?"

"I'm so wet, so ready for you to be inside me. I hate that you're so far away. I want you to love me with your whole body. I want to feel your chest on mine. I want to feel your mouth sucking on my nipples, licking me…down there."

"Christ, baby. I want that, too. Touch yourself. Feel all that heat that I can't be there to touch." He stroked himself in tight, hard moves. She made the sexiest mewing sound, and he knew she was close. "Use one hand to fuck yourself, the other on your clit, baby. Pretend it's my hand and my mouth."

"So good," she said in a heated breath.

"That's it, baby. If I were there I'd bury my cock so deep inside you, you wouldn't know where your body stopped and mine began. I'd suck your nipples so hard you'd feel it burn all the way down to your core."

"Yes…Oh God, Duke…"

"I'm right there with you, baby. You look so sexy when you come. I'm picturing your back arching off the bed, your eyes closed as your thighs fall open wide, then tighten with desire—" Heat burned down his spine.

"More. Talk dirty to me. I'm almost there."

"Christ, baby, that's so sexy. I want to turn you over and fuck you from behind, feel that gorgeous ass of yours against me. I want to kiss every inch of your beautiful back and work my way down to your ass, then flip you over and suck your clit so I can feel every pulse when you—"

"Ohgodohgod. Coming—"

A stream of words left her lips—*So good. Duke. Oh God. Yes*—and drew the come right out of him. Hot ribbons shot across his chest as he groaned out her name.

GABRIELLA CAME SO hard she could do little more than lie there listening to Duke breathe. Her body hummed with pleasure, and she knew it had more to do with Duke's voice and his sexy, loving words than her touch. He had a way of gathering up everything she needed and doling it out at just the right time.

"You still with me, baby? You okay?" he asked with the tenderness he always showed her.

"Yeah. A little embarrassed." Maybe she should be embarrassed by that confession, but she knew he'd understand. And she felt so close to him. There was nothing she wouldn't tell him.

"You're so beautiful, so trusting. Don't be embarrassed by anything we do, baby. I wish I was there to hold you. I'd wrap you in my arms and hold you all night long, so you knew you were safe and loved."

"You make me feel that way even from far away." She pulled the sheet over her naked body. "I've never done all these things before, and with you I want to do it all. Duke, before that night at the lighthouse, I'd never touched myself in front of a man."

"That means you trust me. You feel safe with us. All of this, our talks, our sensuality, our worries, our hopes, that's what makes up a relationship, and that's why we're so good together. I can't wait to go back to the island with you this weekend and experience it as a couple. I want that with you. I want everything with you, and you'll never get anything but honesty from me—in words, actions, and emotions."

"Thank you. We're experiencing a lot of my firsts together, and it's so…I don't know. It feels *big*. It feels good."

"I wish I would have been your first boyfriend, and we would have shared your first kiss."

"I'm not sure you would have liked me back then. I was kind of bossy. My first kiss was with Bill Campbell. He was tall, blond, and the perfect Southern gentleman.”

“Baby, I love it when you’re bossy. Bill’s tall and blond? Did you dance with him at the celebration that night?” His tone was tight with jealousy, and she loved hearing it.

“Yes, actually. But trust me, I wasn’t thinking about our first kiss.” She laughed, remembering her and Bill’s conversation, which revolved around his medical practice in South Carolina.

“You loved the island, and I assume he was from the island. Why didn’t it work out?”

“I was a bossy Greek and he was a quiet Southern gentleman. We clashed like oil and water. Well, that and we were *fifteen*.” She closed her eyes and sighed, wanting to just listen to him talk. How could she be this happy? Was she missing something? A red flag she’d been too swept up in love to see? “Tell me your biggest flaw, and don’t say something like you’re *too loyal*, because that’s not a flaw.”

“The truth?” His tone turned serious.

“Of course.” She laughed. “Otherwise I would have said, ‘Tell me a lie. A really good one.’”

“Okay, well, for starters, I’ve slept with too many women who meant nothing to me.” He paused, and his statement stung. “I’ve always worked too much, wanted too much.”

“Okay,” she managed, still hung up on the sleeping around part. Even though he’d always been honest about it, it didn’t lessen the impact of hearing it said so blatantly.

"Meeting you made me realize *why* I've been doing all those things. I was trying to fill a part of me that I didn't know was empty. I have a great, loving family. A great career. To a lot of people, it must look like I have a perfect life all around. But I lacked what mattered most—loving, and being loved by, the right woman. Someone who loved me for me and not for my assets. Someone bright and interesting, funny and loving. Working so hard for all these years put me in the position to buy the island, and that led me to you. And because I've never felt anything more than physical attraction for any other woman, I know my feelings for you are real and lasting. You're my *kardio mou*, my heart, baby, and we were fated to be together. Can't you feel that?"

Tears burned at the back of her eyes. She wasn't about to tell him that sentences didn't translate verbatim from Greek to English and that he'd sort of misused the endearment. Just the fact that he'd claimed it as his endearment for her meant the world to her and showed her just how much she meant to him. The other women he'd been with might have been more plentiful than the men she'd slept with, but what did that matter? Everything he'd just said was true. His past made him the man he was, and boy did she love that man.

CHAPTER THIRTY

TUESDAY MORNING GABRIELLA stood outside the courtroom waiting for the McGrady case to be called and thinking about Duke. He had called her before she left the apartment to wish her luck. He said the way the meetings were going, he might have to stay until the end of the week. She didn't know it was possible to miss a person as much as she did, but the thought of sleeping without him all week left a lonely ache inside her. She drew in a deep breath and turned her thoughts to Mary McGrady and the trial.

Most of her clients envisioned courtrooms as they saw them on television. Enormous rooms with dark, wood-paneled walls, hardwood floors, and a presence that swallowed them whole when they walked through the door. *If only.* There was wood and there was a presence, but not one of grandeur. Fear, nervousness, and intimidation came from the fact that her clients were doing something they never intended to do. They were walking into moderately sized rooms, some of which looked like they hadn't been remodeled in thirty years, and they were going to be judged for ending a marriage they swore to uphold *for better or for worse.*

Gabriella glanced at Mary, who had taken every ounce of advice Gabriella had given her. From the conservative dark skirt and cream-colored top to the post earrings and stable-not-sexy heels. Her hands were folded in her lap, but Gabriella could see them trembling. Her blond hair was neatly pinned back with a clip at the base of her neck, and her makeup was demure. But it was the lost look in her eyes, in the eyes of every client, even if they were the ones to instigate the divorce, that got to Gabriella every time.

She had prepared Mary to answer as succinctly as possible and answer only the questions that were asked. She'd prepped her about body language and facial expressions. Hurtful things would be flung from both sides, and she didn't want her clients breaking down, or worse, bursting out with a stream of hateful accusations—even if their opposing spouse deserved them. But nothing could prepare them for the inner turmoil over what was really happening and what it meant to their lives. To the lives of their children. Even the clients who treated their children like pawns had to have a pang of guilt and remorse, didn't they? She sure hoped so, because no matter how she tried to divorce *herself* from her clients' situations, the ache of breaking up a family always lingered.

When they were invited into the courtroom, Mary grabbed Gabriella's wrist and said, "No matter what happens in there, thank you."

"Let's hope for the best." Her standard answer at this point.

"He called me this morning and begged me to stay. I wasn't going to tell you," Mary admitted softly, "but I wanted you to know that I stood strong, and I have you to thank for that."

"This was your decision, Mary. I'm just here to help watch out for the best interests of you and your children."

"I know. I just need you to know. He offered me a *lot* of money to stay married, and promised me everything under the sun. But I remembered what you told me about our actions being messages for our children, and…Thank you."

As they walked into the courtroom, Gabriella drew her shoulders back, held her chin up, and readied herself to battle someone else's hell.

THREE GRUELDING DAYS later, Duke was still in Reno, and after too many heated arguments, tears, *should I's*, and long hours spent in the judge's chambers, the McGrady trial was finally coming to an end. Both sides had pled their cases, and the judge was making his final judgment. Gabriella felt the minutes ticking like a time bomb. She didn't want to miss her flight to South Carolina. Her parents' anniversary party was tomorrow afternoon, and come hell or high water, she was going to be there in the morning to help them get ready. That was half the fun, cooking and chatting with all her friends and family.

She wished Duke would be there when she arrived, but he was stuck in Reno until Saturday. At least he'd make the party, and then they'd have one night on the island together before returning to the city. It felt like it had been a month since she'd seen him, even though he'd called her every morning and evening. She'd used the little downtime she'd had to sketch out her garden ideas for his yard, which was how she knew her heart belonged with him. She couldn't deny that she'd also spent the long lonely nights fantasizing about what a future with Duke could be like. Waking up in his arms, raising babies together. He was as close to his family as she was to hers, and that meant so much to her. Everything Duke did came straight from his big, generous heart.

"It is hereby ordered that…"

The judge's voice brought Gabriella back to the moment, and she listened as he outlined his ruling on the division of assets, child support, custody arrangements, and a handful of other items, as he reduced the McGrady family and marriage into a clearly defined list of negotiated items. Mary nodded, pleased with each of his decisions, but Gabriella could tell by her curling fingers and the twitching of her lower lip that her strong face was a thin veil of courage. Unfortunately, it was a veil that seemed to be passed from one divorcing couple to the next.

After dealing with the rest of the paperwork and necessary arrangements, getting the stink eye from Dickhead McGrady, and saying goodbye to Mary, Gabriella felt a huge burden lift from her shoulders. She was one step closer to never handling another divorce case, and nothing could make her happier—except being in Duke's arms.

She zipped off a quick text to Addy as she took a cab to the airport. *One case down, three more to go! Then no more ugly divorces! Go home early. You deserve it for holding down the fort alone.*

Addy's return text came quickly. *Thanks, boss. We'll celebrate when you get back. Have fun on the island! Give your family hugs and kisses for me! Xo.*

She wished she could call Duke, but he'd told her their negotiations had been heated over the past few days, and she didn't want to interrupt. She scrolled to her camera, took a selfie of her blowing him a kiss, and typed, *We survived court, and it ended well. Love you, miss you, can't wait to kiss you. On my way to the airport. Wish you were with me. See you tomorrow afternoon! xox.*

CHAPTER THIRTY-ONE

GABRIELLA STEPPED OFF the boat onto the familiar dock at a little after nine o'clock Friday night. Standing beneath the stars with a smile she couldn't imagine trying to stifle, she kicked off her heels, stuffed them into her bag, and would have whipped off her work clothes and changed into shorts or a sundress right there on the dock if there weren't people walking on the beach. A couple passed by hand in hand, and she thought about how nice it would be to see tourists enjoying the island again.

Dragging her suitcase behind her, she made her way toward the beach. The worn wooden dock was prickly against her bare feet, the air was warm, and the scents of the sea stole the stress of the last few days. *Island magic*, she mused. Oh, how she loved it here. She thought about Duke and hoped things were going okay in his meetings. She couldn't imagine how many people had to come together, how many teams, to buy an island. He'd mentioned his attorneys, land development teams, and financial teams, and that all sounded stressful to her. He'd need this trip as much as she did, and tomorrow they'd finally be reunited.

The welcome center was dark when she went inside and grabbed the keys to one of the golf carts, remembering Duke the first day he'd met her parents, standing in the doorway looking sinfully hot and watching them with amusement in his eyes.

The golf cart rumbled over the familiar dirt roads. When she reached the resort, there were three golf carts outside. They must have hit a rush of guests. All the lights were on, and as she parked the car she saw her grandfather standing in the doorway. It was late for him to be at the resort. She hurried inside, hoping everything was all right. He turned at the sound of the door, and a smile formed on his lips as he opened his arms.

"*Gabrielaki mou*, you got my message. I was worried you might not have heard it." His warmth, and his familiar foody scent, embraced her.

"I didn't get a message. I turned my phone off in the airport. What are you doing here so late? Is everything okay?" She did a quick visual sweep over him, looking for signs of distress, but he was smiling, wearing one of his nicer button-down shirts, slacks, and his favorite sandals.

"We have a meeting. Come." He led her into the confer-ence room, where two men and two women, each very professionally dressed, sat at the conference table. Blueprints were spread out across the table, along with several documents.

Her gut twisted as she scanned the friendly faces of the men and women before her. She turned to her grandfather and spoke in Greek to keep their conversation private. "Who are these people? What is all this?" Was he selling the island to someone other than Duke? *No, no, no, no, no.*

Speaking in Greek, he said, "They are from BRB Enterprises, and they have made a very fair offer for the island."

She felt like a traitor, when Duke was working so hard to put together an offer, but out of respect for her grandfather, she didn't argue. Instead, she tried to extricate herself from the room. If he wanted to sell the island to someone else, that was his business. But she didn't have to condone it.

With her heart in her throat, she once again spoke in Greek. "Why am I here, Grandpa? This is your business deal. I'm tired, and if you don't mind, I'd like to go to my villa."

He draped an arm over her shoulder and surprised her by speaking English.

"Gabriella, they have made a very fair offer for the island, and there has been a requirement written in stating that all designs need your final approval."

Her eyes widened and the air left her lungs. She felt as if she'd been sucker punched. She was *not* going to get tangled up in this new business deal. It was hard enough backing away from it with Duke. She had no intentions of being part of something like this with strangers. She'd almost found her peace. She understood that the island she loved would be wholly changed, but she didn't need to embark on a new journey of discontent. But her respect for her grandfather rose above her own desires, and rather than refuse, she tried to dissuade him.

She stepped closer to him and turned her back to the others, lowering her voice so only he could hear her. "They will never agree to that."

"Not only did we agree; we insisted."

Gabriella's heart stilled. *Duke?* She spun around, her heart hammering against her ribs. Duke stood in the doorway, looking like God's gift to her in a dark suit, light blue tie, and that confident spark in his eyes that had drawn her in since day one.

"Duke…?" A knot rose in her throat as she tried to understand what was happening.

He closed the gap between them and bent to kiss her cheek. "Hi, baby. I missed you." With a hand on the small of her back, he rose to his full height, holding her gaze. "I'm sorry I wasn't in the room when you arrived." He motioned to the table. "These are my partners, Pierce Braden and his sister Emily. And this is Pierce's fiancée, Rebecca, and Emily's fiancé, Dae. We made the switch from Ryder Enterprises to Braden, Ryder, Braden Enterprises when we decided to join forces for this project."

His partners and their fiancés? She was still on cloud nine from seeing Duke earlier than they'd planned, and as she tried to process what he was saying, he continued explaining.

"Emily is a leader in the passive house movement. She's an architect and specializes in green building. Dae is a demolition expert, and he'll be working with us to ensure that anything that needs to be taken down is in the safest, most environmentally aware way possible. Rebecca specializes in acquisitions, and she, Pierce, and I have been working on the business end of the deal."

"It's very nice to meet all of you," Gabriella said, but before they could respond, she added, "I don't understand. What do *I* have to do with this?"

Duke took her hand in his and gazed deeply into her eyes. She felt the room pulse with energy and was sure everyone else could feel it, too.

"Baby, I made you a promise, and I always keep my promises. Nothing, not one single grain of sand, will be moved without your approval. You trusted me, and I trust you. I asked everyone to come with me so you could speak with them, work with them, plan, ask questions, make suggestions and decisions. We're thinking about making the island a walkable resort, just as you wanted."

She could barely hear over the pounding of her heart. She looked at her grandfather, and he nodded his approval.

"We're thinking of a themed island," Rebecca explained. "If you are on board with it, of course, and if you're not, we'll work with whatever ideas you have to come up with an environmentally aware resort."

"We're thinking about keeping the unique Mediterranean and Southern feel," Emily added. "Much like Little Italy, Chinatown, that type of thing, with environmentally friendly buildings, nothing over four stories, and that would only be in certain areas, nowhere near the conservation land, and we'll ensure that no new structures inhibit the views of the existing homes."

"*Ohmygod.*" She gripped Duke's arm. "Duke?" He really was keeping his promise. Tears burned in her eyes. "No roads? But what about emergency vehicles?"

"We were thinking about having a few dedicated roads through the wooded areas to ensure transportation for emergency vehicles, but not in the main areas of the island. The dirt roads would remain dirt, or dirt and gravel." Emily rose and handed Gabriella a packet of information. "There are new experimental roads that can capture kinetic energy and special products and materials that collect solar energy to create electricity, which we'd love to use here on Elpitha. Gosh, I could talk your ear off, and you just got in. I'm so sorry."

"I'm sorry," Gabriella said. "I'm a little blown away."

Duke turned her in his arms and cupped her cheeks between his large, warm, safe hands. "There's no pressure, baby. But I made a promise, and I would like nothing more than for you to be part of this endeavor with us. You'll have final say on everything, but more than that, you'll be an integral part of giving back to the island you love so much."

Tears streamed down her cheeks.

"You won't be in the middle, baby. Just as I promised," he said as he brushed her tears away. "You'll be in charge. That is, if you want to."

Gabriella clutched his arms and forced her voice past the lump in her throat.

"Yes. Yes, Duke. I want this very, very much."

AFTER HAVING A celebratory drink with everyone, they left the others to settle in at the resort. Duke and Gabriella drove her grandfather back to his house, then returned the golf cart at the resort. Duke carried Gabriella's suitcase down the path toward her villa, reminding him of the last time they were there, when he had been carrying his own luggage. He remembered how tormented he'd been when he'd left her that first night, when he'd have given everything he owned to be closer to her.

The villa was just as he'd left it an hour ago, with the porch light on.

"It feels good to be here," Gabriella said as they stepped from the path and onto the grass. She gazed up at the clear midnight-blue sky.

"I started falling in love with you right here on Elpitha Island," she said as she wrapped her arms around his waist, and then she spoke in Greek. "Elpitha cast its spell again."

"It sure did."

She gasped in surprise and met his gaze. "You understood what I said?"

Speaking in Greek, Duke said, "I can't very well ask you to marry me if I don't speak your family's language, now, can I?"

"M-*marry* you?" She spoke in English, too shocked to think.

"I arrived early and had lunch with your family. Your parents, grandfather, and brothers. I've wanted to ask you since you first stayed at my house, when I imagined your belly round with our babies."

Her eyes widened.

"You do want babies, don't you?" He already knew the answer, but she looked so gorgeous standing in the moonlight with a shocked expression on her beautiful face that he couldn't resist toying with her just a little.

"Yes! Yes! I want lots of babies with you." She gripped his shirt, anticipation buzzing like live wires between them.

"And I assume you'll want to move into my place?" he said as nonchalantly as he could.

"Yes! I drew up plans for gardens and everything."

"Okay, well, let's go inside." He picked up the suitcase, and she yanked him back.

"Duke! You can't leave a girl hanging like that!"

He dropped the suitcase and laughed. "Baby, do I *ever* leave you hanging?"

He took a step away, shrugged off his suit coat, and took out his phone.

"Duke…" She laughed and shook her head. "Maybe I won't say yes after all this."

"Maybe not, but I have a good feeling about us."

He flicked on Spotify and turned on "Lose My Mind" by Brett Eldredge. He kicked off his shoes, having removed his socks earlier, and moved around her to the beat of the music, rocking and thrusting his hips, slowly unbuttoning his shirt. As Brett sang about a roller coaster of emotions and knowing when they'd met he'd never be the same, Duke spun around and ground his ass into Gabriella's hips.

"Oh my," she said with heat in her eyes.

The chorus sang of making his screws come loose and driving him wild, and Duke slid his shirt off of one shoulder and leaned in close like he was going to kiss her. She leaned forward and he moved just out of reach as the beat quickened and Brett sung about being driven crazy.

She giggled as he took off his shirt and whipped it around over his head, then tossed it to her. She caught it and pressed it to her nose, inhaling deeply with her eyes closed. Everything she did turned him on, and when she let out an erotic moan, he nearly forewent the rest of the dance to take her in his arms and kiss her. But this was for her, and he wasn't going to do anything short of fulfilling every single one of her wishes, of her fantasies, for the rest of her life.

As the chorus repeated, Duke flicked open the button on his slacks and gyrated his hips, closing the distance between them again. He unzipped his pants and thrust his pelvis against her thigh, making him hard and earning another sexy moan from Gabriella.

"Mm. I wanna make you lose your mind," she said, reaching for him.

"And you will," he said as he moved away and stepped out of his slacks to the beat of the music, leaving him naked, save for his briefs.

He grabbed Gabriella around the waist and pulled her to him, grinding his erection against her hips. Her eyes fluttered closed, and he sang the chorus against her cheek as the song wound down. He reached into his briefs and took out a black velvet bag, dropped to one knee, and removed a ring from the velvet.

"OhmyGod. Duke."

"Gabriella." He paused to steady his breathing and brought her hands to his lips, pressing kisses on each knuckle. "Baby, you're the only woman I've ever loved, and you're the only woman I will *ever* love. I want to make all your dreams, all your fantasies, come true. I want to be there to celebrate your joys and to make sure that you never cry for the same reason twice."

He rose to his feet and gazed into the eyes of the woman whose heart was so big she tried to deny their attraction to save the island and the people she loved.

"Will you marry me, baby? Be mine forever? I promise I'll never leave you hanging."

"Yes, I'll marry you, Duke. I'd marry you right this second."

He slid the ring on her finger as fresh tears spilled down her cheeks. The quartet of princess-cut diamonds encircled with round diamonds glistened in the moonlight. Two rows of diamonds joined together and formed the band, just like their hearts joined together to form their love.

"I might have forgotten to mention one little thing," Duke said with as serious of a tone as he could muster while his heart expanded in his chest.

"What?"

"As my wife you'll be part owner of BRB Enterprises. If you want to move back to the island and manage the projects, I can work from just about anywhere."

She leaped into his arms, speaking so fast it made his head spin—in the very best of ways. "Really? You would do that for me? You'd move here? Away from your house on the water? With me? For me? What about Addy? My practice?

Ohmygod!"

"We'll figure it all out, and of course there's a position for Addy, too. I'd never separate you from your porn-watching partner." Her laugh cut straight to his heart. "I promised to fulfill your every wish. Always and forever, baby. I'll never let you down."

They sealed their vows with a salty, tear-soaked kiss. And as Duke carried Gabriella inside, he felt like the luckiest man on the planet, knowing he'd be kissing her luscious lips every day for the rest of his life.

EPILOGUE

"IT'S STUNNING, SWEETHEART," Gabriella's mother said as Gabriella looked at her sparkling engagement ring for the millionth time since Duke had put it on her finger the night before. "And I'm so glad Duke flew everyone in to help celebrate your engagement."

"And your anniversary," Gabriella added. Nearly the whole town had shown up for the celebration at the big house. It was a familiar, festive scene, with lamb roasting on the spit, laughter coming from all directions, children playing and dancing, and Duke's and Gabriella's families coming seamlessly together. She had been so surprised when she'd seen everyone she'd nearly hyperventilated.

"There's no better anniversary gift than seeing our Gabrielaki happy. He's a wonderful man, sweetheart, and everyone here can feel his love for you. He wears his heart on his sleeve, just like you do." Her mother nodded toward Duke, watching them as he stood with his family and Gabriella's brothers.

Duke blew Gabriella a kiss. His brother Blue nudged him

with his shoulder and said something that made Duke and the others laugh. From the moment she'd met them, she'd loved his brothers Blue and Gage just as much as the rest of his family. Blue's fiancée, Lizzie, was chatting with Addy, Siena, Trish, and Katarina. Addy kept stealing glances at Jake, and it was impossible to miss the way Jake was salivating over her. She wondered how long it would take before her matchmaking relatives noticed the spark. A few feet away, a group of her aunts were huddled together by the buffet table, their eyes trained on Addy and Jake, and she smiled, remembering how they'd glommed on to Duke the morning of the birthday party. Boy, did she love those women. *Boy, do I love Duke.*

Siena lifted Katarina's daughter, Ermione, to her hip. She looked so natural holding the little girl. Gabriella felt a pang of longing. She suddenly had more sisters than she ever dreamed of, and she couldn't wait to get to know them even better, raise babies together, and one day they'd all watch their children as they fell in love and married.

She was getting way ahead of herself, but she and Duke had stayed up all night making love and talking about their future. They both wanted lots of babies.

"Gabrielaki mou."

She'd been so lost in thought, she startled at her grandfather's voice. She took comfort in the scratch of his bushy mustache as he pressed a kiss to each of her cheeks.

"Your future husband, he has given this family a beautiful gift," he said with a serious tone.

"Yes, he has. Emily and Rebecca have incredible ideas, and they're so in tune to nature and the environment, I just know we're in good hands."

"Ah, you see his gift of regenerating the island. I see something else, sweet girl. It takes a special man not to feel threatened by a smart, headstrong girl like you. And it takes a generous, loving heart to want to nurture that strength, to push you outside your comfort zone, instead of tamping it down or trying to control it."

Duke broke away from the others and set a seductive stare on Gabriella. The crowd parted for him as he made his way toward her. Every determined step made her pulse quicken. The rich love in his gaze was layered in lust and desire, and as her breathing became shallow, she wondered how her legs would hold her up if he kept this up. Did her grandfather notice her reaction?

Oh crap! Grandpa!

She turned to face him, and her grandfather leaned in close and said, "Every flower needs sunlight, sweet girl, and Duke has helped you shine. He has given us a much bigger gift than helping the island. He has given our family the gift of your happiness," he said, "and for that I am eternally grateful."

She realized that her grandfather had pushed her past her

comfort zone, too, and in doing so, he'd also helped her spread her wings and shine.

"And I'll forever be grateful to you, too. Everything you've done has led me to Duke. And, Grandpa, he *is* my sunlight, my rain…my *everything*."

DUKE'S HEART FELT like it was going to beat right out of his chest as he approached Gabriella, the woman who would soon be his wife, and hopefully one day, the mother of his children. He was so full of love for her that he could think of nothing beyond reaching her and holding her in his arms.

He watched as her grandfather said something in her ear. Then he and her mother stepped away. Duke reached for Gabriella's hand and laced their fingers together, drawing her in close. The music changed to a slow tune, and as he wrapped his other hand around her waist and brought her body flush with his, they swayed to the music.

"Have I told you lately how much I love you?" he whispered against her cheek.

"Yes." She sounded as breathless as she had after their first kiss, and his whole body took notice.

"Let me tell you again. I love how important your family is to you. I love how you try to do right by everyone and the way you go above and beyond when it comes to us. I love the sexy way you look at me but are a little embarrassed to let me see it." He felt her heart beat faster against his chest. "I love the way you look first thing in the morning, when you're barely awake but your hands are seeking me out. Baby, I love the way our bodies fit together, like we're meant for each other."

"I love that, too."

"What are you thinking of right this very second? How incredible it felt to make love last night?" He lowered his hand to the base of her spine, holding their hips together, and whispered, "Or can you feel how much I want to make love to you again?"

She nuzzled against his neck as they danced. "You're going to turn me to liquid right here in front of everyone."

He glanced at their parents, dancing beside Pierce and Rebecca and Emily and Dae. Cash and Siena were dancing with Ermione between them, and Blue and Lizzie were standing arm in arm, talking with Gage and Trish. Dimitri was leading Addy to the dance floor, and Jake watched on, tracking them like a panther ready to pounce. Duke laughed to himself, remembering how he'd felt when Gabriella had danced with the blond guy at the birthday party. He knew there would be times he'd be jealous in their future. How could he not, when he was marrying such a brilliant, beautiful woman? But he was damn glad she would be coming home to him each and every night forever more.

"Don't worry, baby. If you turn to liquid I'll soak up every last drop and make you whole again. But, with the heat sizzling between us, I think you should just get used to being liquid, because that's never going to end if I can help it."

"You're a little sure of yourself, aren't you?" she teased.

"No, baby. I'm very sure of *us.*"

She gazed up at him with eyes full of trust and love and surety, and when she said, "So am I," he could feel the truth all the way to his soul.

Ready for more Ryders?

Fall in love with Trish and Boone in CHASED BY LOVE

Actress Trish Ryder takes her job seriously and has no time for those who don't. When she's awarded a major role in a new movie featuring America's hottest rock star, Boone Stryker, she's beyond excited. The six-two, tattooed hunk of burning desire is known for his dedication to his craft—but when he ditches their first meeting, she begins to wonder if he's just another rocker with a great PR team.

Sex, booze, women, and music pretty much sum up Boone Stryker's private world. He's coasted through life playing by his own rules with plenty of people willing to cover his tracks, and he's not likely to change—until he meets a woman who refuses to give him the time of day, much less anything more.

Sparks fly from the first moment Trish and Boone meet—Tensions run hot and desire runs hotter when they're trapped together on a remote location with no place to hide. Will sparks ignite, or will a hurricane douse the flames?

To continue reading, buy **CHASED BY LOVE**

Love the Ryders?

The Ryders are just one of many families in the Love in Bloom big-family romance collection. Characters from each family series make appearances in future books so you never miss an engagement, wedding, or birth. If you love to binge read, download the Love in Bloom series checklist and start at the very beginning of the series with SISTERS IN LOVE.

Free Love in Bloom series checklist here:
www.melissafoster.com/SO

Get **free** first-in-series Love in Bloom ebooks and see my current sales here:
www.MelissaFoster.com/LIBFree

Have you met sinfully sexy Sam Braden?

Fall in love with Sam and Faith, in RIVER OF LOVE

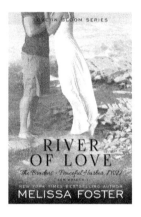

Chapter One

A MAN COULD take a wedding for only so long before he drank too much booze or left with a warm, willing woman to wash away all that purity. Sam Braden stood with a drink in one hand and a greedy itch in the other, debating doing both.

"I'll take the redhead if you want the brunette." Ty, his youngest brother, lifted his chin in the direction of the bar. In addition to being a world-renowned mountain climber and photographer, Ty was also Sam's carousing partner. "Unless you're double-dipping tonight, in which case I'll go for one of the Staley sisters."

Sam scoffed. *Been there, done them.*

He spotted two blondes slinking across the dance floor toward them. He'd hooked up with the one who was currently eye-fucking him last month, and the redhead Ty had been ogling moments ago had joined them in their hot, sweaty romp. His gaze shifted to the sexy brunette standing by the bar looking like she wanted to jump over it and hide behind it but she couldn't quite figure out how. *Faith Hayes.* He'd been trying *not* to look at Faith all night, but he was losing that battle. Faith worked in Cole's medical practice. She was sweet, and good, and smart, and...Sam should not be thinking about laying her on the bar and doing dirty things to her gorgeous body.

No. He definitely should not.

Every time he looked at her, every time he thought of her—*which was every damn day*—that feeling of wanting more than a few quick hookups resurfaced. He not only wanted to lay her down on the bar, but he wanted to take her home. That was bizarre, too, since as a rule Sam never took any woman to his cabin. But half his *visits* with Cole at his office were merely made-up opportunities to get a glimpse of Faith. He didn't fully understand his fascination with her, considering he usually preferred the kind of woman who wanted to jump *him* and damn well knew how, but there was no denying the stirring inside him every time she was near. He forced himself to look away and focused on the dance floor, where their eldest brother, Cole, danced with his new wife, Leesa, and just beyond, their younger brother Nate and his fiancée, Jewel, were gazing into each other's eyes. Weren't they always? Sam used to get hives just thinking about being tied down—*unless, of course, it was to a bed*. But he couldn't deny how happy his brothers seemed since they'd fallen in love, and lately he'd begun feeling as if he were missing out on something.

The tall blonde sidled up to Sam, blocking his view of Faith and blinking flirtatiously, while her friend joined Ty. "You boys look lonely."

"Ladies," Sam said smoothly, bringing his attention back to the pretty girls who definitely knew how to use their bodies for the good of mankind.

"Care to dance?" she asked, and like a puppy with a bone, Sam followed her out to the dance floor.

Music and dancing ranked right up there with white-water rafting in Sam's book. As the owner of Rough Riders, a rafting and adventure company, he rarely slowed down, but a strong beat calmed his internal restlessness. And Sam was always a little restless.

The blonde moved sensuously in his arms, reminding him of all the reasons a woman should win out over booze tonight. On that thought, his eyes drifted back to Faith, still standing by the bar, holding a drink he'd bet was soda, and nervously running her finger up the side of the glass as she...*watched him?* Sam's lips curved up and Faith's gaze skittered away. She became adorably flustered whenever he visited Cole at the office, and though he probably shouldn't,

Sam got a kick out of flirting with her.

Cole stepped into his line of sight, blocking his view of Faith and casting a threatening look at Sam, sending the message, *Don't even think about it.*

There were no two ways about it, Sam loved women and everyone around him knew it. He loved the way they smelled, the feel of their soft bodies against his hard muscles, their delicate features, the sounds they made in the throes of passion. But his mind refused to play the *any woman* game these days. It was drenched in thoughts of Faith, and he wanted to experience all those things about her firsthand.

"Sam!" Cole chided.

He shook his head to clear his mind, laughing under his breath, as he turned his attention back to the woman he was dancing with. His hands sank to the base of her spine. *Mm.* She felt good. His eyes were drawn to Faith again, who was staring into her drink. *Bet you'd feel even better,* was his first thought, but it was the second—*I wonder what you're thinking*—that took him by surprise.

I SHOULDN'T HAVE come to this wedding. Faith checked her watch for the hundredth time that evening. She'd told herself she had to stay for an hour after dinner. That was the respectable thing to do at her boss's wedding, even though she'd rather leave right this very second. Work obligations outside of the office were uncomfortable enough, but now she was not only surrounded by people she barely knew, but her stupid hormones were doing some sort of *I Want Sam Braden* dance. God, she hated herself right now. *Look at him, getting all handsy with the town flirt.* He'd been dancing all night with every other woman in the place. They practically lined up to be near him. Why shouldn't they? He was not only nice to everyone, but he was tall, dark, and distractingly handsome. The kind of handsome that made smart girls like Faith forget the alphabet. His arm was the most coveted spot in all of Peaceful Harbor, and damn it to hell, she did *not* want to be there.

Too badly.

I seriously need to dive into a tequila bottle. Or leave. Since driving home after drinking a bottle of tequila posed issues, she decided leaving was a better option.

She had the perfect excuse to cut out a little early, too. She was hosting a car wash tomorrow to raise funds for WAC, Women Against Cheaters, an online support group she'd started for women who had been cheated on.

By guys like Sam.

Sam glanced up and—*Oh God, shoot me now*—caught her staring. *Again.* She turned away, hoping he hadn't really noticed, even though his eyes were like laser beams burning a hole in her back. Of course he saw her. How could he not?

She was practically drooling over him. She didn't want to have this stupid crush on the man who, if she believed the rumors, had slept with most of the women in Peaceful Harbor. If she took away his devastatingly good looks, he was the exact opposite of the type of man she wanted or needed.

Unable to resist, she stole another glance, and like every other set of female eyes in the place that weren't related to him, she was drawn in like a fly to butter. He was *gorgeous*. Manly. Rugged. And that smile. *Lordy, Lordy.* She fanned her face. His smile alone caused her toes to curl. All the Bradens were good-looking, but there was something edgy and enigmatic about Sam. *Dangerous.*

Too dangerous for her, which was okay, because she didn't really want him. Not in the *try to keep him* sense. A man like Sam couldn't be kept, and she wasn't about to be the idiot who tried. She'd be happy with leering and lusting, and pretending she wasn't.

Except, *oh shit*, he was coming over. He moved across the dance floor like he owned the place, confident, determined, focused, leaving the blonde, and a dozen other women, staring after him. If looks had powers beyond the ability to weaken Faith's knees, Sam would have eaten her up before he even reached her. His dark eyes were narrow, seductive, and shimmering with wickedness. His broad shoulders looked even wider, more powerful, beneath his expensive tuxedo. The top buttons of his shirt were open, giving her a glimpse of his tanned skin and a dusting of chest hair. He looked like he should be lounging on a couch with women fawning over him. Godlike.

Godlike? I am pathetic.

Faith was not a meek woman without a man in her life. She was single by choice, *thank you very much*. She stunk at choosing men, and besides that…men sucked. They cheated, they lied, and eventually they all tried to put the blame back on her. Ever since JJ, her last boyfriend, made good on the unspoken All Men Must Cheat promise their gender seemed to live by, she'd confined her dating pool to include only boring, slightly nerdy men.

"Faith."

Sam's deep voice washed over her skin and nestled into her memory banks for later when she was alone in her bed, thinking about him. She hated that, too. Why, oh, why, did he have to be a player? Couldn't he be like his brothers Cole and Nate? Loyal to the end of time?

He touched her arm, burning her skin.

"Oh. Hi, Sam." That sounded casual, right? He was so big, standing this close, and he smelled like man and sunshine and heat all wrapped up in one big delicious package.

Great. Now I'm thinking of your package.

"Would you like to dance?" he asked.

Yes. No! Stick to your boring-man rule, Faith.

Sam was anything but boring, taking every outdoor risk

known to man and out carousing every night of the week. Nope, she wanted no part of that.

"No, thanks." She sipped her drink, wishing it were tequila instead of Jack and Coke. Wishing she were home instead of standing beside the human heat wave.

His brows knitted. "You sure? I haven't seen you on the dance floor all night."

"Have you run out of girls already?" *Holy Jesus, did I say that out loud?*

An easy smile spread across his face, like he wasn't offended, but...*amused?* He looked around the room and said, "No, actually. There are a few I haven't danced with." Those chocolate eyes focused on her again. "But I want to dance with you."

She downed her drink to keep the word *Okay* from slipping out and set the empty glass on the bar. "Thanks, but I'm actually getting ready to leave."

"Now, that would be a shame." His eyes dragged slowly down her body, making her feel vulnerable and naked.

Naked with Sam Braden. Her entire body flamed, and he must have noticed, because his eyes turned midnight black.

"You look incredibly beautiful tonight, and it's Cole and Leesa's big day. You should stick around." He leaned in a little closer. "And dance with me."

It wasn't like her jelly legs could carry her out of there anyway. *Incredibly beautiful?* Faith had been told she was pretty often enough to believe it, but *incredibly beautiful?* That was pushing it. That was smooth-talking Sam, the limit pusher.

She had to admit, he had this pickup thing down pat. His eyes were solely focused on her, while she felt the gazes of nearly every single woman in the place looking at her like they wondered what she had that they didn't—or maybe like they wanted to kill her. *Yup.* That was probably more accurate.

"The wedding was lovely," she managed. "I'm happy for Cole and Leesa, but I'm hosting a car wash at Harbor Park tomorrow afternoon. I should really get going so I have time to prepare."

Sam stepped closer. His fingers caressed the back of her arm, sending shivers of heat straight to her brain—and short-circuiting it.

"Harbor Park?" The right side of his tempting mouth lifted in a teasing smile. "Surely you won't turn into a pumpkin this early. You can't leave without giving me one dance. Come on. Think of how happy it'll make Cole to see you enjoying yourself."

He was obviously not going to give up. Maybe she should just give in and dance with him. She had no desire to be another in the long line of Sam's conquests, but it was just one dance, and then she could leave, and he'd go back to any of the other women there. That idea sank like a rock in her stomach.

Her stupid hormones swam to the surface again. *You did ask nicely.* Maybe she was reading too much into this dance. It was just a dance, not a date.

But his eyes were boring into her in that *I want to get into your panties* way he had. She'd seen him give that look to several other women tonight.

Several. Other. Women.

Ugh! Why was she even considering this?

It was his hand, moving up and down her arm, making her shivery and hot at once. And those eyes, drawing her in, making her feel important. She wasn't important to Sam. She knew that in her smart physician assistant brain, but her ovaries had some sort of hold on that part of her brain, crushing her smart cells.

Faith glanced at the dance floor and caught sight of Cole whispering something in Leesa's ear. They were such a handsome couple, and Cole was such a kind boss. Maybe she should stay a little longer. She didn't have to dance with Sam. She could just talk with him until he got bored and moved on.

Cole's eyes turned serious, and Leesa looked over, too. He said something to her and headed in their direction with a scowl on his face and an angry bead aimed at Sam. *Shit.* This was not good. He was her *boss.*

Oh my God. What was she thinking? She shouldn't

dance with her boss's brother!

"Actually…" Panic bloomed inside her chest as Cole neared. Cole respected her, but she knew he'd noticed the way she got flustered around Sam. He'd seen her turn beet-red with Sam's compliments when Sam visited him at the office. She didn't need him seeing her all swoony-eyed over him now.

"I really have to go, but thanks for asking, Sam." She spun on her heel and hurried away before she could lose her nerve.

To continue reading, buy **RIVER OF LOVE**

Have you read the Remingtons?

Fall in love with Boyd and Janie in TOUCHED BY LOVE

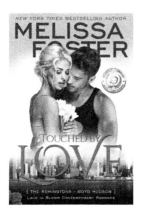

Blaine's mouth blazed a path up her inner thigh. His hot breath teased over her wet flesh. Kenya fisted her hands in the sheets, dug her heels into the mattress, and rocked her hips, aching for his talented tongue in the place she needed him most. Blaine lifted smoldering dark eyes, a hint of wickedness shining through, as his tongue slicked over his lips. He was a master at seduction, but Kenya didn't give a shit about seduction. She wanted to be fucked hard. Now. She needed his—

A large hand landed on Janie Jansen's desk beside her braille device. She nearly jumped out of her skin and nervously yanked out her earbuds. *Holy shit.* She was supposed to be finishing a technical editing assignment, not listening to the latest hot romance audiobook.

"Nice article in the newsletter this week, Jansen. *The Oxford Comma Revolution.* Catchy." Her boss, Clay Bishop, was slightly less arid than a desert, but Janie didn't mind. He'd hired her to work at Tech Ed Co, or TEC, on a trial basis, and four years later, her respect for him had only grown. He was a fair and equitable boss, and was currently considering her for a promotion.

It was difficult to spice up a weekly column geared toward grammar and editing, but Janie tried. It was just one more step toward the promotion of technical writer she'd been vying for, a nice step up from editor.

"You're here late. Trouble with the ARKENS handbook?"

"I'm just catching up on a few things. The handbook is almost done." Well, technically not *almost* done, but she'd meet the deadline. She had yet to miss one. She loved editing, but she hadn't set out to be an editor after college. She'd wanted to be a journalist, but that door had closed and she'd tabled her dream and settled for editing. Usually the intensity of her job didn't get to her, but after weeks of grueling revisions on this particular medical equipment handbook, she'd needed a short mental break. But Clay would never think to take a break. He was all business all the time, even hours after their workday officially ended.

"Perfect. Don't forget, Monday afternoon we have the peer review of your writing sample. If that goes well, your promotion will be in the hands of the management team. I'm not worried—you're always on top of your game."

"Yeah, she is." Boyd Hudson's amused voice brought a smile to Janie's lips.

Boyd consulted at TEC only a few days a month, and though Janie didn't know him well, he was quippy and flirtatious, bringing a spark of amusement into her otherwise quiet days.

"Hudson," Clay said dryly. "Okay, well, it's late, so…"

"See you Monday, Clay." Janie listened to his retreating footsteps and let out a relieved sigh.

"He almost caught you again, didn't he?"

She heard the smirk in Boyd's voice. "He didn't *catch* me last time. I was on my lunch break last week. And besides, I was just studying the nuances of the romance genre."

"If by *study* you mean *getting swept away in the sexy fantasy life of some fictional, ridiculously unattainable hero*, then yeah, I'd buy that."

"Why do you trash the genre when you know it's my favorite escape?" She began gathering her things to leave for the day.

"Because it's fun. You're too smart to be a cliché, Janie. You know that, right? Girl who's blind whiles away hours of her youth reading romances because her parents are too controlling. Grows up wanting a fictional life that can never exist. Break free from it." His voice rose with excitement. "Let it go. Romance isn't real. It's crap writing about fake people."

She never should have revealed that tidbit about her parents in the break room last month. They'd been talking about their childhoods, and while others had fun stories of hanging out at the mall, or going on spur-of-the-moment outings with groups of friends, Janie had very few spur-of-the-moment anything to share. Her parents worried about every step she made, questioning her safety and whether this or that location would be difficult for her to navigate without them to hold her hand. They'd been a noose around her neck, and it had often been easier to escape into fictional worlds than to battle for the chance to go out.

"And your sci-fi adventures are more real than romance? Ha!" She hefted her bag over her shoulder. "I bet you've never even read a romance."

"Don't need to. It's crap."

"It's not crap. I bet I could write a romance that you'd not only read, but love." Janie turned off her computer and braille device.

"Not unless it's got a heroine who likes sci-fi, is smarter than me, *and* is into kinky sex."

"God, you're a pig. Fine, sci-fi and kinky sex. It shouldn't be hard to make her smarter than you." She lifted her brows with the tease. "But if I write it, you not only have to read every single page of it, but you also have to go to the Romance Writer's Festival with me in October and stay all day. Plus," she added, getting excited about the bet, "you have to buy me every romance book I want for a month."

He placed Janie's cane in her hand. "A little greedy, aren't you?"

"Hey, if I'm writing a whole novel, it's got to be worth it."

"Fine, but I'm not buying you romance books for a month."

"Whatever. Torturing you with the festival for an entire day will be worth it. It's Friday night. What are you doing here so late?" It was after nine o'clock, and a group of people from work had gone down to NightCaps, a local bar where they often hung out.

"Had a busy day before coming here," Boyd answered.

"Are you going to NightCaps, or are you going to *while away the hours* with your nose in outer space?" Janie loved the constant vibration of laughter, hushed whispers, and the hum of sexual tension at NightCaps, but her best friend, Kiki Vernon, was out of town, and she didn't like to go to bars without her. She'd planned on spending a quiet weekend at home, but she assumed Boyd would want to go.

"I've got a date, so I'm pretty sure my nose won't be anywhere near space, but I'll walk with you. I'm headed that way anyway. But first, shake on our bet."

"Game on, dude," she said as she shook his hand. "And you're *so* gonna owe me, but I'm not going to NightCaps. I was going to read, but now I think I'll start plotting my romance. *Hm.* What should I call it? *Sci-fi Sexiness?*" She couldn't wait to tell Kiki about the bet. She loved the genre as much as Janie did, and she'd get a kick out of Janie actually trying to write a sexy story.

"That doesn't even sound romantic," Boyd said. "I'm going to win the bet, and when I do, you have to attend Comic Con with me. You'll make a hot Catwoman."

Janie laughed. "Yeah, that's *so* not going to happen. I'm writing this book and you're going to spend an entire day meeting romance authors and male cover models."

Boyd hooked his arm in hers as she touched the tip of her cane to the ground.

"You know what that cane does to me," he said in a seductively low voice.

"I know what it's going to do *to* you if you don't stop teasing me."

As they left the office, the crisp night air rolled over Janie's skin. The sounds of people walking by, cars moving along the road, and horns honking were familiar and comforting. The smell of exhaust tangled with what Janie had come to know as the dark scents of the city. Tension was thicker at night in New York City, as if everyone was shrouded with awareness. Janie felt that awareness prickling her skin.

"Want me to flag down a cab?" Boyd asked.

"No thanks. I hate riding in cabs here. The drivers petrify

me. I like the subway better." She'd ridden in cabs with Kiki when they'd first moved to the city after college, and the constant stopping and starting and traveling alone when someone else was in complete control of her end destination made her feel unsafe. Navigating the city alone presented enough of a challenge. She didn't need to end up in some back alley with a cab-driving killer.

"The subway? To each their own, I guess."

Janie's phone rang as they made their way down the sidewalk.

She stopped to dig it out of her bag. "Sorry. We can keep walking as long as you can guide me. It's a little distracting to use my cane and talk on the phone."

Boyd placed a hand on her arm. "Sneaky way to get me to touch you."

Janie shook her head and answered the phone, immediately greeted by Kiki's excited voice.

"Hey, just wanted you to know that since you blew off coming home with me this weekend, I'm not going to tell you about the date I had last night." Kiki had been her best friend since the third grade, when Kiki had put a boy in his place for teasing Janie about using a specially lighted magnifying device to read large-print books. Not that Janie needed protecting. Even back then she'd known some people were just too self-centered to care about other people's lives. Not Kiki, though. As soon as she'd finished with the bully, she'd wanted to know everything about Janie's eye condition: Cone-Rod Dystrophy, a degenerative eye disease. The disease had varying degrees of severity, from mild to complete loss of vision. So far Janie was lucky. She still had some light perception. If there were very bright lights, large planes of bright colors, or if the contrast was just right, and she looked out of her peripheral vision and got up super close, she could still sometimes make out shapes.

"Was it your headboard I heard banging the wall at three in the morning?" She loved teasing Kiki about her sexual proclivities.

"I wish. Anyway, when I come back, we're having a girls' night for sure," Kiki said. "I need to touch up your roots, so we'll do margaritas and hair dye. A great combination." Ever since they were little, Kiki had insisted on helping Janie with all things girly, which included not only hair and makeup, but also clothing and manicures and anything else Kiki put into the *girls must do* category. Kiki was the only person who had ever *not* been afraid to jump into those personal aspects of Janie's life, and Janie loved her even more for it because Kiki accepted and pushed and made sure that Janie missed out on nothing.

"Last time we did drinks and dye you blonded me out, which is why I *have* roots."

"You're a hot blonde," Kiki said.

"You also said I was a hot brunette. I gotta run. Have fun." She ended the call.

Boyd chuckled and said, "You'd be hot no matter what color your hair was. Careful stepping off the curb."

Janie was used to his flirty comments and knew better than to take them seriously. He doled them out in the office like she dotted her i's and crossed her t's, adding a touch of humor to their otherwise stoic workplace.

"Curb, careful," he said as she stepped back onto the sidewalk.

She liked that he knew enough to warn her to the change in her footing. Not everyone did, which was why she continued to use her cane, especially if guided by someone she didn't know very well. She knew they were nearing the subway and shifted her bag to her other shoulder, dropping her phone in the process.

"I've got it." Boyd stopped to pick it up. "So, you're really going to try to write that novel?"

"Darn right I am." She resituated her cane and bag, and they continued walking.

"You sure you want to take the subway?" Boyd asked again. "I'll even pay for a cab if you're worried about the money."

"It's not the money. It's the freakishly fast driving and then slamming on the brakes thing that New York cabbies do. I'm fine, really. Have fun on your date. I'll see you the next time you're at TEC."

Janie made her way down the steps to the subway, mentally playing with ideas for her romance story. At twenty-seven, she had only a few sexual experiences to draw from, although they'd never fully lived up to the sexual exploits of the heroes and heroines in the novels she'd read. She also knew absolutely nothing about sci-fi, or for that matter, kinky sex, other than what she'd read about. She might not have experience, but she was a master at research.

The subway platform was eerily quiet. She tried to focus on the bet instead of the fact that every *tap* of her cane echoed in what she assumed was an empty station. She'd boarded trains alone plenty of times, but as much as other people feared strangers, in the subway, she relied on auditory cues from them. Tingles of anxiety prickled through her chest as the heels of her shoes echoed chillingly.

She tapped her way to the bumpy strip along the edge of the platform, which was designed to let people who were visually impaired know they were nearing the edge. Her bag slid down her arm. She twisted sideways, trying to catch it. Her toe caught on a bump, sending her sprawling forward. In the space of a breath, her cane dropped through the air, and suddenly she was falling. Fear gripped her seconds before she landed on her right side with a painful *thud*. She sucked in air as pain spiraled through her. Something sharp dug into her cheek. *Rocks?* The pungent smell of grease and gasoline permeated the cold, dank air, and she realized she'd fallen off the platform.

Her heart thundered in her chest, battling with the blood rushing through her ears as she frantically searched for her cane, listening for a train. Tears streamed from her eyes as fear consumed her. *Get up. Get away from the tracks. Move. Move. Move.* Finding her cane, she clutched it to her aching chest and pushed up to her knees. A blood-curdling pain shot through her ankle. Fighting light-headedness, she clenched her teeth together and forced herself upright, bending her right knee to keep from putting pressure on her ankle. She gripped the cold, hard edge of the platform and tried to pull herself up.

"Help!" Her voice echoed in the empty station, magnifying her fear.

Her ankle rolled on the rocks, sending her tumbling down to the ground again. *Get up. Get up.* Pushing past the pain, she rose again, determined to get to safety. Her fingers moved over the platform's bumpy ridges that had tripped her up. Her fingertips grazed the smoother concrete just beyond. She used her left, uninjured foot for leverage as she pulled, pushed, and climbed her way onto the platform. Vibrations rumbled beneath her, and the sound of the train squealed in the distance. On the platform, she rolled onto her back, gasping for air and clutching her cane to her chest. The concrete vibrated as the train approached. Sobs wrenched from her lungs, and miraculously, she felt herself smile, because *goddamn it*, she wasn't going to get run over by the stupid train.

To continue reading, buy **TOUCHED BY LOVE**

MORE BOOKS BY MELISSA FOSTER

River of Love
Crushing on Love
Whisper of Love
Thrill of Love

THE BRADENS & MONTGOMERYS at Pleasant Hill – Oak Falls

Embracing Her Heart
Anything For Love
Trails of Love
Wild, Crazy Hearts
Making You Mine
Searching For Love

THE BRADEN NOVELLAS

Promise My Love
Our New Love
Daring Her Love
Story of Love
Love at Last
A Very Braden Christmas

THE REMINGTONS

Game of Love
Stroke of Love
Flames of Love
Slope of Love
Read, Write, Love
Touched by Love

SEASIDE SUMMERS

Seaside Dreams

Seaside Hearts

Seaside Sunsets

Seaside Secrets

Seaside Nights

Seaside Embrace

Seaside Lovers

Seaside Whispers

Seaside Serenade

BAYSIDE SUMMERS

Bayside Desires

Bayside Passions

Bayside Heat

Bayside Escape

Bayside Romance

Bayside Fantasies

THE RYDERS

Seized by Love

Claimed by Love

Chased by Love

Rescued by Love

Swept Into Love

THE WHISKEYS: DARK KNIGHTS AT PEACEFUL HARBOR

Tru Blue
Truly, Madly, Whiskey
Driving Whiskey Wild
Wicked Whiskey Love
Mad About Moon
Taming My Whiskey
The Gritty Truth

SUGAR LAKE

The Real Thing
Only for You
Love Like Ours
Finding My Girl

HARMONY POINTE

Call Her Mine
This is Love
She Loves Me

THE WICKEDS: DARK KNIGHTS AT BAYSIDE

A Little Bit Wicked
Wicked Aftermath

WILD BOYS AFTER DARK (Billionaires After Dark)

Logan

Heath

Jackson

Cooper

BAD BOYS AFTER DARK (Billionaires After Dark)

Mick

Dylan

Carson

Brett

HARBORSIDE NIGHTS SERIES

Includes characters from the Love in Bloom series

Catching Cassidy

Discovering Delilah

Tempting Tristan

More Books by Melissa

Chasing Amanda (mystery/suspense)

Come Back to Me (mystery/suspense)

Have No Shame (historical fiction/romance)

Love, Lies & Mystery (3-book bundle)

Megan's Way (literary fiction)

Traces of Kara (psychological thriller)

Where Petals Fall (suspense)

ACKNOWLEDGMENTS

There are so many people who helped me with this story. Every fan, every street team member who pushed to make Duke unique, every friend who listened to my endless chatter about the story, and of course, my family, who lives and breathes characters and fictional worlds with me on a daily basis. But this story could not have been as rich without the help of my friend and loyal fan Aphrodite Pipilis and her sister, Katarina. Thank you, Dite, for your endless answers about the Greek culture, terms, food (OMG the food!), and for being gracious enough to read the early rendition of the story. I think Elpitha belongs to you as much as it does to Duke and Gabriella. (Please note that Elpitha Island is a fictional location.)

Lynn Mullan, thank you for the word *undercrackers*, which is sure to become a household term among my readers. Christine Dyc, I hope you enjoyed Duke's obsession with Gabriella's luscious ass(!). Oh, how much joy we have in our fabulous street team! If you haven't joined us yet, dear readers, please do!
www.facebook.com/groups/MelissaFosterFans.

Remember to sign up for my newsletter to keep up-to-date with new releases and special promotions and events: www.MelissaFoster.com/Newsletter

If you don't yet follow me on Facebook, please do! We have such fun chatting about our lovable heroes and sassy heroines, and I always try to keep fans abreast of what's going on in our fictional boyfriends' worlds.
www.Facebook.com/MelissaFosterAuthor

Thank you to my awesome editorial team: Kristen Weber and Penina Lopez, and my meticulous proofreaders: Jenna Bagnini, Juliette Hill, Marlene Engel, and Lynn Mullan.

Meet Melissa

www.MelissaFoster.com

Melissa Foster is a *New York Times* and *USA Today* bestselling and award-winning author. Her books have been recommended by *USA Today's* book blog, *Hagerstown* magazine, *The Patriot*, and several other print venues. Melissa has painted and donated several murals to the Hospital for Sick Children in Washington, DC.

Visit Melissa on her website or chat with her on social media. Melissa enjoys discussing her books with book clubs and reader groups and welcomes an invitation to your event. Melissa's books are available through most online retailers in paperback, digital, and audio formats.

Melissa also writes sweet romance under the pen name, Addison Cole.

Printed in Great Britain
by Amazon